Francis William Bain

**Christina, Queen of Sweden**

Francis William Bain

**Christina, Queen of Sweden**

ISBN/EAN: 9783337324322

Printed in Europe, USA, Canada, Australia, Japan

Cover: Foto ©Raphael Reischuk / pixelio.de

More available books at **www.hansebooks.com**

# CHRISTINA,

# QUEEN OF SWEDEN.

BY

## F. W. BAIN, B.A.,

LATE JUNIOR STUDENT OF CHRIST CHURCH, OXFORD.

LONDON:

W. H. ALLEN & CO., 13 WATERLOO PLACE,

PALL MALL, S.W.

1890.

# PREFACE.

WITH the exception of the interesting, but somewhat slipshod 'Memoirs of Christina,' by Henry Woodhead (2 vols., 1863), now out of print and hard to get, there is nothing like a complete or trustworthy account of Christina in English. In addition to some very old translations of foreign lives (French and German libels), and various more or less unsatisfactory notices in encyclopædias and biographical dictionaries, those worth naming are, that by Mrs. Jameson in her now antiquated 'Celebrated Female Sovereigns;' the section devoted to her in Ranke's 'History of the Popes;' and an essay by Hardinge, the Lothian Prize Essay for 1880. Occasional allusions in historical and other literature show that little or nothing is commonly known about her.

And yet she was, to say the least, one of the most original and extraordinary women in her own or any age. It is indeed not an easy thing to write a short life of Christina, and this not merely because her country, her father, her precocious political genius, the strength of her character, her learning, her court, her abdication, her conversion, her travels, her connection, more or less direct, with the most celebrated names of her time, tempt one to be continually turning aside to dwell on subsidiary points; but also because the manner in which her history has hitherto been written necessarily compels her would-be biographer to adopt a half-polemical tone. Never has any historical character been more hardly dealt with than Christina. It has been her lot to meet either with the most outrageous calumny, or more rarely with extravagant panegyric, seldom or never with her due meed of justice. Her conversion made all Protestants her violent enemies, and some Catholics her equally violent admirers; her abdication destroyed the hopes of all kinds of interested persons, offended sober people, and insulted her own subjects, who have never forgiven her; it has been persistently misrepresented accordingly. The political complications and jealousies between the French, the Spaniards, and the Pope, drew her into their quarrels, and each party hated and libelled her according as it suspected her of growing favourable to the other. Lastly, her own peculiar character, and her neglect of conventionalities, offered an appropriate subject for scandal. She is still viewed through the distorting medium of French and Protestant seventeenth-century gossip and slander, and measured by commonplace standards; though it is with genius as with crime, which, says a great Russian, cannot be judged correctly if we come to it with ready-made opinions.

The chief authorities for her life, used for the present work, are first, the 'Mémoires de Christine, Reine de Suède,' by Arckenholtz, in four volumes, quarto (1751–1770). The large collection of her letters and writings, and laborious reference to a multitude of authorities, make these 'Mémoires' of primary importance for any life of Christina; but they must be very carefully used and searchingly criticised, for the author is a rampant Swede and Protestant, entirely devoid of impartiality, though he supplies the means of correcting his bias. Roman Catholicism is synonymous in his eyes with "depraved morality," and he never loses a chance of blackguarding the French and proving his Swedes to be in the right. Later writers, as will presently be seen, trust quite unsuspectingly to his judgment. Next come the 'Mémoires de Chanut,' French Resident at the Court of Sweden (edited by Linage de Vauciennes, 1674). These are of great value in the early part, as long as Chanut was in Sweden; after he left, and was succeeded by Picques, they are almost worthless, the French being then spitefully jealous of Christina: she complains

herself of the insult to Chanut's memory in
publishing such libels under his name (see
page 329). Whitelocke's 'Journal of the Swedish
Embassy,' in 1653–4, is of great value, and very
amusing into the bargain; only it is to be
carefully recollected he has the orthodox Puritan
horror of pleasure, which most of Christina's
biographers have forgotten. Count Galeazzo
Gualdo's ' Istoria di Christina,' 1656 (in English
by Burbery, 1658), gives her travels and conversion at inordinate length, but the author is an
enthusiastic Catholic. Puffendorf's ' De Rebus
Succicis ' gives the history of her reign. There are
various short lives, as those of Lacombe, Catteau
Calleville (a very excellent one). Other special
authorities are Burmann's ' Collection of Letters
of Learned Men ' (*Sylloge Epistolarum*); the
' Mémoires ' of Richelieu, Madame de Motteville,
Mademoiselle de Montpensier, and the works of
other French writers of that age, named in the text.
To modern authors, Geijer, Ranke, and Fryxell
(' Berättelse ur Svenska Historien,' vols. 9, 10),
I am indebted for many special particulars and
extracts from state records. Grauert's 'Christina
und ihr Hof,' the best of all lives of Christina,
has been of great service. Other minor sources
are named as they occur. A large quantity of
so-called lives, mostly in French, or translations
from that language (of which a list may be found

in Arckenholtz, vol. 1), have been read through
to no purpose; they are all nothing but baseless
libels, from which come the imputations on
Christina's good fame. Those who care for a
specimen may consult the 'Histoire de la Vie de
la Reyne Christine de Suède' (Stockholm : chez
Jean, Pleyn de Courage, 77 [1677]), a collection
of ten anonymous pamphlets on her; nothing will
be learned from it but a lesson in the language of
abuse, as well as in the way in which Christina's
character has been handled by this sort of person.
It may be stated here, once for all, that there is
not the shadow of a basis for the multitudinous
imputations on her morality; they all sprang
from the union of French jealousy and French
prurience.

Lord Bolingbroke once observed that it had
been his lot to suffer more from his friends than
his enemies. Such has also been the lot of
Christina. Her worst enemies have been her
apparent friends, or those who had no reason to
depreciate her. To deal fully with all of them
would require a volume, but it is necessary to
examine some.

The French writers of the eighteenth century
are principally answerable for the prevalent
impression that her conversion was merely a
means to other ends. Voltaire, above all, goes
and leads astray in this matter; his eye saw what

it brought the power of seeing. He will have it
that she was a *philosophe*, that she "quitted the
throne for the fine arts." This will be shown
hereafter to be entirely wrong. When he asserts,
however, "that if she had reigned in Italy, she
would never have abdicated," he is certainly
right, but only accidentally. It was not the fine
arts, but religion, which drew Christina from her
throne.

Fryxell, again, stumbles in this respect and
others. Nothing, he asserts, can be *proved* about
Christina's conversion; he himself believes she
was indifferent, if not atheistical: "at the beginning of her reign Christina spoke of God; later,
of Providence; last, of Fate:" this represents, in
his view, the course of development and the final
result. Now, it may be positively asserted, in
opposition to this, that there is nothing more
certain in all history than that Christina's conversion was sincere. The pages of this book will
prove it irrefutably. Elsewhere Fryxell suggests
she was insane. Nothing is harder to refute
than such a charge, for it is *almost* impossible to
define insanity. There was certainly in her
some of that madness which is akin to genius;
but the madness which Fryxell means is not
that. His charge will be found entirely without
foundation, but what it is important to notice is
how he came to make it. The fact is, that

Fryxell has woven up into one unified narrative
all the preserved evidences, whether sound, baseless, or contradictory, and presented them to his
readers as all standing on the same level.  This is
to place the story of the apple on a level with
the theory of gravitation, to adopt all the statements of Victor Hugo about the third Napoleon,
and so on.  Why, certainly, in this way Christina
will strike us as insane, insane to a degree that
throws all Bedlam into the shade.  To give but
a single instance, Fryxell incorporates in his
account of Monaldeschi's execution the remark
attributed to Christina: "Give him a stab, and
make him confess."  What a cold-blooded cruelty
does not this suggest!  Now this is strange, for
there is ample evidence of Christina's large-
hearted humanity.  The fact is, the words quoted
do not occur in the authentic accounts of the
scene; they are nothing but a libellous invention
of her enemies.  This is merely one instance out
of scores.  Fryxell shows a complete incapacity,
or unwillingness, to discriminate between good
and bad evidence; and mixes things up in the
most absurd way.  Thus, in his account of her
religious views he confuses a philosophical dictum
with a religious opinion, and attributes a religious
meaning to Christina's remark (à-propos of philo-
sophies old and new), that " the ancient follies were
as good as the new ones."  And so on continually.

Both Fryxell and Geijer give an entirely
erroneous impression of the last years of her
reign. Their pictures are highly coloured with
the misrepresentations of the ousted *savans*,
the recitals of Puritans and rancorous Lutherans;
they tell of "the decay of morality," "youth `
showing no respect to its superiors," and so on.
All this is simply ridiculous. There was no
other difference between the beginning and end
of Christina's reign than is amply explained by
the state of her own health, which required her
to abstain from the excessive labour she indulged
in, and the comparative cessation of business
after 1648 and 1650; there is not a particle of
evidence justifying Geijer's assertion that "from
this period dates the ruin of pure and decorous
morality," which is based upon Whitelocke's
puritanical criticisms, and an old prejudiced
Swedish-Lutheran extract he ought to have
known better than to accept. As to the general
discontent of the country, Geijer is equally short-
sighted. Christina deserves all blame for her
reckless alienation of Crown lands; but this was
not the cause of the distress: that had been
accumulating for fifty years, and was due to the
war and the nobles, as will be shown. It was
against them, and not Christina, that the popular
odium was directed. Geijer's whole portrait of
Christina is falsely coloured; every line betrays

the dark influence of her enemies. The following instance taken at random will show the *way* this is done. He refers to her "atheism and frivolity," and then adds, "representations from her mother were ill received." This gives the impression that her excellent mother made expostulations on her evil courses, and she persisted in them. Now, any one who will refer to page 183 of this book will open his eyes wide, when he sees these "expostulations" there presented in their true light. The fact is, Maria Eleanora was the mouth-piece of the insolence of the Lutheran clergy, who *suspected* Christina of lukewarmness in the Swedish faith, fixed upon Bourdelot as the cause, and had the impertinence to send in a petition for his dismissal, which they did not dare to present to the Queen themselves!

Even Ranke himself, to whom, let me say, this book is indebted on every page, must nevertheless stand convicted of careless acceptance of baseless charges against her. Here, again, it would require a pamphlet to expose fully all his errors. Some instances must stand for the rest. In his examination of her conversion, he says, "she repeatedly (*oft*) declared that she had not discovered any essential errors in Protestantism, but, &c." Now, *first,* this "repeatedly" is Ranke's own addition to the original charge, which only says she did so once. But, *secondly,* Grauert

shows [vol. ii., p. 62] that the whole statement is
false, and rests on a mere mistranslation of a
Latin passage in Wagenseil! What a basis for
an important statement damaging Christina's
sincerity! Again, speaking of her secrecy in
the negotiations for her conversion, Ranke says,
" the charm of this affair to Christina was principally in the certainty that no one had the slightest suspicion of her proceedings." But there are
absolutely no grounds for attributing such a
small-minded love for hide-and-seek to Christina,
whose character was not of that kind. She had
the best of all reasons for preserving absolute
secrecy; her abdication and her revenues, nay,
her crown and life itself, would have been
seriously endangered, had there leaked out the
slightest inkling that she was meditating
becoming a Catholic.

That Ranke was not writing carefully, or at
first hand, in this part of his book, is proved by
a thing in itself of small moment. At the conclusion of the ceremony of her abdication, he
states that the Peasants' deputy returned to his
seat, *without having said one word.* Now, in fact,
he made a long and very peculiar speech, which
is fully reported in the very passage in Whitelocke's journal, to which Ranke refers.

Mr. Hardinge, again, while he recognizes the
sincerity of Christina's conversion, has based his

view of her character far too readily on the statements of her enemies, on whom he permits himself to improve. For instance, Montpensier asserts that Christina "used to swear. by God" at Paris. Other observers deny that they ever heard her swear. Still, Christina herself admits that she used to swear, adding that she learned the habit in Sweden,* where at that time all, both men and women, were accustomed to do so in conversation; but she adds that she had since entirely broken herself of that bad habit. Hence she certainly swore, if at all, very little. That is all the evidence as to her swearing. But see how Mr. Hardinge improves this. "Cromwell," he says, "did not wish to have Christina in England. Christina, let loose among the Pharisees of Whitehall, *swearing like one of Rupert's troopers, jesting profanely at the expense of the elect* . . . . would have shocked feelings which, &c." (The Italics are ours.)

In this way do casual hints and unfounded

* Observe an instance of how Arckenholtz, whom later writers follow, falsifies history for his ends. Christina herself says she learned the habit of swearing from her own countrymen and women; and it is matter of history that her statement is correct. But Arckenholtz, who always tries to screen his Swedes, says, that *since* Bourdelot was *said to be* one of the best swearers of his time, "it is *therefore* this wicked man that was the cause of her failing in this respect." This is a good specimen of the way in which Bourdelot has been maligned.

misrepresentations grow into definite charges.
The process of time does it all. Christina's
last biographer, Gustafson, in his 'Bidrag till
Historien om Drottning Kristina's afsägelse och
Riksdagen,' 1654, speaks as follows, on page 66 :
"It has been asserted that Christina determined
to quit the Swedish throne in consequence of
her inclination to the Catholic faith. But she
had, at the end of her reign, principally through
Bourdelot's influence, arrived at such a view of
life that it was all the same to her to which
religion she belonged. That she subsequently
adopted the Catholic faith rests on this, that it
appealed more to her love of display, and was
more convenient for her residence in foreign
Catholic countries. We must not overlook the
sensation that would be aroused by such a conversion, nor that it was just Christina's highest
wish to excite remark, and get herself talked
about. For the rest, she herself considered her
solemn conversion as a farce."

Any one who will read the following pages
through, will not only convince himself that all
this is entirely false, but will even wonder how
any man professing familiarity with the subject,
could ever make statements in such glaring contradiction with all the facts. It shows, at any
rate, that the Swedes have never forgiven her for
turning her back upon them. What, however,

is worth noticing about it is, the evidence he
adduces in proof of accusations so sweeping.  For
confirmation of all, we are referred to Arckenholtz, in his account of her conversion, which
happens to be exactly that part of his work which
is worth nothing at all.  The story of her calling
her conversion a farce is a foolish libel due to
Chevreau, who is entirely unworthy of credit.
But the world believes what it likes ; the amusing
always gets in before the true.  In Christina we
have the best possible illustration of the aphorism
—*interdum fucata falsitas in multis est probabilior
et sæpe rationibus vincit nudam veritatem.*

With regard to the present little book, its aim
is to present facts instead of fiction.  It lays
claim to no beauties of style; its only merit, if
any, lies here—that whereas the received method
of dealing with Christina is to abstract her from
her relations, and compile her history in the
light of mere tittle-tattle and hostile *on-dits*, the
method attempted here is to view her in the con-
crete, replace her in her circumstances, and then
see how the charges brought against her agree
with the facts.  One absurd charge will then be
found to disappear—the perpetual charge of
"inconsistency and fickleness," which in nine cases
out of ten proves nothing but the laziness of those
who make it.  Time, place, and " circumstances,
which with some gentlemen pass for nothing,"

*b*

are the important matters. "The time, the time," cries Michelet, "let us replace our man in his time ; *laissez là vos systèmes.*"

It is quite possible for different persons to take different views of Christina when they are acquainted with the facts. But what is not to be allowed is, that people should go on abusing her, without knowing anything about her.\* And a biographer is not called upon to paint imaginary portraits, or say what character he might or might not possibly admire or dislike ; it is better to praise people for what they are than abuse them for what they are not.

No space could be given to Gustavus Adolphus ;

---

\* In the recently published collection of ' Instructions aux Ministres de France' from 1648, M. Geffroy, Membre de l'Institut, who writes the introduction to the volume on Sweden, speaks thus of Christina, *à-propos* of her motives to abdicate : "On a signalé à bon droit *son peu de capacité aux grandes affaires,* ses difficultés en présence d'une aristocratie, et même de ministres assez peu flexibles, et les embarras financières que des guerres incessantes causaient à la Suède. Toutes ces raisons doivent être comptées assurément ; mais il faut ajouter l'inconsistance d'esprit, *et cette sécheresse de cœur* qui allait jusqu'à la cruauté." (The italics are ours.) Where did M. Geffroy get his information about Christina ? From Dumas' ridiculous play ? One can forgive the " *sécheresse de cœur,*" though how can that possibly be a motive to abdicate ? But what are we to say of his assertion as to her want of political capacity ? Even her bitterest enemies never disputed her remarkable political genius. Such ignorance, or something worse, in a Membre de l'Institut, is no credit to French literature. *On la signale à bon droit.*

as to relate his life after 1626, the period of his most important activity, would be to write his history as well as Christina's. Military events, useless unless fully detailed, have only been considered in so far as they had influence on politics.

While every effort has been made to be at once full and succinct, the book does not profess to be a complete history of Sweden or any other country. Of its manifold shortcomings I am deeply conscious, and would fain have seen some more redoubtable champion coming forward on behalf of the truth and of Christina; but none such has appeared. I can only venture to hope that in this instance too the old Greek axiom may be verified, that the half is more than the whole.

My best thanks are due to the kind friend by whose encouragement the book was written.

OXFORD, 1889.

# CONTENTS.

---◦◇◦---

## CHAPTER IV.

## CHAPTER V.

## CHAPTER VI.

## CHAPTER VII.

[NOTE.—*For an explanation of the medal on the back, see p.* 328.]

# CHRISTINA, QUEEN OF SWEDEN.

## CHAPTER I.

IT is not necessary, in order to understand Christina and her time, to go back into the mists of Scandinavian antiquity. The modern history of Sweden begins with Gustavus Vasa. And of all national histories, that of Sweden has been most dependent upon, and conditioned by, the personal character of its monarchs. "As I write the history of Sweden," exclaims Geijer, "I feel as strongly as may be that it is the history of her kings." The sublime genius of some among them is not more wonderful than the sustained elevation of all ; they are a gallery of heroes, which it would be difficult to parallel elsewhere. The family characteristic, from Gustavus Vasa to Charles XII., is a fiery energy of will and impatience of restraint, combined with the highest intellectual power. These qualities are pre-eminently illustrated in Christina, who is well worthy to take her place in the series,

B

although a woman; and perhaps her story gains additional interest on that very account.

In 1397, by the Treaty of Calmar, Denmark, Norway, and Sweden had been combined into a great Scandinavian monarchy by the " Semiramis of the North," Queen Margaret of Denmark. This union, however, was always more of a name than a fact, for it had no foundation in popular sympathies; in addition to the Danish monarchs, Sweden continued to have rulers of her own. In 1513, Christian II., " the tyrant," succeeded to the throne: his violent and impolitic despotism sounded the knell of the Act of Union. It was his aim to break the power of the Swedish nobles; but if he designed thereby to conciliate and benefit the popular element in the nation, his massacre of the principal nobles on November 8, 1520, " the blood bath of Stockholm," was as foolish as it was inhuman. By this gross blunder, he roused the Swedish national feeling to the necessary pitch; and nothing was wanted to assure their independence but a man. The Swedes found him in the young Gustavus, son of . Eric Johanson, with whom begins the history of Sweden and the house of Vasa.*

Though only twenty-two years of age, he had already made himself known. He had borne the

---

* The name comes most probably from the faggots, or *wisps*, in the family arms.

Swedish banner in the battle of Brennkirk in 1518, in which Christian was defeated by Steno Sturè. Sent as a hostage to Denmark, and carried away captive to Jutland, he remained there a year, brooding over the condition of his country; thence he escaped in disguise, to learn soon after of the Stockholm massacre, in which his own father perished, and swear a terrible revenge; a price was set on his head, and he had to fly to Dalecarlia, where his escapes and wanderings became historic; till at length with a growing band of peasants and patriots he came forward to liberate his country. He took Westerås and Upsala, and laid siege to Stockholm. Fortune favoured him; for at this critical moment, Christian was expelled from his own country by the Danes (1523). The garrison in Stockholm withdrew, and Gustavus was shortly after crowned King of Sweden by his grateful countrymen.

Like all inaugurators of a new era, he found that the initial victory was but the beginning of his difficulties. Before him lay long struggles with all orders in the State. The nobles, gradually regaining their courage and position, regarded him as merely one of themselves, and an upstart; the peasants had wanted a liberator, and found to their disgust they had got a master. But the greatest difficulty of all lay with the clergy. It has been asserted that the Reformation in Sweden differed from that in other countries, in that here it was introduced by the Government for political ends before being preached to the people, instead of spreading from below upwards. This is true enough, but it must be remembered that Gustavus could never have forced it upon an entirely reluctant people; moreover, the initial cause, or rather occasion, of the Reformation in all places, the vices and abuses of the clergy, existed in Sweden as strongly as elsewhere. By its scandalous self-seeking and unpatriotic action, the Church, represented by Gustavus Trollè, had "got itself regarded as a foreign power in the State," and Gustavus Vasa made use of this state of things for his own ends. He studiously avoided positively declaring that he was introducing the Lutheran religion (though he was in correspondence with Luther); but aimed at depriving the clergy of temporal power, for the purposes of his own absolutism, and in order to get their wealth into his hands. He effected this most difficult step very diplomatically at the Recess of Westerås, in 1527, which marks the establishment of the Reformation in Sweden. But its principles and spirit did not achieve a complete victory over old customs, and gain a definite hold, till the time of Charles IX., when, just as in

England against Spain, politics combined with
religious views to make Catholicism abhorred in
the eyes of the nation.

Gustavus lived long enough to accomplish his
threefold task, of liberating his country, founding
it anew in a religious and political sense, and
leaving the kingdom as an heirloom to his
descendants, by the hereditary settlement of
1544.   He had to use all means to his end, from
demagogic cajolery to masterful despotism; and
in the process he gave full evidence of his most
striking characteristics, " strong endurance and
great sagacity." The wisdom that lies in biding
one's time, and knowing when  to strike, was
never more strongly exemplified than in him.
He was of all his house the one who had most
pre-eminently the qualifications of a builder.

Under  his  two  immediate  successors  the
anarchy seemed beginning again; and this is
not to be laid entirely to their charge; such is
always the case during the reaction from a great
impulse, before the new mould has had time to
fix itself.   But they were by no means equal to
their father.   We need not dwell upon Eric XIV.,
who has been called the Swedish Caligula, and
who resembles his Roman prototype not only in
his madness, but in the  remarkable intellect
which was clouded by it; a certain mystery
hangs over his life and his end; he was deposed

and poisoned by his brother, John. The story
of his son—the unfortunate Gustavus Ericson—
and his lifelong exile, is among the romances
of history, but must not detain us; yet we
may note, that he too showed the hereditary
abilities of his race, and possibly by his sojourn
at the Russian Court with Boris Godunoff, where
his legend and his wanderings made a great
impression on the popular mind, prepared the
way for the false Demetrius.

The reign of John III. is memorable chiefly for
his designs towards a restoration of Catholicism
in Sweden. His marriage with Catherine Jagel-
lonica, an ardent Catholic, by which the crowns
of Poland and Sweden were united, had the
most important results. Catherine had probably
great influence on his policy; for at the
beginning of his reign and during her life he
worked energetically in the Catholic interest;
published his Red Book, or Liturgy, in 1576,
and seemed on the point of establishing
Catholicism, or something closely akin to it, in
Sweden, aided by the Jesuits, who came from
Rome to assist him. But after her death he
turned completely round, and even persecuted
the doctrines he had endeavoured to spread.
There was no further chance for the Counter Reformation till his death.

His son, Sigismund III., a devout and eager

Catholic, soon succeeded, by his religious, vacillating, and impolitic conduct, in identifying in the Swedish mind the ideas of Catholic and anti-national; the Lutheran cause found its champion in Duke Charles, his uncle, the third son of Gustavus Vasa, and the "second founder of Protestant Sweden." Charles stood in exactly the same position as his great son Gustavus Adolphus did at a later time; in his person centred the opposition to the Catholic schemes. The crisis was one of those which determine the history of the world. Sigismund was in fact conquered and expelled from Sweden; his heirs were excluded from the throne, to which Charles was raised in 1604 as Charles IX. The Catholic reaction was lost in the North, and Lutheranism, till now indefinite and wanting cohesion, was suddenly crystallised into the unalterable political faith of Sweden.

Sigismund expelled, Charles set himself to reorganise the State, which had been falling asunder under his brothers, and especially to crush the power of the nobles, who were again becoming formidable to the Crown. He was the greatest of the sons of Gustavus Vasa, "and perhaps," says Geijer, "the greatest of all his house; his spirit was full of the hereafter; in him, more than any of his contemporaries, laboured the burning future, which burst forth in the Thirty Years' War." He left the Protestant cause to his son, nothing doubting he would accomplish the work he himself had to leave undone. "*Ille faciet*," he would say, laying his hand on the head of Gustavus Adolphus; "he will complete it."

The life of Gustavus Adolphus, a perpetual conflict, fulfilled the prophecy and carried out the policy of his father. His history, his early wars with Denmark, Russia, and Poland; the gradual evolution of the Swedish hero into the champion of the Protestant cause; how, in the short interval between his landing in Pomerania in 1630 and his death at Lutzen in 1632, he turned the tide of victory on the Catholics, and established the ultimate result, though he did not live to see it, must be sought elsewhere. Here, we can but notice the essential features of his character. He presents the most remarkable analogies to Cæsar, and to him alone. In both, the highest creative military genius was combined with a humanity quite unknown to all the other generals of their time. Both were remarkable for that "marvellous serenity, which never deserted them in good or evil days." Like Cæsar, Gustavus was "prodigal to recklessness of his great life," and, like Cæsar, it was owing to his recklessness that he came by his end. Both, again, died leaving their work incomplete; and hence in both cases speculation has been busy as to their designs, yet without being able to determine what was the ultimate plan which was nipped untimely in the bud. In both cases, an untimely death, the greatest of misfortunes for the world at that time, has canonised its victim in the eyes of posterity.

These were Christina's ancestors. "The special feature in Charles IX. is his inborn striving to grasp across every limit; beyond every goal set to another." This imaginative striving after ideal objects, this poetical dissatisfaction with ordinary goals, and inability to sit still, is, in fact, the keynote in the Vasa character. It is the explanation of Christina's strange career.

On November 25, 1620, was celebrated the marriage of Gustavus Adolphus with Maria Eleanora, eldest daughter of John Sigismund, Elector of Brandenburg. Her father died before it took place, and her brother was not anxious for it, fearing the preponderating influence of Sweden in North Germany; but he had to accept it with what grace he could muster.

"This princess," says Christina herself in her Memoirs, "who was beautiful, and possessed all the good and bad qualities of her sex, lived with the king in an affectionate union, to which nothing was wanting but an heir." Their first child, a daughter, died in her fourth year; a second died also in a few months. During a journey to Finland, the queen found herself in an interesting situation for the third time. All signs, aided perhaps by hopes in so anxious a crisis, led her to expect a son. The court returned to Stockholm, and the king was summoned from Poland, where he had just been victorious. Both king and queen dreamed dreams, forecasting the happy event. Astrologers, whose influence was still strong in Europe, presented themselves with confident predictions. They affirmed that the crisis must of necessity be fatal either to the king, or the queen, or the child that was to be born. Should it, however, live twenty-four hours, then it would eventually become great.

On November 8, 1626, Christina was born. " I came into the world all over hair ; my voice was strong and harsh. This made all the women think I was a boy, and they gave vent to their joy in exclamations, which at first deceived the king, prepared as he was to wish for an heir. When the mistake was discovered, they were afraid to undeceive him. At last his sister, the Princess Catharine, for whom he had always had a great affection, undertook the task. She carried me to him and let him see for himself what she did not dare to tell him. The king, without

showing any surprise, took me in his arms, saying
composedly to her: 'Let us thank God, sister;
I hope this girl will be as good as a boy to me;
may God preserve her now that He has sent her.'
The princess, wishing to please him, tried to
remind him he was still young enough to hope
for an heir; but the king replied instantly, 'My
sister, I am quite satisfied; may God preserve her
to me.' So saying he sent me away with his
blessing. Every one was surprised to see that he
seemed pleased. He gave orders to celebrate the
event with the customary rejoicings for male heirs.
I was called Christina." The king afterwards
said of her, with a laugh, " She will be clever,
she has taken us all in." It is hardly necessary
to add that the predictions of the astrologers came
to nothing, unless we give them credit for their
assertion that the child was destined to be great.

The queen, who was not undeceived so soon as
the king, when she discovered the mistake was
inconsolable. " She could not bear to see me,
because she said I was a girl, and ugly to boot;
and she was right enough, for I was as tawny as
a little Moor." This dislike had important consequences for Christina later on. Her father, on
the contrary, loved her, and she reciprocated his
affection; she was indeed her father's child. She
seemed instinctively to discover the difference
between the way in which she was regarded by

her father and mother. Christina herself asserts that various means were tried to make away with her, such as dropping her, letting beams fall on her. We shall be slow to believe this, but, however that may be, she bore all her life the marks of one of these untoward accidents, in that one of her shoulders was always higher than the other; "a defect that I could have cured if I had taken the trouble," she says—but she never did.

To make up for this want of affection on the part of her mother, Gustavus seems to have been very fond of her. In an assembly of the Estates summoned for that purpose on December 24, 1627, he caused them to swear allegiance to her, and recognise her as heir to the crown. And although during her early years the Polish war and affairs of State gave him little time for less important matters, he showed in many ways his care and love for her. Hearing that she was taken dangerously ill, when he was on a visit to the mines, he came back to her, "quicker than any courier could," to find her at the point of death.; his inconsolable grief was however changed to extraordinary joy when she recovered, and he ordered Te Deums to be sung in the churches for her escape. Another time he took her with him to Calmar, when she was not as yet two years old, and subjected her to a test, the result of which increased his affection for her. They were hesitating to fire a salute with the guns of the fortress in his honour, according to the custom, for fear lest it might frighten a child of such importance as the little heiress to the throne of Sweden. The governor sent to ask for an order. The king, after weighing the matter a little, said, " Yes, fire, she is a soldier's daughter, and must get accustomed to it." Accordingly they saluted in due form. "I was with the king in his carriage, and instead of being frightened, like any other child, I laughed and clapped my hands; not being able as yet to speak, I expressed my joy as well as I could in my fashion, signifying by signs that they should fire again. This little event increased the king's tenderness for me ; he hoped I might be naturally as intrepid as himself." Since that time he took her with him to the reviews of his troops ;—" he used to jest with me,—' Come, I'll take you one of these days to a place that will please you.' But unfortunately," proceeds Christina, " death prevented him from keeping his word, and I had not the happiness of serving my apprenticeship under so good a master."

The time, however, approached when he was to leave Sweden never to return. On the 19th May, 1630, he bade farewell to the Estates in an affecting speech. He presented to them the little Christina, at this time not four years old ;

commending her to them, as the heiress of the kingdom, and his daughter. Then he went on: "Seeing that many perchance may imagine that we charge ourselves with this war without cause given, so take I God the most high to witness, in whose face I here sit, that I have undertaken it, not out of my own pleasure, nor from lust for war; but for many years have had most pressing motive thereto, mostly for that our oppressed brethren in religion may be freed from the papal yoke, which by God's grace we hope to effect. And since it usually comes to pass that the pitcher which is carried often to the well comes to be broken at last, so will it go with me too, that I who in so many trials and dangers have shed my blood for Sweden's welfare, and yet until now escaped, through God's gracious protection, with life unharmed, must lose it one day; therefore will I before my departure at this time commend you, the collective Estates of Sweden, both present and absent, to God the most high, wishing that after this wretched and burdensome life we may by God's good pleasure meet and consort in that which is heavenly and imperishable." "On this occasion," says Christina, "they had taught me a little complimentary speech to recite to him; but as he was so busy that he could not attend to me, I, seeing that he was not listening, pulled him by his buff coat, and made him turn round to me. Perceiving me, he took me in his arms, and embraced me, unable to restrain his tears, as those who were present at the time have told me. They tell me, that when he was gone, I cried so hard for three whole days without stopping, that my eyes were seriously endangered, and I came very near losing my sight, which, like that of the king my father, was very weak. They took my tears as a bad omen, all the more as I naturally cried little and very rarely."

Before his departure Gustavus Adolphus did not forget, in the midst of the multitudinous cares and business of State which demanded his instant attention, to provide for the future well-being of his daughter. He consigned her to the care of his sister, the Princess Catharine; her husband, John Casimir, the Prince Palatine, he left in charge of his finances. This office he was deprived of after the king's death, being feared by the Regency on account of his Calvinism, and suspected of designs on the monarchy. The queen objected strongly to this arrangement; she detested the princess for reasons of her own: but " the king would be obeyed in this matter," and he was. He caused the Estates and the Army to swear fealty to Christina and acknowledge her as lawful heir. The five great officers of the State were to be her guardians. The queen was specially excluded alike from the State and the

Government. This certainly seems to us hard, but Gustavus, though he was fond of his wife, and liked, says Chanut, to see her well dressed, considered her unfit to hold any position in State affairs, and we must suppose he had good reasons for his actions. This was not at all to the taste of the queen; we shall have occasion to recur to the troubles which arose out of her antipathy to the Regency further on. It is worth while to notice that Christina says herself, she could justify her father in this matter if she chose, though she has not done so.

The care of Gustavus for his daughter did not stop here—he chose further for her two governors and a tutor to superintend her education. "He was as fortunate in his choice," says Christina, "as he could be, restricted as he was to men of Swedish nationality." This caution he thought necessary, it is said, because it had been predicted to him that Christina would not die in the faith of her fathers, and he wished to guard against this by his choice of men who were least likely to lead her astray. Whether this was so or not, her governors and tutors were Swedes. The first was Axel Baner, senator and grand master of the Royal House, a clever courtier, a man of the world, and very dear to the king. He was brother to the celebrated Baner who did so much to retrieve the fortune of the Swedes after the king's death. Under Charles IX., who was hostile to the nobility, his father lost his life on the scaffold. Gustavus had reconciled the family to himself, and, as the event showed, it was well for Sweden in her hour of need that he did so. Axel Baner was good at all physical exercises, but very ignorant, knowing no language but his own; much given in his youth to wine and women, and headstrong and violent in character; he seems never accordingly to have been a favourite of Christina's, though she calls him a very honest man. He died in 1639.

As additional governor the king chose Gustav Horn, also a senator; a man of great culture, who knew all the foreign languages, which he spoke well; had travelled in France, Spain, and Italy, was versed in diplomatic affairs, and the manners of foreign countries, and bore a high character. But more important than either of these for Christina's education was her tutor John Matthiæ, Doctor in Theology, previously Professor of Poetry in the University of Upsala, then Rector of the College at Stockholm, and chaplain to the king; a man whose varied culture and wide and tolerant spirit formed a striking exception to his class and time. His admirable character, kindly without being weak, acquired a great and lasting influence over Christina. In spite of her change of religion, she always retained her old

C

veneration for him ; she made him later Bishop of Strengnäs. His favourite scheme of a general reconciliation in religion, and the consequent suspicion that he had a leaning to Calvinism— the worst of crimes in the eyes of the Swedes of that age—brought him, after her abdication, into disfavour with the bigoted ecclesiastics who ruled the country, and he had to resign his bishopric.

Leaving the government in the hands of the senate, the king embarked on the 30th May, 1630.

There are still preserved two letters written by Christina to her father in Germany some time during the next three years, which are worthy of notice as being the earliest letters we have from her pen. The style, and the fact that Gustavus had strictly enjoined her tutors to let her write her letters alone, declare them to be her own composition. They are interesting, further, as showing that she was already acquainted with German. Here is the second :—

" MOST GRACIOUS AND BELOVED FATHER,—As I have not the good fortune of being with Your Majesty, I send Your Majesty my portrait. Will Your Majesty please to think of me by it, and come back to me soon, and send me meanwhile something pretty ? I will always be good and learn to pray diligently. I am quite well, praise

God. May He send us always good news of Your Majesty. I commend you to Him always, and remain,

"Your Majesty's dutiful daughter,
"CHRISTINA."

And the king on his side, in the midst of his affairs, did not forget his family. In 1630 he writes to Oxenstiern : "Though the cause be good and just, the event of war is nevertheless uncertain by reason of sin. We cannot count on the life of man . . . . If anything happens to me, my family are worthy of compassion on my own account as well as for other reasons. They are but of the weaker sex—the mother, without capacity; my daughter, a young and helpless girl; unfortunate if they govern themselves, in danger if others govern them. Love and natural affection cause me to write these lines to you, an instrument God has given me, not only to aid me in great affairs but also to guard them against all misfortunes that might happen to me, and all that I hold most dear in this world."

A sentiment akin to the old Greek notion, that "the divinity is jealous," and is wont to visit too great prosperity with its wrath, seems to have haunted Gustavus in his last years. "On his return to Saxony in 1632, shortly before Lutzen, the people received him with such

c 2

extraordinary acclamations, that he said to his
chaplain : "I fear lest God should punish me for
the madness of the people. Would not one think
these people look on me as their divinity ? He
who is named the jealous God might well bring
it home to them that I am but a weak mortal." ·

His presentiment did not deceive him. On
November 6th, 1632, was fought the fatal battle
of Lutzen, and "the Lion of the North, the
bulwark of the Protestant faith," was found dead
on the field; though he died, as his daughter
said, in the arms of victory.

The death of Gustavus caused a profound
sensation throughout Europe. By the Imperialist party it was received with manifestations
of joy : at Rome, Brussels, Vienna, and Madrid
it was celebrated with rejoicings that lasted
for days; even in Paris people could hardly
restrain their satisfaction at being delivered
from a too powerful ally. "This Goth," said
Louis XIII., after Leipsic, "must be arrested in
his career." At the moment when the balance
Richelieu schemed for seemed to be on the
point of disappearing in the · might of a great
Northern Empire, Fortune played into his
hands.

It was very different with the Protestant party.
The death of their champion dashed their hopes

to the ground.   On the Swedes the news fell like a thunderclap.  " First came tidings," says Count Peter Brahé, " that the battle had had a prosperous issue.  The next day after, which was the 8th of December, at half-past nine in the forenoon, word was sent me that I should come into the treasury chamber.  When I entered, I saw all the councillors mightily troubled, some wiping their eyes, others wringing their hands.  The Palsgrave came to me at the door lamenting. My heart misgave me, and I knew not what to fear, till I heard to my sore grief what had occurred.  Both strangers and countrymen were in great woe and perturbation, despaired of the public welfare, and deemed that all would go to wreck and ruin.  We of the council, as many as were here present, agreed to a well-considered resolution before we parted—to live and die with one another, in defence and for the weal of our Fatherland ; and not only here at home to uphold our cause with all our power and in unity, but also to finish the war against the emperor and all his party, according to the design of the king of happy memory ; and for a secure peace."

It was a moment analogous to that when the news of the disaster at Syracuse came to Athens. Like the Athenians, the Swedes did not despair. They forgot their internal differences in the face of the common danger.  Above all it was necessary

to determine the succession. King Ladislaus, who
had succeeded his father Sigismund on the throne
of Poland, thought that now or never was his
chance of regaining the Swedish throne. "The
partisans of Sigismund said openly, in various
parts of Sweden, that his children showed more
inclination for the Protestant religion than that
of Popery, in which they had been brought up;
and that should one of them in good faith embrace
the confession of Augsburg, there was nothing to
hinder him from regaining his rights on the
crown." It was further to be feared that at any
moment the old enemy, Denmark, might discover,
that Sweden's weakness was her own opportunity.

It was a dangerous moment for the monarchy.
Christina asserts in her Memoirs, and the fact is
by no means improbable, that 'it was debated in
certain circles whether it would not be well to set
aside the infant heir, and establish a Republic.
It is certain, however, that such a course was impossible; the lower orders and the army would
have insisted on the queen's rights. It was accordingly determined for the security of the State
immediately to proclaim the queen as heir; John
Casimir led the way in giving the young queen
his support, and the nobles followed his example.
In the beginning of 1633 the Estates convened at
Stockholm declared that, in conformity with the
decrees of the Diet in 1604 at Norköping, and at

Stockholm in 1627, Christina, daughter of the late King Gustavus, called the Great, should be Queen-elect, and hereditary princess of Sweden —with the reservation, however, that when she came of age, she should confirm all the rights, liberties, and privileges granted by former kings.

Hereupon there occurred an amusing incident. When the Marshal of the Diet proposed it to the Estates, a member of the Order of Peasants, named Laurent or Larsson, interrupted him, asking, " Who is this daughter of Gustavus ? we do not know her, and have never seen her."

The Commonalty all began to murmur, and the Marshal answered, " I'll show her to you—if you will." And thereupon he went to fetch Christina, brought her into the assembled Estates and showed her to the Peasants, especially to the said Larsson. He, after having looked at her and considered her closely, cried, " 'Tis herself—'tis the very eyes, nose, and forehead of Gustavus, let her be our queen." Accordingly she was proclaimed by the Estates Queen of Sweden, and placed upon the throne.

Leaving the form of government to be settled in accordance with the advice of the Chancellor, Oxenstiern, who was absent in Germany, it was determined that the five highest officers of the State should be Regents during the queen's minority ; the war in Germany was to be carried

on with all possible assistance of means and
forces; while the exclusion of Sigismund and his
house from the throne of Sweden was reinforced.

"The problem presented to Gustavus Adolphus
had been to reconcile finally to the hereditary
monarchy as soon as possible that nobility which
his father had oppressed.    To their power he
opposed that of an official class dependent on the
sovereign.    The FORM OF GOVERNMENT of 1634
in this respect merely develops the fundamental
principles laid down by his administration.    That
this official class rose to be a new aristocracy was
occasioned by circumstances inevitable to a
government of guardians."

This remarkable document is said to be the
earliest known example of a written constitution.
Its main provisions are as follows : After requir-
ing the king and his subjects to profess the
Lutheran faith, and the confession of Augsburg,
and directing that the succession shall be regu-
lated conformably to the hereditary settlement of
1544, it enacts that the king shall govern with
full powers, but according to law; assisted by a
senate of twenty-five members chosen by him
from the nobility, including the five great officers
of the State, who were to be *ex officio* members—
namely, the High Steward, the High Marshal,
the High Admiral, the Lord Treasurer, and the

Lord Chancellor, the heads respectively of the five Colleges or Departments, of Justice, War, Admiralty, Exchequer, and Foreign Affairs. In the absence, illness, or minority of the king, the whole administration was to be in their hands. For judicial purposes there were hereby constituted four Palace Courts; in addition to the principal Court of Justice, at Stockholm, presided over by the High Steward, assisted by four councillors of State, and twelve others, of whom half were to be noble, there were provided " by reason of the size of the kingdom," three other courts, at Jonköping for Gothland, Åbo for Finland, Dorpat for the Transbaltic lands, each presided over by a member of the council with twelve assistants, half noble. In cases where, by reason of the nature of the matter or rank of the parties, the ordinary courts did not suffice, a special supreme court was to be constituted of the whole of these courts, together with the Senate and one burgomaster from each of the towns of Stockholm, Upsala, Gottenburgh, Norköping, Åbo, and Wiborg. To each of the four other colleges was assigned a certain number of assistants, chosen principally from the nobility. All five were to sit, except in special circumstances, at Stockholm. The Treasury alone had the power of disposing of any public funds.

The country was further divided for judicial

purposes into fourteen "assizes," and for administrative purposes into twenty-four "districts,"
under as many prefects; the town of Stockholm
retained its own jurisdiction under its own town
reeve. Special regulations are laid down touching
the tenure of each particular office. All public
functionaries, in every department, are to render
account once a year at specified times to the
particular college to which they belong; at
which yearly conventions exact account is to be
taken of the whole state of the realm. In the
absence, illness, or minority of the king, all new
laws made, privileges, liberties, patents of
nobility, &c., conferred, crown dues or taxed
estates alienated or discharged, are legally null
and void, unless they receive subsequent ratification by him.

From this outline of the main features of the
form of government, it will be seen that the
whole power of the State is placed in the hands
of the nobility. Although there is little reason
to doubt that the general idea received the
approbation of Gustavus Adolphus before his
death, yet the filling in of the details may be
confidently ascribed to Oxenstiern. It was at
the time feared by some, that under the pretext
of relieving him of business, this was but a scheme
to reduce the sovereign to the position of a
Venetian doge, and not without reason; for such a

result was more than probable, even with a king
of strong character ; how much more was it likely
to be the case with a mere girl ?  When accordingly we observe that the social power of
the nobles, not less than their political power,
increased greatly during her minority, it will
impress us as no slight proof of her commanding
intellect and force of character, that she could
acquire so speedy and so absolute a sway over
the Senate on taking the reins of government
at eighteen.

The five great officers of State, who were also
the guardians of the young queen, were : Baron
Gabriel Oxenstiern, younger brother of the
Chancellor, High Steward; "a very honest
man," says Christina; popular with the people
and the nobility, but of no special ability :
Baron Gyldenheim, High Admiral, a natural
son of the late king, a true Swede, "cast in the
antique mould ; " his powers had been sorely
tried by a captivity of twelve years in Poland ;
"he loved me," she writes, "as if I had been his
own child : " the Treasurer, Gabriel Oxenstiern,
cousin of the Chancellor, "a worthy man, with
abilities equal to his position " (as we have seen,
the Regents removed John Casimir from this
post, in spite of his excellent fulfilment of his
duties, because they suspected his Calvinism, and
feared he might entertain designs on the throne) :

Count Jacob de la Gardie, High Marshal, originally
of French extraction, a man whose merit had
raised him to the honours he enjoyed; his family
will come before us again; and last, Axel Oxenstiern, Chancellor, the chief man in Sweden,
and one of the first statesmen in Europe.

He will play a large part in Christina's life;
we must pause to describe him. No one knew
him better than Christina herself, and she has
left us her own estimate of him. "He had
studied much during his youth, and continued
to do so in the midst of business; his capacity
and knowledge of the world's affairs and interests
were very great; he knew the strong and weak
points of every State in Europe. His assiduity
and attention to business were indefatigable;
when he took relaxation, he found it in working.
He has often told me that when he went to rest,
he stripped off his cares with his clothes. He
was ambitious, but faithful and incorruptible,
withal a little too slow and phlegmatic,"—so
much so, indeed, that, as he said himself, the
manifold cares of State never spoiled his night's
rest, except on two occasions, the death of
Gustavus and the disaster of Nordlingen.

A very close observer has painted him for us—
Cromwell's ambassador, Whitelocke. "He was
a tall, proper, straight, handsome old man, of the
age of seventy-one years; his habit was black

cloth, a close coat lined with fur, a velvet cap on his head furred, and no hat; a cloak; his hair grey, his beard broad and long, his countenance sober and fixed, and his carriage grave and civil. He spoke Latin, plain and fluent and significant, and though he could, yet would not speak French, saying he knew no reason why that nation should be so much honoured more than others as to have their language used by strangers. In his conferences he would often mix pleasant stories with his serious discourses, and take delight in recounting former passages of his life, and actions of his king; and would be very large in excusing his *senilis garrulitas.*"

He began his career under Charles IX., abandoning theology for politics; he had been the right hand of Gustavus Adolphus all through his life; we are still to see his government during the Regency, and what befell him during Christina's own reign, which he outlived. Thus his whole life was bound up with the house of Vasa. Although it is as a Foreign Minister he is chiefly known, yet Axel Oxenstiern was not only a diplomatist, but a statesman: especially were his ideas on trade in advance of his time. In a memorial addressed to the senate on the affairs of Sweden in 1633, he says, speaking of certain regulations made by Gustavus Adolphus, "Although at the time there were grounds for them, it is

now clear and manifest that trade, which ever
loves freedom, suffered under them : since the
towns do not increase by one, two, or three
persons only having liberty of dealing and traffic,
but their growth comes from multiplication of
inhabitants, and in their concourse, whence all
the burgesses of a town derive advantages ; therefore the greatest part of the corporate bodies
and their rigorous laws, especially the needless
cost, should be abolished. Generally it were
advisable to open Stockholm also, at a convenient
season of the year, both to inlanders and out-
landers . . . and although some hucksters should
set themselves against it, and it should have the
appearance of impairing by free trade the maintenance of the burgesses, yet he who observes
the matter with intelligence and without bias,
and considers the welfare of the whole, will find
that our inland wares will thereby only be more
in request."

Such was the minister to whom it fell to deal
with this difficult crisis ; the situation in Germany was one which demanded all his energies
and his utmost skill. The death of Gustavus
had resolved the Protestant party into a chaotic
confusion. Judicious people were of opinion that
" the union of Sweden and the allies would soon
go out in smoke." Oxenstiern foresaw that the
internal discord was far more likely to be fatal to

their plans than all the efforts of their enemies, though the King of Spain was raising new levies in Italy, and had obtained from the Pope permission to make use for the war of the tithes in his country. That obedience which all had been willing to yield to Gustavus Adolphus would, he foresaw, not be continued to himself. The various Powers were united only in their distrust and hatred of Sweden. "They hate us," he wrote, at a later time, "for the very thing that ought to make them love us,—they cannot do without us." With the short-sighted policy which has distinguished German potentates in every age, the Northern Princes were unwilling to continue a war of which they were thoroughly weary to benefit a foreign Power. Moreover, although Austria was their enemy, they distrusted equally the overbalancing power of Sweden. " I fear there are some of them," wrote the Chancellor, " who have their eyes turned to the Emperor. They are entirely ignorant how to adapt their steps to these dangerous times," "they nourish vain hopes ; long?orations, and reasons for doubting, with many ceremonies, are not wanting." Elsewhere he speaks contemptuously of "princes with their heads full of ancestors, and fancies many hundred years old."

The Elector of Saxony, unmindful of all that Sweden had done for him (he actually spoke of

the heroic efforts of Gustavus to free Germany as
" the troubles which arose in the year 1630 "),
and furiously angry to see a simple foreign
gentleman like Oxenstiern taking the direction
of affairs—a position which he thought ought to
belong to himself—not only refused to act with
him, but even did his best to render all his
efforts towards a firm consolidation nugatory.
The Elector of Brandenburg was little better :
Oxenstiern in vain endeavoured to rouse him by
the prospect of a marriage between Christina and
his son Frederic William : he contented himself
with expressing his great and permanent affection for Sweden.  The Princes of Lower Saxony
indulged in pleasing dreams of neutrality.  In
spite of all these obstacles, however, Oxenstiern
concluded, on March 8th, 1633, a treaty with the
four Upper or Southern Circles, at Heilbronn :  by
which they agreed to carry on the war under the
lead of Sweden ; the direction of affairs was to be
entrusted to Oxenstiern, aided by a council of
six ; no separate treaty was to be concluded by
any one of the allies.  The French court seized
the opportunity to try and enter this alliance ;
its minister Feuquières, who had been instructed
to conciliate the Chancellor, made various overtures to him, assured him of the favour and
assistance of the king, his master, in any schemes
for his own private advantage, and even offered

to negotiate a marriage between Christina and his son Eric; (this report contributed not a little at a later time to the dislike of Christina towards the party of Oxenstiern). The Chancellor, however, who knew Richelieu, and suspected, under these insidious proposals, his design of making a catspaw of Sweden to gain his own ends, declined; he contented himself with a renewal of the previous alliance between France and the late king.

Into the details of the war we can only enter in so far as they are subsidiary to politics. After Lutzen, confusion reigned in the Swedish army. Deprived of its leader, it lost also its unity, and the enthusiastic spirit which had placed it so far above the mercenary bands of the great military juggler, Wallenstein. Duke Bernard of Weimar, who had been mainly instrumental in gaining the victory of Lutzen after the death of the king, now claimed the lead. Mutiny arose, instigated, Christina asserts, by Bernard himself. The colonels drew up their complaints in writing, and refused to serve unless their claims were granted. Oxenstiern had to grant letters of investiture to German lands and estates amounting, together with money, to the value of 4,900,000 rix dollars. The Duke himself received the Duchy of Franconia, and the two bishoprics of Bamberg and Wurzburg, though

D

the title which he coveted of Generalissimo of the Forces was sternly denied him, and given to Horn.

All this soon found its natural result in the disaster of Nordlingen, September 6th, 1634; the Swedes were defeated with the loss of 6000 men, and Horn taken prisoner. The consequences were well nigh fatal; Oxenstiern passed his second sleepless night, and even began to doubt whether Sweden had not taken upon itself too heavy a burden; Saxony speedily concluded a separate peace, at Prague (by which the Elector gained Lusatia); to this peace almost all the Protestant States, except the noble little Hesse, came over. The Swedish Government was terribly disheartened; the truce with Poland was drawing near its term, and apprehensions were entertained from the quarter of Denmark. The finances of the State were in a desperate condition. The clergy stubbornly refused to be taxed, though the nobles were more patriotic; the country was exhausted by the length of the war and the hard times. King Ladislaus began to make the most extravagant demands; he styled himself King of Sweden, completely ignoring Christina; Charles I. even promised him assistance should he proceed to arms. Under all these circumstances, a truce was concluded with Poland at Stumsdorf for twenty-six years, at the sacrifice of Prussia, on September 2, 1635. It went to the heart of the Chancellor to see all that his master had gained, at so great a cost, the result of years of warfare, annihilated by a stroke of the pen.

The league of Heilbronn now " threw itself into the arms " of France ; Bernard of Weimar bound himself to French interests, hoping thereby to promote his own. The opportunity was one for which Richelieu had been waiting ; without delay he sought to use it in gaining the provinces on the Rhine. Oxenstiern met the Cardinal at Compiègne, and arranged a treaty in April, 1635, by which the French were to have Alsace, and ſubsidize the Swedes.

This marked, however, the lowest point which the Swedish misfortunes were to reach. Irritated by the arrogant pretensions of the King of Poland, and the selfishness of the Elector of Saxony, the Swedes decided, in the Diet of 1635, to have nothing to do with the peace of Prague ; their renewed resolution, led by the genius of John Baner, once more regained them their lost reputation. Banèr had been named by Gustavus Adolphus as the man most capable of supplying his place, should anything befall himself ; but till the present moment he had been laid up by a wound received at Nuremberg. He now came forward to prove that he resembled Gustavus not merely in personal appearance. After quelling with prompt energy a mutiny at Magdeburg, he overran Saxony, giving the country of the perfidious Elector to the flames; and gave the decisive turn to his operations by completely defeating the allied Saxon and Imperial forces at Wittstock (September, 1636). By this victory the moral effects of Nordlingen were effaced.

# CHAPTER II.

In July, 1633, the widowed queen returned to Stockholm with the body of Gustavus. It was her nature to rush into extremes, and she showed her grief for his loss to an excessive degree. She had his heart enclosed in a gold box, which she kept by her bedside, and visited every day with mourning and lamentation. Though the bigotry of the Senate and the clergy afterwards compelled her to place this box in his coffin with his body, she found other ways of commemorating his death; she instituted an Order, with a badge in the shape of a heart, on which was engraven a coffin with the letters G. A. R. S. (*Gustavus Adolphus Rex Succiæ*), and a Latin motto, to this effect, " In death I conquer."

New complications between her and the Regents soon ensued. As has been related, Gustavus Adolphus had left particular directions that the queen-mother was not to have any part in the education or up-bringing of her daughter. But whenever the Regents tried to approach the subject, Maria Eleanora burst into such a storm of sobbing and crying, that they had to abandon

the attempt. They accordingly determined to
wait till the Chancellor returned from Germany.
He did so in 1636, and it was then decided,
though not without considerable discussion, to
remove Christina from her superintendence, and
entrust her to the Princess Catharine, her aunt.
This may seem harsh on the part of the Regents,
yet it would certainly have been a bad thing for
Christina to have remained with her mother.
The gloomy effect of her room, hung with black
from ceiling to floor, into which no light was ever
allowed to penetrate; the wax tapers always
burning, and the unceasing wailings of the
queen began to work seriously on Christina's
spirits; not that there was now any want of
affection for her; on the contrary, the death of
Gustavus had changed her mother's aversion into
immoderate affection. "By dint of loving me
she drove me to despair," writes Christina;
"she said I was the living image of my father,
and would never let me out of her sight;"
hardly would she let her go on with her
studies, and more than this, "she began to find
fault with the education I had hitherto received,
and had several quarrels with the Regents on
that point." Though they might have over-
looked much else, the Regents felt this was
going too far; and accordingly in 1636 Christina
was removed from the charge of her mother.

This last and worst affront brought the quarrel between Maria Eleanora and the Regents to a climax : at all times hostile to the Swedes, whom she abhorred, and especially to the Regents, whom she was perpetually bothering for money, at a time when the financial condition of the State made such appeals particularly obnoxious, she now openly broke with them and retired to Gripsholm in Sudermania in disgust. We shall see further on how her conduct was the immediate occasion of the war with Denmark. Christina returned to the house of Princess Catharine, with whom she remained till her death in 1639.

The important matter of the education of their young queen was considered by the nobles and clergy in a document drawn up in the diet of 1635. In this they recommend that, in view of the fact that she is one day to reign over them, she shall be brought up in a careful understanding of the reciprocal duties and relations between herself and her subjects; that she shall be instructed in the manners and customs of other nations, but more particularly those of Sweden ; to this end great care is to be used in the selection of her tutors, who are to pay special attention to the formation of her character and morals ; above all she is to be well grounded in the articles of her faith and the Christian virtues ;

the art of government, and, as the groundwork thereof, history, especially that of the Bible, are to be carefully studied, as well as foreign languages, mathematics, and other branches of learning; great caution is to be used that she be not imbued by the reading of improper books, or the hearing of improper conversation, with the opposite errors of Popery or Calvinism.

Her tutors have already been described; they began her education as soon as they were appointed in 1631, with the exception of Matthiæ, who was away till 1633.

There is still preserved a little statement written by her in Latin when she was ten, and entitled "Obligatory Letter." It runs as follows :—

"We, the undersigned, promise and bind ourselves by this one bond that in future we will speak Latin with our tutor. We promised before, but did not keep our promise. Henceforth, with God's help, we will do what we promise. Next Monday, God willing, we will begin this our task. For future certainty we have written this letter with our own hand and signed it.

"CHRISTINA.

"Given at Stockholm, October 28, 1636."

The king had enjoined them to give her the

education of a man. "He declared very positively he would not have them instil any
feminine sentiments into me, except those of
honour and virtue; in all other respects he
would have me a prince, and instructed in all
that a young prince ought to know: in this my
inclinations marvellously seconded his designs,
for I had an invincible antipathy to all that
women do or say. I was utterly unable to learn
their handiwork : never could any one teach me
anything of it. To make up for this I learned
with marvellous facility all the tongues, sciences,
and exercises they would teach me. These I
knew at fourteen; since which time I have
learned many others without a master; certain it
is I never had a master either for German, French,
Italian, Spanish, or my own native Swedish. It
was the same with physical exercises. I learned
to dance and ride ; I know, besides, however, all
other exercises, and can use arms well enough,
though I was never taught their manage-
ment. . . . I was further indefatigable. I often
lay without grumbling on the hard ground. I
ate little, and slept less. I went often two or
three days without drinking, as they would not
give me water, and I had an invincible repugnance to beer or wine. My mother whipped me
one day when she caught me secretly drinking
the dew water in which she used to wash her

face: as to eating, all was indifferent to me, except ham or pork, which I could never touch. I could endure heat and cold, walk long distances on foot, ride without getting tired; the life I led was extraordinary, but, though they did what they could to prevent it, they had to let me have my own way. I was passionately fond of study, but no less of hunting, running, or sport. I loved dogs and horses, yet all this never drew me away from my studies for a moment; the men and women who attended me were tired out. I gave them no rest, night or day; if they attempted to turn me from so wearisome a method of life, I would say, ' Away ! go and sleep, I have no use for you.' Though I loved hunting, I was not cruel; I never killed an animal without feeling pity for it."

With Matthiæ, her tutor, she applied herself eagerly to her studies; she read with him Justinus, Livy, Curtius, Sallust, Terence ; and combined the study of languages with a special attention to the political and moral lessons conveyed. A very rapid advance in learning was not attended in her case with any want of judgment, for which two instances may suffice. We have a quantity of letters written by her at this time in Latin. In 1639, referring to the eagerness which the various parties showed in Germany to gain possession of Brisach, left ownerless by the death of Bernard of Weimar, she writes to her uncle :—

" MOST SERENE AND ILLUSTRIOUS PRINCE, AND DEAR COUSIN,—I received from your lovingness two letters yesterday, to which I think it worth while to send an answer. I understand from ordinary letters that the Count Palatine is to take Weimar's army (an excellent plan). Mr. Treasurer wrote to me yesterday, and told me amongst other things this—in a word, that Brisach has many lovers. Kings and princes are quite mad for love of her ; the King of England wants her to be set aside not for himself, but his nephews the late Frederic's sons, and to that end has handed over large sums to the officers of Weimar's army. The French king is promising them likewise mountains of gold, provided they give him Brisach, who like a bride has lured them all on to love her, so that it is doubtful which of all these rival princes will enjoy the nuptial couch. I couldn't refrain from letting your lovingness know this, to let you see how fond they all are of that city."

A strange letter from a girl of thirteen !

In another she tells him in a postscript : " Mistress Beata Oxenstiern and her daughter have just arrived, *quo plures, eo pejus.*"

She spent six hours in the morning and six in

the evening at her studies, taking holidays on
Saturdays and festivals.  With this application
it is no wonder she made progress.  From time
to time two senators examined her.  Before she
was eighteen she could read Thucydides, Poly-
bius,* and Tacitus with ease in Latin.  After the
Chancellor returned from Germany he used to
pass three or four hours every day with her,
instructing her " in her duty."  " 'Twas from
him that I learned whatever I know of the art
of government.  I took extreme pleasure in
listening to him ; there was not a study, game, or
diversion of any kind I would not gladly quit to
come to him.  He on his part took great pleasure
in instructing me, and if I may say so, this great
man had often occasion to wonder at the talents
and capacity of such a child as me."

Under such conditions as these, the precocious
intellect of Christina, " a tender plant in a
moral hothouse," speedily developed.  Gradually
as the Regents began to discern her astonishing
aptitude and predisposition for politics, they
admitted her to a closer familiarity with State
affairs.  In May, 1643, Oxenstiern introduced her
to the Senate with a speech ; since then she
attended regularly at all its meetings, and

* She did not read Greek at this time, though it is often
stated in her biographies that she did : she learned it later,
when she knew Vossius.

immediately showed, girl as she was, that in administrative capacity she was inferior to none of them, not even the veteran Chancellor him-self; that she was moreover fully conscious of her own powers, and determined to be Queen not only in name but in fact. Circumstances soon afforded her an opportunity of proving her tact and independent judgment.

These are well illustrated in two letters she wrote to her uncle the Prince Palatine, in 1641, when she was fifteen, expressing her concern for the death of Baner. In the first she says:—

"I cannot keep your lovingness in igno-rance of the sad news lately arrived, that Baner is dangerously ill, and in all human probability will die . . . . People here don't bother much about it; they suppose they can easily get somebody else, but such men are not shaken out of one's sleeve. If Baner dies, all will go ill there. Salvius is eager for peace, but that is not what the C—— has at heart."

And again, a few days afterwards, she writes that the King of Denmark has sent a ship to fetch her mother away, though the news is not quite certain; the officers of the army have written for a sum of money, which unless they get, they will take their departure; demanding in addi-tion that the general appointed in place of Baner shall not, like him, take his own counsel, but command according to the advice of all; she hears that the French are trying to debauch the Swedish army, "a thing easy enough."

In order to explain the allusions in these letters it is necessary to take up the history of the war in Germany which we left at the victory of Wittstock. In the interval, Baner's genius had regained for Sweden all the prestige lost at Nordlingen, and established his claim to be considered one of the first generals of the age. We have seen the allusions of Christina to the struggle for Brisach; this place, reputed impregnable, had been seized by Bernard of Weimar, entirely to the satisfaction of France, in whose interests he was acting. It was the design of the Duke to establish himself as an independent chief in Germany, after the fashion of Wallenstein; he had even began to negotiate his marriage with the Princess of Hesse, the celebrated Amalia Elizabeth, when he suddenly died, in 1639. This left the Imperialist forces opposed to him free to join those engaged with Baner; and France seized the opportunity to gain possession of Brisach, and take Bernard's army into her pay.

The difficulty Baner found in conducting a campaign with vastly inferior forces was increased by the want of money and his own ill health. Owing to the state of the finances, Oxenstiern had to write to him that the war must pay itself;

nor could the Government listen to his repeated demands for furlough. "Baner on a sick-bed is worth more than any other man on horseback;" "Sweden requires John Baner's services, and John Baner must serve." We cannot enter into the details of his operations, but at his death, in 1641, Christina's forebodings only proved too well grounded. Just as after Lutzen, so after the death of the "second Gustavus" at Halberstadt, the Swedish cause seemed falling to pieces; mutiny again arose in the army; the officers refused to obey a Swedish general any longer, and sent home a deputation with their demands; some even began to treat with the enemy. The distress was terrible; troopers and soldiers bartered their horses and accoutrements for provisions. The desperate condition of affairs is well shown in an extract from a letter written by General Wrangel to his son : "Mind that ye lay hands upon somewhat, as the rest do; he that takes it has it."

It seemed, indeed, as if at this moment nothing could save the cause. But it was the fortune of Sweden to possess in this hour of need yet another general trained in the school of Gustavus Adolphus; she found in Leonard Torstenson a man worthy to redeem the loss of Baner; "his equal in genius, his superior in energy : mastering by the greatness of his soul a body wasted by captivity and disease." The extraordinary pace at which he flew about from place to place, even when unable from sickness to mount a horse, gained him among the soldiers the nickname of "Blixten," "the Lightning." Arriving from Sweden in the autumn with fresh troops and money, he infused a new spirit into the army, and, though so ill that at times he had, to be carried in a litter, succeeded in closing a brilliant campaign with the decisive victory of Leipzic (October 23, 1642).

By a series of complications now to be related, the war was transferred to a new scene.

Since her exclusion from all share in the government or education of Christina, Maria Eleanora had continued to reside at her castle of Gripsholm, on the Lake Malar, in Sudermania. For some time she had been secretly negotiating with Denmark to make her escape from the country. All preparations being at length completed, she prepared to carry her design into execution on July 29, 1640. Dismissing her attendants on pretence of keeping a fast, she descended in the night into her garden, crossed the lake, and posted to Norkoping; thence being transported in a Danish ship to the isle of Gothland, she found two Danish men-of-war waiting to receive her, in one of which she was conveyed to Denmark, and proceeded subsequently to her native country, Brandenburg.

It seems impossible to discern how far the queen-mother or the Swedes were to blame for the hatred they entertained for one another; she was certainly harshly treated, and it has even been hinted that the Chancellor was instrumental in compelling her to fly from Sweden; it has further been asserted, with little probability, that the ancient King of Denmark had motives of a very tender character to induce him to lend her aid. In any case, her flight to the country, and by the aid, of their hereditary enemy, roused very sore feelings in the Swedish people. Though her flight has been most erroneously termed the cause of the war which followed, it was certainly one of the primary occasions of it. The cause lay deeper. The jealous national hatred of Denmark had recently been violently excited, not only by the action of that country with respect to the Sound dues, which Christian IV., in 1639, when the Swedish prestige was low, had raised, but also by the attempts of that monarch to constitute Denmark a mediator in the peace negotiations, behind which pretext he was suspected of concealing dangerous machinations. On the bad feeling thus created the circumstances of the Queen-mother's flight fell like a spark. Sharp recriminations passed on both sides; but a war with Denmark now appearing inevitable, and being moreover thoroughly

E

popular, and the Dutch further urging Sweden
to fight, the Regents determined to forestall the
enemy in commencing hostilities.  Accordingly,
without any distinct declaration of war, secret
orders were sent to Torstenson to invade Holstein;
(these were to be disavowed by the Government
should any accommodation be arrived at in the
meantime).

In 1643, Torstenson, after succeeding in throwing Gallas off his guard by feigned proposals for
an armistice, hastily burst into Holstein, defeated
the Danes at Kolding, occupied Jutland up to
the Skaw, and threatened Fyen; at the same
time Horn entered Scania with twenty thousand
men, and made himself master of Helsingborg,
Lund, Christianstad, and the isle of Bornholm.

On the sea, however, fortune was not at first
on the side of the Swedes ;  De Geer's thirty ships,
manned by Dutch volunteers, were unsuccessful
against the Danes, commanded by Christian
himself.  In the great sea fight next year, on
July 6, which was four times renewed, both sides
claimed the victory : the old king of sixty-eight
years fought like Hector, and was badly wounded,
as well as having his eye knocked out.  On the
Swedish side, the High Admiral Klas Flemming
was killed in his cabin, three weeks later, by a
spent ball.  But, in spite of his tremendous personal efforts, Christian was unsupported by his

factious aristocracy, and taken entirely unpre-
pared; his allies failed him; the attempts of
Gallas to create a diversion in his favour were
foiled by Torstenson. In the sea fight of October
13, 1644, the Swedes and Dutch combined obtained a decisive victory: their prestige was
moreover increased by the recent victory of Torstenson at Jankowitz, and the taking of Bremen
by Königsmarck. Denmark had no choice left :
Oxenstiern came to Bromsebro to negotiate a
peace, under the mediation of France, through its
ambassador, de la Thuillerie.

The Chancellor, whose diplomacy was always
more coloured with national prejudice than that of
a statesman ought to be, was personally inclined
to press hard terms upon the vanquished; he
bore a grudge against the Danes, and would have
been supported in this policy both by Senate and
people. But the young Queen thought very
differently. She felt esteem for the heroic old
King, and was unwilling to press a fallen enemy
too hard ; she foresaw, too, that fortune might at
any moment take a turn in Germany, and that
the other interested Powers might side with the
Danes, in their fear of Sweden gaining too great a
preponderance on the Baltic. She was unquestion-
ably right, and showed in this preliminary peace
how much more tact she possessed than the Chancellor, as she was to show it on a larger scale in

the peace of Westphalia. The letters which she wrote him at this moment will not easily be paralleled among those of statesmen of nineteen.

On April 12 she writes that she is well aware of the difficulties, and of the necessity of obtaining good guarantees; still the moment seems to have arrived for pushing things to their conclusion ; " we must be careful not to let slip the opportunity, and so leave posterity reason to complain. Perhaps it would be as well not to hasten the treaty too much, just at present, so as to be able to dispute over the guarantees, and so gain our ends." Oxenstiern on his part was in no degree inclined to let slip, by wax and paper, what had been won by arms. Christina writes again, on the 20th June, " I agree with you, we ought to demand Holland and Blekingen, and certainly insist on good security, without which we must not even think of peace ; but amongst other reasons, which have made me recommend you to descend some steps in your demands, this is not the least, that most of the Senate are of quite a different opinion from you or me. . . . Should the affair come off unsatisfactorily, people will say the whole thing was begun by certain unquiet heads, and continued by my own and certain other's ambition ; my youth will be subjected to this calumny, that it was not capable of taking good counsel, but that, transported with ambition of empire, it has led me into mistakes; my fate is such that if I do anything carefully and after ripe thought, others will reap the honour. Should, on the contrary, anything be neglected, which others should have looked to, the blame will be mine." She bewails the loss of time, but hopes for better progress when the fleet has arrived. On the 24th, however, she writes more decisively. . . . "I see further so many difficulties in carrying on the war, that I fear we shall have much trouble in attempting so great a task with means so small: and that it would be [leaving too much to chance to refuse the conditions offered. We must recollect that, in case peace should be broken off, every one at home or abroad will lay it to the charge of our unmeasured ambition, based on injustice, and with the sole object of empire. And as I don't rely too much on the co-operation of the Dutch, I fear lest, if the proposed conditions are not accepted, they may try to become arbitrators, so that their jealousy may cause them to attempt something untoward; not to mention what the Poles might do. In short, we must make it plain before God and all the world that we applied ourselves to all reasonable means for obtaining peace."

The peace was finally concluded on August 13, 1645. By it Sweden obtained complete freedom

from tolls on the Sound and the Belts; the
provinces of Jemteland and Hartjedale, with the
islands of Gothland and Œsel; Halland she was
to hold for thirty years, after which time she was
to keep it unless some equivalent territory
was given her in exchange: she also retained
Bremen, which had been taken by Königsmarck
from King Christian's son.

On his return, Christina rewarded Oxenstiern
by conferring on him the title of Count, then the
highest dignity in Sweden, and endowing him
with the territory of Sodermœre in Smaland.
The flattering speech which she addressed to him
in the senate added to his honour, inasmuch as
it not only awarded him high praise, but proved
by the admiration it extorted even from himself,
that the commendation came from one capable of
judging.

For the sake of continuity, the war with
Denmark has been related up to its close, in
1645: meanwhile Christina had come of age,
and assumed the direction of affairs. On her
eighteenth birthday,* December 8, 1644, the
Estates were convened at Stockholm. The ceremony took place in the Great Hall. Christina
sat on a silver throne, surrounded by the chief
men in the State. After promising to maintain

* Or perhaps the day before; the date is not certain.

the national religion, and the ceremonies of the
Church and the Senate, and to observe every
man's privileges and the Form of Government
agreed to by the Estates, she took the oath as *King*
of Sweden—being the first of her sex to sit on the
Swedish throne ; a precedent followed in 1719
in the case of Ulrica Eleanora. The Regents
presented an account of their administration,
wherein, after recounting the difficulties of their
position, they alluded among other matters to
the alienation of the Crown lands, as forced upon
them by the necessities of State. The nobles
also pressed her for a confirmation of their
various privileges and exemptions from taxation.
The Queen gave her assent and ratification to
all their demands. The full consideration of the
Form of Government, " seeing that by reason
of the many pressing embarrassments we have
not leisure to examine it accurately," was postponed till her coronation.

The internal affairs of Sweden were at this
moment in a very dangerous condition. The
minority of the Queen, and the eternal war, from
which only the nobles derived benefit, aided by
the aristocratical tendency of the constitution,
had placed all the power in their hands. They
used their privileges and all the means in their
power to grind down the lower orders with the
most oppressive exactions. The peasantry, on

their side, worn out by the taxes and conscriptions, and completely powerless, in a country
where land was still the chief source of wealth,
were ripe for revolution. The State was divided
into two hostile nations. Among the chief
causes of complaint against the Government was
the alienation of crown lands. The action of
Christina in giving her confirmation to all the
demands of the nobles, destroyed the last hope of
the democratic party, always ready to put their
faith in the king; serious disturbances were
at hand, had not the attention of the country
been diverted for the moment by the recent
victories to foreign politics. We shall go more
fully into the whole question further on: for the
present it is to be observed, that however ready
Christina might have been at the moment of
her accession to the throne to play the Patriot
Queen, it was morally impossible for her at
eighteen, surrounded by the members of the
oligarchy, among whom she had been brought up,
to have broken through educational trammels
and made enemies of all her friends by espousing
the cause of the people to the extent required.
But on the other hand, in the history of the
ten years that follow, up to her abdication in
1654—years marked by an extraordinary diligence and activity on her own part, and the most
striking contrast between the brilliant glitter of

the court and foreign relations, and the dull
background of domestic discontent—we shall find
that Christina showed in this exact respect the
one great want and blot on her character as a
statesman and lover of her country. Neither her
own character nor the necessary circumstances
allowed her to enact the part afterwards played
by Charles XI.

But if in this point of her domestic policy,
Christina, like many another great man, was to
seek, it is quite otherwise with her foreign policy,
for which she deserves a great deal more praise
than she has ever received. Nowhere has the
share she took in promoting the peace of Westphalia been adequately recognised. To this we
must now turn, postponing the consideration of
the domestic difficulties till the end of the war,
after which the internal troubles were free to
come to the front.

Relieved, by the peace of Bromsebro, from
obstacles in the quarter of Denmark, Sweden was
now able to devote all her energies to the final
settlement of the war in Germany, to which the
Danish war was related as a fragment to the whole.

For a time, indeed, it seemed as though the
negotiations for peace were to be as eternal as
the war itself, which was "pressing on the nations
involved in it with the weight of an inevitable
necessity." Years had been passed in fruitless

haggling over preliminaries, and when at length the congress was finally determined upon in 1641, other years flew by in sterile disputes about questions of precedence and futile formalities. At length, in 1644, it did actually assemble, the Gordian knot of the difficulties being cut by the arrangement that Sweden should send her plenipotentiaries to Osnaburgh, and France hers to Munster, preliminaries being carried on under the mediation of Venice and the Pope. But it was not till 1645, after the victorious campaigns of Torstenson and Condé, that there was any serious effort towards the actual furtherance of peace. That it was finally brought to a successful issue, when it was, is to a great extent due to the personal energy of Christina.

To this end she laboured with all her heart and soul. The reasons that determined her were many, both political and personal. She thoroughly understood the terrible evils of the most appalling war which has ever been waged, which is saying a great deal ; and longed with a large-hearted humanity to deliver Germany from the ghastly vampire that was draining her blood not slowly, but in gulps. She saw, moreover, how her own people were being ruined chiefly by the burdens and conscriptions necessarily entailed upon them, as well as by the increasing power of the nobles, who flourished by the national decay, were the only gainers by the war, and wished to continue it, on behalf of their country's glory and their own interests, at the expense of the State. Though she well foresaw the troubles that would at once start into dangerous promin- ence the moment peace was concluded, she did not shrink from them; moreover, at any moment Fortune might desert them again, as she had so often done in the course of the war, rich in instances of the see-saw of victory and defeat; then would all the advantages gained at the expense of so much blood and toil and treasure be lost. The troubles of the Fronde were looming on the horizon in France, and that cloud looked then more dangerous than it afterwards proved.

"Now or never," she exclaimed, " is the time." But to these motives were added others of a per- sonal nature. She longed to signalise her reign by other glories than those of war: visions of a brilliant and intellectual court in which she should move as the central luminary, dispenser of benefits, and patron of the arts and sciences, floated before her. She had only just mounted the throne, and fired by ambition and the con- sciousness of great abilities, longed to be supreme not only in title, but in fact. All this could only come to pass by putting an end to the war; for as long as it continued, the European fame of the Chancellor, to whom all the credit for whatever happened in Sweden would be ascribed, would throw her, young, and a woman, completely into the shade.

In order then to gain strength to work her will, Christina found it necessary to form a party to balance the influence of that of the Chancellor. The situation is sketched in the words of the French ambassador, Chanut: " All the ministers were so much on their guard that one could draw from them nothing but conjectures as to the present state of the Court, which was as it were divided; on one side the Queen, the house of the Constable de la Gardie, the Palatine Princes (*i.e.* Charles and Adolphus), and Marshal Torstenson; on the other the Chancellor Oxenstiern, Marshal Horn, General Wrangel, and all those of the Senate who looked upon the Princes and the Constable as strangers. This latter party was less disposed to peace than that of the Queen."

We have already had hints of Christina's growing distrust of the Chancellor; she now became more definitely antagonistic to him. This rested on various grounds. Not only, as stated above, did his established position stand in the way of her fame, but her sympathies and his were diametrically opposed. He belonged to the party of the nobles and the war; not that he was, like many of them, and the generals, definitely opposed to peace; but he was lukewarm in its cause. He had indeed a genuine love of his country, and its honour was his first consideration ; but just for this reason would his policy at this conjuncture have been fatal to Sweden.  Now in his old age he remained faithful to his traditions and the maxims of the old religious war era that was passing away, and found himself unable to remodel his views to suit the changing circumstances of the time.  It is impossible to say what might ultimately have become of Germany had the Swedish councils been dominated at this moment by the stubborn and unyielding patriotism of Oxenstiern.

He belonged to a vanishing system : Christina to the new.  In nothing was this difference more significant than in their attitude towards the French.  The Chancellor, true to his traditions, looked upon France with distrust, and for this there was some reason.  Up to the last years of the war, one main cause of the want of genuine success on the Protestant side had been the lack of hearty co-operation between the French and Swedish forces ; the French, directed by the calculating policy of Richelieu and Mazarin, never threw themselves heartily into the struggle till the appearance of Condé and Turenne.  Hence the Swedes regarded France with distrust, and this traditional attitude was now maintained by Oxenstiern.  Christina, on the contrary, was

strongly inclined to the French, both from policy
and personal motives. With a truer instinct
than the Chancellor, and the tact of a woman,
she perceived that to gain her ends it was
incumbent upon her to establish friendly
relations between the two Powers. She was
also drawn in that direction by her relations
with several members of her court. The French
resident in Sweden already mentioned, Pierre
Chanut, a man of very unique ability and sterling
worth, of whom more anon, had made a deep
impression upon her, and enjoyed her confidence
to a great extent. She had a great admiration
for Condé and Turenne, and wrote them letters on
more than one occasion, expressive of her regard.

In order to promote the best relations between .
France and Sweden at this conjuncture of affairs,
she determined to send as ambassador to the
French court the man whom she delighted to
honour, Count Magnus Gabriel de la Gardie.

The contrast between this man and his predecessor in France is typical of the old and new
style. The celebrated Grotius, author of the
' de Jure Belli et Pacis,' after escaping from his
imprisonment in his own country, had gone to
France, and enjoyed for some time a pension from
Cardinal Richelieu ; for some reason or other
this was suddenly withdrawn, and Grotius
retired to Hamburg. This became known to

Gustavus Adolphus, who admired Grotius immensely; one of his aphorisms was *unum esse Grotium;* he used to keep the '*de Jure Belli et Pacis*' under his pillow, though he was fond of saying that if Grotius was engaged in actual warfare, he would find that many of his fine theories would not admit of being carried into practice. He ordered Salvius, his minister at Hamburg, to engage Grotius in his service. The same year Gustavus died; but Oxenstiern here and elsewhere set himself to carry out his master's plan. He sent Grotius as ambassador to Paris: it is difficult to see why; though we need scarcely suppose it true, as is asserted, that he did so on purpose to pique Richelieu, who might certainly not care to see the man from whom he had withheld his pension return as ambassador. Whatever else he could do, Grotius was the last man to be an ambassador. From various stories told of him we can see that the stiff pride of the philosophical student, combined with his want of diplomacy, did not improve the relations between the two countries; and though the breach between the cardinal and himself was subsequently mended,* Grotius still remained unsuited for his post. After Richelieu's

---

* Grotius' epigram on Richelieu is well known: "*Christianos principes mutuis armis exercuit: aulam homuncionibus implevit: lusit Europam.*"

death he was delicately recalled in 1645, and well treated by Christina, who purchased his library when he died, and sent a kind letter of condolence to his widow. His successor, Cerisante, " a man fitter for the theatre than great affairs," left his post of his own accord. Christina determined to replace him by De la Gardie.

His father was Jacob de la Gardie (son of that *émigré* from Languedoc, who "formed Gustavus Adolphus for ten years in the wars of Denmark, Russia, and Poland"), who had risen step by step to be Count, Senator, Marshal, High Steward, and one of the Regents and Guardians of the Queen. His mother was the beautiful Ebba Brahé, who had refused to marry Gustavus himself, then desperately in love with her, because she detected him in a *liaison*. Count Magnus combined the beauty of his mother with his father's French vivacity. He had just returned from travelling abroad, among other places in France, where he had made a great impression, and now commended himself by his intelligence and courtly graces to the young Queen. She took him into favour, made him Captain of the Guards, with a handsome pension, betrothed him to Marie Euphrosyne, daughter of the Palsgrave, and, both on his own account and hers, selected him in 1646 as exactly the man to send as ambassador to France. The avowed object of his mission was merely complimentary; the secret object to establish friendly relations with the French.

The embassy was unusually splendid (it cost 100,000 rix dollars); three ships of war conveyed it to the French coast. Chanut wrote privately to say that the Count was likely to enjoy the Queen's favour to a greater extent than any one else; nothing could gratify her more than to give him a cordial reception. The hint was taken; on his arrival Count Magnus was fêted and caressed with balls, plays, and similar diversions; his character and brilliant suite, added to his glowing praise of Christina, created a great sensation, and the lively Parisians drew their own inferences. The gossip of Paris is reflected in the pages of Madame de Motteville: " He spoke of his queen in terms so passionate and respectful, that it was easy to suspect in him a feeling more tender than that which he owed her as a subject; " then, alluding to his betrothal : " Some say that had she followed her own inclinations, she would have taken him for herself." All this is indeed nothing but the scandal in which Paris delights; but the Count succeeded in his object, of creating a favourable inclination towards the court of Sweden, and returned home the following year. His last relations with Christina were destined to be very different from his first.

F

By means such as these did the Queen endeavour to pave the way towards peace, and form a party in opposition to the Chancellor. To the various motives determining her dislike of him must be added her close connection with the Palatine house, which the Oxenstiern party viewed with suspicion and dislike as a foreign element. Further reports had got about of an intended marriage between her and his son Eric—with how much truth we cannot determine. The Chancellor, however, wrote a long letter to his son, recommending him to still the disadvantageous rumour by marrying someone else.

The course of the negotiations for peace still further widened the breach. The plenipotentiaries for Sweden were John Oxenstiern, son of the Chancellor, and Adler Salvius. The former, a stiff, pig-headed man, full of his own importance, yet distrusting his own capacity, and devoid of diplomatic skill, was a creature of his father's, and at daggers drawn with his partner, Salvius. The latter, his complete antithesis alike in character and policy, was devoted to the Queen, who, with her usual keen insight into character, had recognised in him an instrument well suited to her ends. The son of a citizen of Strengnäs, he had raised himself by his abilities to a high position under Gustavus and Oxenstiern; his diplomatic talents and knowledge of the world were great, and he had a supple capacity of "working all men to the desired end," as Christina describes it.

Between the two delegates there was bitter hostility. The arrogance of Oxenstiern offended Salvius, who, relying on the support of the Queen, despised him, and set him at naught. Of this difference Christina was well aware and made use. John Oxenstiern was quite unable to cope with his delicate position, and knew this himself. He even endeavoured to shirk the duty altogether, pleading inability; the old Chancellor's reply has become a proverb : " *An nescis, mi fili, quantillâ prudentiâ regitur orbis ?* " And during the course of the proceedings he had repeatedly to reprove his son for his small-mindedness in attaching importance to little things, his want of tact in writing to the Queen, his impolitic loss of temper. The division in the Swedish camp was not unknown to the French. " The Swedish counsels are not so united as they are supposed to be," wrote the French ambassador; " the split comes from above." The French plenipotentiaries were no better; D'Avaux and Servien were at open enmity. The Duc de Longueville had to be despatched to preserve concord between them. With this condition of affairs, the main business did not get along; peace was not the matter, but following and party.

Even without all these personal animosities it
would have been no easy matter to adjust the
difficult complications and rival claims of the
various parties. The recent victories of Torstenson
and Condé enabled the Swedes to take a high
tone; they demanded principally Pomerania,
Camin, Wismar, Bremen, Verden, and Silesia,
and twenty million thalers for the army. France
required above all Alsace. But these demands
were scouted. Brandenburgh refused to let
Pomerania go; the Emperor would not hear
of giving up Alsace, and contented himself
with trying to sow dissension among the rival
claimants. Additional difficulty was caused by
Bavaria. The Swedes hated Bavaria, even more
than they hated the Emperor, and refused to
allow its neutrality; Mazarin, on the other hand,
was not inclined to press Bavaria hard. The
French were distrusted, as not acting for the
general good, and in fact, were not zealous for
the preponderance of Sweden in the north, or the
Protestant interest. (In the instructions sent to
the French delegates in 1646 we read: "The
pretensions of the Swedes are exorbitant and cause
the Queen great pain, because she sees that they
tend to raise the Protestant party by lowering
the Catholics"; whereas Oxenstiern laid stress
on the religious point of freedom for the Estates.)
Further negotiations resulted in the ultimatum

of the Swedes; for Pomerania, Rügen, Wollin, and Stettin, and some other places.

Throughout the transactions, the Chancellor and his party were haughty and unyielding, hating and hated by the French. "With you, I see," wrote Oxenstiern to his son, " the treaty of peace slumbers, and is pursued with hardly any other mind than *pro forma*." The Queen on the other hand, in the face of such obstacles, did not despair; aided by Chanut and Salvius she worked hard to make friends of the French, and bring matters to a conclusion. She corresponded personally with D'Avaux and Servien, Louis XIV. and his mother; chiefly to her exertions was it due that France made common cause with Sweden against Bavaria, and supported her in her claims for satisfying the army.

Her letters to Salvius during the period throw a strong light on her policy and character. In December, 1646, she writes:

" I thank you for the trouble you take in conducting this great matter to a successful conclusion, and your communication : I beg you not to grow weary, but continue in the zeal you have manifested till now in my service and that of the kingdom. In return I assure you that though many should attempt, perchance, to blacken you here, I will permit none of them to do you wrong in any respect; on the contrary, should you by the grace of God return in good health and successful, I will let you know by solid results that I am and remain always disposed to favour you.

"CHRISTINA."

February, 1647.—"I have received two letters from you which have pleased me greatly. I have not time to answer them as they deserve; accordingly, I beg you to thank M. D'Avaux for the essential service he has done me, and make my very particular excuses to him for not being able to write to him to-day. I have so much to do just now, that time is not sufficient for all my business. I hope he will never doubt my gratitude. I will not fail to thank him by the first courier. As to the Treaty of Peace, I have declared to both of you my opinion and my determination. Push matters on as best you can. I expect to have plenty to attend to here, so much so that I shall thank God if I am able to obtain, by hook or by crook, a good peace. You know better than me, *quam arduum quamque subjectum fortunæ regendi cuncta onus!* Nothing more at present; only this, please give me your advice as to whether I can, without prejudice to myself, gratify Count Magnus with Benfeld . . don't tell anyone about this, but let M. D'Avaux know it, *sub fide silentii;* and don't say anything about it to the Graf Gustafson [i.e., Oxenstiern].'

In another letter (without date) she begs him to see to a particular matter, also touched on in the first, the borrowing of a hundred thousand crowns by Count Magnus, which, in the present state of the finances and the army may be seized on by malicious persons eager " *nova imperia reddere odiosa* "; she wishes everyone to know it was done by her express command; should Salvius perform his duties satisfactorily, there is no position in the State, however high, to which he may not aspire.

4th Sept., 1647.—" I see that the Treaty is in the same condition as if it had stopped, and that everybody is waiting for the end, nevertheless I hope that on your side you will use your utmost diligence to conclude this long business, which may the Almighty graciously accord. . . . I enclose a letter for M. Servien, send it to him as soon as possible : civility compels me to answer his letter, otherwise I should be the rudest person in the world, since he offers himself so cordially to my service, and speaks too much in my favour in his quarter ; thus it behoves me to assure him of my good will and keep up a good correspondence with him, for you must recollect he is a creature of the Cardinal.   I know, too, the French ways, and that their manners consist chiefly in compliments ; but one loses nothing by being civil, and one pays them in their own coin. The compliments that they and others make me are pure flattery, I do not deserve such praises; nevertheless I find myself obliged to return their civilities in kind, therefore be courteous to him and others; bear witness of my affection for the Queen, as well as for the Cardinal, for he it is that governs all, that is why you must *faire bonne mine* to his creatures. Please get me a copy of the enclosed, as I have none here."

The peace, nevertheless, still dragged its weary length along. On 10th April, 1647, Christina sent the following final manifesto to the two colleagues, enclosing at the same time a private letter to Salvius, whereby it is obvious that the angry displeasure of the first was meant for John Oxenstiern alone.

10th April, 1647.—" Gentlemen: I add these few words to my public despatch, to discover to you with my own hand the fear I entertain lest this treaty, so earnestly desired, and for whose happy conclusion we have till now had reason to hope, should be arrested by causes not yet sufficiently well known to me. Therefore, to let you perfectly understand my will, you must thoroughly persuade yourselves that before all things I desire a sure and honourable peace. And since the *satisfactio coronæ* is already determined, and there remain only those of the soldiers and the *gravamina* of the Estates of the Empire, I will that you keep matters in good course till Erskein arrives and communicates to you his commission. Then without any further dawdling you must bring the negociations to a satisfactory conclusion by securing the best condition of the Estates, satisfaction of the Crown, and contentment of the soldiery that may be possible without breaking the peace—and no longer drag matters out as at present; otherwise, you will have to look to it how you will answer it before God, the Estates of the realm and me. Let not the phantasies of ambitious men turn you from your goal, unless you wish to incur my extreme disgrace and displeasure, and stand accountable to me blushing and blanching: you may be sure that in that case, no authority nor support of great houses shall hinder me from showing all the world the displeasure I feel at insensate procedure.    I am convinced that if things go ill with the Treaty your errors will have placed me in a labyrinth, whence neither you, nor the brains of those who foment such plans, will ever draw me. Therefore it behoves you to look well to yourselves," &c.

The letter to Salvius alone was as follows:—

"From all circumstances, I see how a certain

person, not being able entirely to break the Treaty, seeks to put it off. . . . I will let all the world see that the C—— cannot turn the whole world round his finger, *sapienti sat.* . . . My letter herewith is addressed to both of you, give it immediately to G. J. O.; though I attack him and you equally in it, 'tis meant for him alone—let D'Avaux know the contents, that the French may not think ill of me, but see who is to blame. . . . If by God's grace you come back here after the Peace, I will reward you *Senatoriâ dignitate.* You know it is in our country the highest honour to which an honest man can aspire—were there any higher *gradus honoris* I would not stick at conferring them upon you. But though that cannot be without drawing on you many envious persons, you can say with Marius in Sallust—'*contemmunt novitatem meam, ego illorum ignaviam, mihi fortuna, illis probra objectantur*'. . . . as to Count Gustafson, look to it well what you let him know—'*nec res magnæ sustineri possunt ob eo, cui tacere grave est.*'

"P.S.—Mind you let me know what grimaces G. J. O. makes, on reading my letter to both of you."

This letter deeply wounded the Oxenstierns. The Chancellor requested leave to retire from Sweden; the Queen granted it immediately, but

the remonstrances of the Senate, and the representations of Jacob de la Gardie, added to her
own indulgent respect for her old master, changed
her mind ; she begged him not to quit her service, and the wound was outwardly healed, though
Oxenstiern's power and influence over her were
gone for ever. On his part, John Oxenstiern
wrote her two letters, giving vent to the deep
mortification he felt at the slight put upon him,
and his rancour against Salvius. For him, however,
the Queen had no pity, and wrote shortly afterwards to Salvius, saying, " I enclose a copy of
G. J. O.'s letter to me, you can judge thereby of
his feelings to yourself.  Do not be disconcerted,
however, as I am more than pleased with you."

Again on November 27, 1647, she writes, " The
Ch——r *fait fort le souple, sed quidquid id est timeo
Danaos et dona ferentes.*  I observe every day in
him what Tacitus says of Tiberius, '*jam Tiberium
corpus, jam vires, nondum dissimulatio deserebat, sed
dabit deus his quoque finem.*'  Yet far be it from
me to wish him ill."

At length in July, 1648, it seemed as if the peace
was really at hand ; the Queen writes to Salvius :

21st July, 1648.—" I cannot express to you the
joy your pleasant news gave me. . . . what I
desire most of all and place above everything
is to give peace to Christendon.  When the

*instrumentum pacis* is drawn up, you will bring it yourself. . . . If God grants us peace I hope to compass all my desires, then we shall see some long faces here, and may say, *victrix causa Deis placuit, sed victa Catoni :* a word to the wise."

The campaign of Wrangel and Turenne in 1648 put an end to the obstinacy of Maximilian of Bavaria, and the finishing impulse came from the capture of Little Prague by Konigsmarck, on July 31, whereby he took an enormous booty ; though all his efforts and those of Charles Gustavus, who had come to assist him to take the rest of the town, were unsuccessful. On the 24th October, 1648, the Peace of Westphalia was actually signed ; though it was not till the Recess of Execution at Nuremberg, two years afterwards, that all the details were finally and definitely completed.

" Sweden received Hither Pomerania, including the island of Rügen ; from Further Pomerania the island of Wollin and several cities, with their surroundings, among which were Stettin, as also the expectancy of Further Pomerania in case of the extinction of the House of Brandenburgh. Furthermore it received the city of Wismar in Mecklenburgh, and the Bishoprics of Bremen and Verden, with reservation of the rights and immunities of the city of Bremen. Sweden was to

hold all the ceded territory as feudal tenures of
the Empire, and be represented for them in the
Imperial Diet. The Bavarian, Burgundian, and
Austrian circles were to be released from contributions to make up the five millions to be paid to
the Swedish army, for which only the seven other
circles were to be responsible."

In the settlement of the religious difficulties, a
compromise was arrived at. Full recognition was
now given to Calvinism as well as Lutheranism.
New Year's Day, 1624, was fixed as the limit,
after which Catholics and Protestants were to
hold whatever benefices they then possessed. In
the Imperial Diet, the two opposing creeds were
placed upon an equal footing. Thus the final
blow was given to Imperial claims in Church or
State, and a new system inaugurated, whereby
for the already antiquated universal supremacy
was substituted the balance of political power and
the rights of individual nations. The Peace thus
forms an epoch, a date dividing the old and
new. This is of more importance to us now than
the particular acquisitions of Sweden. But in
this connection it is to be noted that the Baltic
became, by these provisions, a sort of "Swedish
inland lake;" and 1648 marks the culminating
point of Sweden's fame. Her position among the
European states was, however, based on mere
externals, and not justified by her intrinsic capa-

bilities; this, even more than the relative rising of her neighbours, such as Russia and Prussia, is the explanation of her subsequent decline.

The Queen kept her promise to Salvius; she made him a senator, in spite of the keen opposition of the nobility, always jealous of extending their privileges, and with additional reasons [to increase their dislike of this *novus homo*. But Christina overruled all their objections. " When it is a question of good advice and wise counsel," she said in the Senate, " we do not ask sixteen quarterings; but what it is necessary to do. Salvius would no doubt be a capable man, if he was of good family." The new senator was in some apprehension of what his enemies might attempt against him; he wrote to the Queen a long and very diplomatic letter of thanks, recounting his services and explaining his fears. He came shortly after to Sweden, and was graciously received by the Queen, though he did not live long to enjoy his new honours, dying four years later.

Christina was extravagantly delighted when at length the Peace was actually signed; she gave the courier who brought the news to Sweden a gold chain, worth 600 ducats, and raised the secretary who brought the instrument to the nobility. *Te Deums* were sung in the churches, cannons fired, and public rejoicings held by her order. But the Chancellor and his war party were by no means so much pleased; they had no such exact perception of the needs and exigencies of the time as the wise young Queen, and looked only to the fact that less gain had accrued to Sweden than in view of all her efforts they thought might and ought to have been the case. Most of the nobles even regretted the war for its own sake. Themselves first, Sweden next, and Germany to take care of itself was their policy: whereas Christina exactly reversed that order, and placed the wants of Germany and the Swedish people above everything else. When some expressed in her presence their opinion that the Peace would not be of long duration, she replied, "I know well that there can be no eternal peace in this world; but that same Providence which has brought freedom to Germany will watch over it to preserve it."

By the clergy, again, it was not so well received; it stank in their nostrils that Calvinism should be recognized, or any disposition shown to half measures with Catholicism. In the pulpits they preached against it; one bigoted preacher exclaimed that the cause of Lutheranism had been deserted, and delivered an invective against the Catholics. Christina had him summoned before her, and rebuked him so sharply that the poor man lost his wits, and denied that he had ever uttered what had been heard by four thousand people.

We must carefully remember these things when we listen to abuse of Christina; it was just by such actions as these that her large mind and catholic toleration gained her the rancorous abuse and hatred of pitiful religious and political sectarians who could not comprehend her. Nobles and Swedish Lutheran patriots bore her a grudge for the Peace of Westphalia. It is exactly in this reference that Christina showed a keener political insight than the Chancellor. " It was," says Geijer, " the beginning of a new order of things, which in its operation set him aside; in this, more than in the weakness of age, lay the secret of his powerlessness; his political life terminated with the Peace." From this moment he stands aside, and the Queen does everything by herself. " She did without him on several occasions," says Chanut, " consulting him only like the other ministers, without marking the wide distinction there was between his experience and that of her other advisers."

And this is the moment at which she reaches her greatest elevation. To understand the benefits conferred on the world by the peace it is necessary to be familiar with the horrors of the Thirty Years' War. Fortunately this is not the place to dwell upon them; yet something must be said to help us to realize the situation. It was no longer a war of man against man, but brute against brute. Human nature was *disappearing*, in every sense of the word. Military license, famine and cannibalism, plague and pestilence ruled over Germany; the initial stages of rage and despair had long passed away, and only apathy remained to the miserable remnant of the population. A few more years, and this too would have vanished, and Germany have become a desert. " Almost all the country below Leipsic," wrote the Chancellor in 1643, " is a waste." " In the two armies," wrote Gronsfeld in 1648, " there were certainly more than 180,000 men, women, and children, who must all live as well as the soldiers; provisions are distributed every twenty-four hours for 40,000 ; how the remaining 140,000 are to live passes my comprehension, if they are not to pick up a bit of bread for themselves ; there is not a single place where the soldiers if they have money can buy anything : I say this, not as approving exorbitancies, but to show that all was not done out of insolence, but much out of mere hunger."

The imagination, brooding however deeply over that picture, will notwithstanding never be able to reach the appalling misery of the actual facts. What wonder that Germany took long to recover, and that her civilization

G

was thrown back for a century. That a period was put to this desolation, she has to thank Christina more than any statesman of that age; we shall not err in asserting that but for Christina the Peace might have been retarded indefinitely. But for her, the policy of the past, the policy of religious uncompromising antagonism and national antipathy, the policy of the war party and Oxenstiern, would have carried the day; Sweden and France would never have united, and the rest would have been chaos. The Peace of Westphalia, with all its consequences, even the existence of Germany as a nation, is entirely due to the unflagging energy and unwearied labour of Christina. And when we consider what was the strength of the opposition through which she carried it by the force of her genius and tenacity of her purpose, working, amidst a multitude of other business, from eighteen to twenty-two, harder than any under-secretary, to master all its minutest details, which she knew better than any paid official—never allowing herself to be absent from the Senate, even though frequently " suffering from fever, and obliged to be bled," till she had attained her end—we shall recognize that her claims to the admiration and gratitude of posterity are of quite another kind than those of many of its painted idols.

## CHAPTER III

BEFORE turning to Christina's personal and domestic history, we must dismiss two foreign events which immediately concerned her.

Immediately after the conclusion of peace, the Pope, Innocent X., published a Bull, dated November 26th, 1648, fulminating against the treaty, with special condemnation of the delivery of ecclesiastical benefices to heretics, and the increase in the number of electorates—an eighth having been created for Charles Lewis, son of Frederic V. Throughout this ill-advised instrument Christina was studiously ignored, reference being made only to Sweden and the Swedes. But the Bull only succeeded in making the Pope ridiculous: the Emperor refused to allow it to be published in his dominions; and a special refutation was composed by Herman Conring, pointing out the folly of attempting, among other matters, to put this slight upon a monarch recognized by the Emperor and the other powers, and alluding with a satiric touch to the answer once made by Pius II. to the ambassador of Frederic III., that it was the custom of the Holy See to recognize as king the person who sat on the throne. He might have added with reference to

Christina that it was with her fame as with that of Brutus and Cassius in the funeral procession described by her favourite Tacitus : " Their lustre shone forth all the brighter, for that their images were not seen."

Thus the Bull proved a complete fiasco ; the second affair was more important. Just before the negotiations terminated, King Ladislaus of Poland died. The news of his death was not unwelcome in Sweden, always in an embarrassing situation with regard to him. His arrogant claims and constant hostility had been a thorn in her side, nor did the dubious twenty-six years' truce of Stumsdorff, in 1635, set the Swedes at rest. Hence it became of great moment to endeavour to ensure the election of a king friendly to Swedish interests. Of the candidates, rumour assigned to the late king's brother-in-law, the Duke of Neuburg, the best chance of favour with the Poles. Of the two remaining sons of Sigismund, Charles Ferdinand was preferred in Sweden for his pacific disposition, while France on the other hand supported the claims of John Casimir, fearing the Austrian proclivities of his brother. The Emperor's candidate, Ragoczy, being a man of warlike disposition, was viewed by both powers with equal dislike. Christina was strongly determined not to allow the Polish crown to pass out of the royal house, not only because neither of the brothers were likely to give Sweden any trouble, but also to avoid the possibility of their renewing their claims to the Swedish throne, should she die without heirs. Nevertheless it was dangerous to show decided preference for any candidate without ascertaining who was most popular in Poland; since to do so might make a dangerous enemy of the king who should be actually elected. Under these circumstances she despatched Canther, one of her secretaries, into Poland—nominally to discuss the conditions of a peace ; principally however to try and discern the temper of the Poles, and the chances of success of the various candidates. It was reported that the party of Casimir was most likely to carry the day, and accordingly the Queen, who had written on the point to the Chancellor, and found that their opinions herein coincided, sent letters of recommendation to Poland on behalf of John Casimir, with orders not to present them without consulting the French ambassador, and unless the tide seemed to be setting in his favour ; otherwise they were to make use of similar letters on behalf of his brother. John Casimir was in short elected in December 1648.

When Christina on this occasion asked Chanut whether the King of France, in writing to the late King of Poland, had not given him the title of King of Sweden, he answered no, not knowing, it is said, anything to the contrary. But it is certain that the French Court gave him this title, and when the Court of Sweden complained, France replied that the title had been given to the King of Poland as *in petitorio*, to the King of Sweden as *in possessorio*, of the kingdom.

Christina had by this time attained a wide renown, and the French, by reason of this and her readiness to conciliate their goodwill, no less than by the embassy of De la Gardie, and his glowing descriptions of his Queen, were eager to gain a more accurate knowledge of her.

"To judge by the picture he gave us," says Mme. de Motteville, "she had neither the face nor the beauty nor the inclinations of her sex. Instead of making men die of love for her, she makes them die of shame and despair. . . . . She has no need of ministers, for she herself, young as she is, manages all alone. . . . She afterwards caused the death of Descartes, by not approving his method of philosophising" (here, as not infrequently, Madame romances a little). "She wrote to the Queen, to Monsieur, uncle of the King, to the Duc d'Enghien, and the ministers, letters which I have seen, and which were admired for the graceful humour of the thoughts, the beauty of the style, and the ease she showed herself to possess in handling our language, with which, as with many others, she was familiar.

People attributed to her all the cardinal virtues, placing her on a level with the most illustrious women of antiquity. All pens were employed in her praise; they said that the depths of science were for her what needle and distaff are for our sex. Fame," Madame aptly concludes, "is a great talker."

To satisfy the curiosity of the French, Chanut drew up her character, and sent it home; (her portrait, which they had asked for, Christina herself, as soon as she knew of it, undertook to send them). We have already spoken of Chanut. Pierre Chanut was a man of no ordinary stamp. To judge by the accounts we have of him, he appears to have been not unlike David Hume. It was not only by his deep studies and varied accomplishments that he attracted the attention of Christina—though his travels in Italy, Spain, England and the North of Europe, his know-ledge, no superficial one, of Latin, Greek, and Hebrew (he could speak Italian, Spanish, English, Swedish), and his love of philosophy, in which he was a follower of Descartes—were well calculated to make an impression on her mind; but his calm wisdom, and the simplicity of his cha-racter, gained her confidence in an extraordinary degree. Richelieu said he knew of three men of pre-eminent capacity in affairs, and named Chanut as the first. Séguier said of him that he

had never known a man who had had more
opportunities of making himself rich and powerful, who yet preferred the reputation of a good
servant; if he had lived, said Oxenstiern, in
ancient Greece or Rome, they would have erected
a statue to him. He came to Sweden as French
resident in 1644, and immediately exercised
great influence on politics, through the Queen:
we shall see in the sequel to what an extent she
honoured him with her friendship.

"The fine qualities of the Queen of Sweden
made at that time so great a noise throughout
Europe, that their majesties ordered *M. Chanut*
to send them a portrait of her: but as this portrait could make known only the exterior linea-
ments of the body, he sent them in advance one
which represented not only the beauties of the
body, but also the finest qualities of her mind:
but as curious people might remark therein
various defects, not existing in the original, he
said, to excuse himself, that he never took the
liberty of looking fixedly or attentively at the
beauty of this princess; if, however, he might
be permitted to trust to the report of another, he
could assure them that the first time one looked
at her one saw not in her so much to wonder at
as if one considered her more at leisure; he said
that one portrait was not sufficient to paint her
face, which was subject to such sudden changes,

according to the various emotions of her soul,
that it was not recognisable from one moment to
another. Usually she appears somewhat pensive,
yet passes easily and often to other expressions.
Her face, whatever be the revolutions of her mind,
yet retains always a certain agreeable serenity;
though certainly if, as but rarely happens, she
disapproves of what is said to her, a sort of cloud
may be seen to spread over her face, which
without disfiguring her yet causes terror in
those who see it. The tone of her voice is as
a rule very soft, and however firmly she pro-
nounces her words, they are clearly recognised
as those of a girl : sometimes, however, yet without affectation or apparent cause, she changes
this tone for one stronger and louder than that
of her sex, which little by little sinks back to its
ordinary pitch. She is rather below the average
height, which would not have been obvious, had
this princess been willing to make use of shoes
such as ladies are wont to wear ; but, in order to
be more at ease in her palace, or in walking or
riding, she wears only shoes with a sole and little
black heel similar to those of a man.

" If we may judge of the inside by the external
signs, she has lofty opinions of the Deity, and a
sincere attachment to Christianity ; she does not
approve, in ordinary scientific discourse, of leaving the doctrine of grace in order to philosophize

after pagan fashion; what is not in harmony
with the Gospel she considers as pure dreaming.
She shows no bitterness in disputing on the
differences between the Evangelicals and the
Roman Catholics; she seems to be less anxious
to gain insight into these difficulties than into
those presented to us by philosophers, Jews
and Gentiles. Her devotion to God appears in
the confidence which she manifests in His protection, greater than in any other thing; for the
rest, she is not scrupulous, and does not affect an
outwardly pious ceremonial. Nothing is more
constantly in her mind than an incredible love
for a lofty virtue, wherein lies all her joy and
delight: to this she joins an extreme passion for
glory, and, as far as we can judge, her desire is
for virtue coupled with honour. Sometimes it
pleases her to speak, like the Stoics, of that ' plat-
form of excellence ' which constitutes our sovereign good in this life; she is marvellously strong
on this subject, and when she is talking to persons
with whom she is familiar, and begins to discuss
the true estimate which we should make of the
things of this world, it is delightful to see her
putting the crown beneath her feet, and announcing virtue as the only good, to which it
behoves all men to apply themselves, without
making capital of their rank; but during this
avowal she soon recollects she is a queen, and

therefore again assumes the crown, of which she
is sensible of the weight. She places the final
step towards acquiring virtue in doing one's duty,
and in fact she is largely endowed by nature
with the qualities necessary to enable her to perform her part worthily; for she has a marvellous
facility in understanding and seeing into affairs,
and a memory which serves her so faithfully that it
may be said she often abuses it. She speaks Latin,
French, German, Flemish, Swedish, and is study-
ing Greek; she has *savants* by her who discourse
with her in her idle moments of all the most
curious details in the sciences; her mind, greedy
of knowing all things, seeks information on all.
No day passes that she does not read in her
history of Tacitus, which she calls her game at
chess; this author, who makes *savants* puzzle over
him, she understands easily in his most difficult
passages, and where the most learned pause,
hesitating as to the meaning, she translates well
in our tongue with extraordinary facility. Yet
she avoids or at any rate does not study to seem
learned or *savante*. She takes great pleasure in
listening to the discussion of problematic questions, especially by learned people of different
opinions; her own opinion she never gives till all
have spoken, and then only in few words, the whole
so well considered that it may pass for a formal
and positive decision. . . . Her ministers, when

she is in council, can with difficulty discern to
which side she leans; she preserves the secret
faithfully; and as she never lets herself be prejudiced by what people tell her, she seems mis-
trustful, or difficult of persuasion, to those who
gain access to her. . . . 'Tis true she is inclined
to be suspicious, and sometimes she is a little too
slow at seeing the truth, and too ready to infer
*finesse* in others. . . . She asks no one's advice in
her private affairs, but she deliberates in the
Senate in all matters concerning the State. It
is incredible how powerful she is in her council,
for she adds to her position as Queen, grace,
credit, benefits, and a power of persuasion, such
that the senators themselves are often amazed at
the influence she wields over their opinions, when
they are assembled. Though some attribute this
to the secret influence of her sex, yet to say truth
this authority arises from her personal good
qualities. A king of like virtue would be absolute
in his senate; in any case that would be less
surprising than to see a girl turning as she will
the minds of so many old and wise councillors.
It is no wonder that she displays the prudence
of a man in the Senate, seeing that in action
Nature has refused her none of those qualities,
of which a young cavalier would brag. She is
indefatigable in field exercises, and will even
when hunting be ten hours in the saddle. Cold

and heat are indifferent to her ; in eating she is
simple, careless, and entirely without epicureanism.
No one in Sweden knows better than her how to
knock over a hare in its course with a single
ball; she can put a horse through all its
paces, without pluming herself on it. She rarely
speaks to the ladies of the court, since her exercises, or the cares of state which keep her, give
no opportunity for conversation, and they do
not even see her, except by way of a visit; and
then after the necessary civilities she leaves them
in a corner of the room in order to go and converse with men. If she is with those from whom
she thinks nothing is to be learned, she cuts down
the conversation to the absolute *minimum ;* accordingly her servants say little to her—still they
like her, since, however little she addresses them,
it is always with sweetness, and she is a good
mistress, liberal even beyond her means. Sometimes she amuses herself by jesting with them,
which she does with good grace and without
bitterness, yet it might be better if she abstained
[Christina adds in a note,—' Right ; raillery procured me many enemies '] because this always
leaves a suspicion in those who have been its
objects that they are despised ; still business
and study leave her little time for this. Of her
time she is very avaricious, for she sleeps
little, and usually stays in bed only five hours

[Christina annotates 'three hours']; this not being sufficient, however, to restore her forces, she is sometimes obliged, principally in summer, to sleep an hour after dinner [Christina says, 'No']. She cares little about dressing and adornment; we must not reckon it in the division of her day. She dresses in a quarter of an hour, and, excepting on great occasions or festivals, the comb alone and a knot of ribbon constitute her headdress. Nevertheless this negligent method of doing her hair suits her face very well; but so little care does she take of it that neither in sun, wind, rain, town or country, does she wear hat or veil. When she rides, she .has for protection against the weather only a hat with feathers in it, so that a stranger who might see her hunting in her Hungarian habit with a little collar like a man's would never take her for the Queen. Perhaps she carries this too far . . . but nothing is important in her eyes except the ambition of making herself renowned for extraordinary merit rather than conquest; she loves to owe her reputation to herself, rather than to the worth of her subjects."

The character of the author, and its .obviously careful delineation, added to the fact that it was never meant for the eye of the Queen, are a guarantee for the general accuracy of this portrait; we may supplement it by some

interesting details from the description of Father
Mannerschied, confessor to the Spanish Ambassador Pimentelli.

"She is a prodigy, and the incomparable
marvel of this century. I will say nothing
of her of which I have not been ocular witness.
Her forehead is broad, her eyes large and
piercing, but her look is mild, her nose aquiline,
her mouth small and pretty. There is nothing
feminine in her but her sex. Her dress is
very simple; never have I seen her wear
gold or silver, on her head, clothes, or neck,
except a gold ring on her finger. . . . I have
sometimes observed, when talking to her, that
she had spots of ink on her cuffs, from
writing. She only spends three or four hours in
sleep; when she wakes she spends five hours in
reading. It is torture for her to eat in public;
she never drinks anything but water; never has
she been heard to speak of her food, whether it
was well or ill cooked. . . . I have often heard
her say that she lived without disquiet or discontent, and that she knew nothing in the world
great, harmful, or disturbing enough to trouble
the tranquillity of her mind. It is her boast that
she fears death no more than sleep. She attends
her council regularly; one day after being bled
she was five hours with her ministers: another
time, during a fever of twenty-eight days long,

she never neglected her state affairs. She
says that God has given her the government of
her kingdom, and she will do her best thereby—
that though she may not always succeed, she
may have nothing to reproach herself with.
Public affairs all pass through her hands; she
arranges and despatches them all alone—ambassadors and foreign delegates treat only with
her, without even being passed on to secretary or
minister. When ambassadors harangue her in
public, she answers herself. . . . She reads all
treatises on domestic affairs, many and copious
though they be. I know that one day she read
and explained in Latin one of these to a foreign
ambassador in a very short space of time. She
approves of all nations, esteeming virtue wherever
it is to be found. . . . According to her, the whole
world is divided into two nations, honest men
and knaves. . . . She cannot bear the idea of
marriage, because she says she was born free and
will die free. . . . She knows ten or eleven languages,—Latin, Greek, Italian, French, Spanish,
High German, Flemish, Swedish, Finnish, and,
unless I am mistaken, Danish also. She can
read Hebrew and Arabic, and understands them a
little. She reads and knows very well the ancient
poets. She knows modern poets, French and
Italian, almost by heart. She has been through
all the ancient philosophers, and has read a great

number of the Fathers—as, S. Augustine, S. Ambrose, S. Jerome, Tertullian and Cyprian; but these are not to her taste, she prefers Lactantius, S. Clement of Alexandria, Arnobius, Minutius Felix, some of S. Jerome and S. Cyprian; above all she prefers Gregory Nazianzen.* One cannot make use of some ancient poet's thought without her perceiving the theft.

To these eulogies may be added the accusations which she brings against herself: "I was distrustful, suspicious, ambitious to an excess. I was hot-tempered, proud and impatient, contemptuous and satirical. I gave no one quarter. I was, too, incredulous and little of a devotee."

The fame that Christina acquired by her personal qualities, her generous and universal patronage of learning and the learned, and her commanding position as head of the leading Protestant power, brought numerous suitors into the field for her hand. This had long been the subject of anxious consideration. Of these aspirants, the two sons of Christian IV. of Denmark are first to be noticed, Prince Ulric and Prince Frederick. Their alliance was supposed

---

* Christina's preference for this Father, whose erratic life and copious rhetoric furnish a commentary upon his own remark, that he had put away all ambition, save that of eloquence, is highly significant.

H

to have been favoured by the Queen-mother; we have already seen her close connection with Denmark. But however eagerly their suit might have been pressed, there was never the slightest probability that it should succeed : the relations between the two countries put such a match out of the question—Oxenstiern himself assured the Senate that any attempt to press this matter might lead to civil war, and endanger the life and crown of the young Queen, who never showed, moreover, the slightest inclination for it.

More important were the proposals of the Elector of Brandenburgh. This had been a project dear to the heart of Gustavus Adolphus. In a letter of the Chancellor's to the Senate, dated Berlin, February 4, 1633, he writes: " His Majesty of Christian memory, when he was a year ago at Frankfort-on-the-Maine, himself proposed to the commissioners of the Elector of Brandenburgh a match between his daughter and the young Elector, and commanded me to communicate further regarding it with the envoys, as I have also done several times. . . .. The principal reason was that His Majesty would not cede Pomerania, and yet found that it could not be kept without notable detriment and great umbrage to the Elector of Brandenburgh ; next that the King also perceived that if Sweden and Brandenburgh with their dependencies could be conjoined, hardly such a state could be found in Europe, and they might offer the headship to whom they would." This fine scheme was viewed with great jealousy and disapproval by all the Powers except England and Holland: but the soldiers in the Swedish army were already drinking healths to the young couple when Gustavus died, and the project died with him.

Under the pretext of settling the difficulties connected with the Queen-mother's escape to Denmark, the Elector sent an embassy to Sweden in 1641 to make final proposals. The Regents, however, who had no longer any intention of pursuing the design, fearing the foreign influence of German Princes, put him off with fine words; and although from time to time he made various attempts to reopen the subject, at length, in 1646, he recognised his suit was hopeless, and married a Princess of Orange. It was hinted by the Chancellor's enemies that he had expressly prevented this marriage in order to make the way clear for his son Eric; we have already seen that, whatever truth there might have been in these malicious insinuations, the only effect of them was to sow dissension between Christina and the Oxenstierns, and that the Chancellor had to write to his son, recommending him to marry in order to give the lie to scandal.

Besides these, there were at different times

proposals, more or less serious, set on foot in favour of Philip IV. of Spain, King John of Portugal, the three sons of Sigismund, King of Poland, the King of Hungary, Don John of Austria, and others, all of which were, for obvious political or religious reasons, palpably absurd, and came to nothing. But of all the suitors of Christina, the one who seemed to be most in favour, both with herself and the Swedes, was Charles Gustavus, the Prince Palatine, her cousin. Brought up as she was by his mother, the Princess Catharine, for whom she always had a great affection, Christina had from her'youth up been accustomed to consider Charles as her future husband; in their children's play, they would call themselves husband and wife; Christina promised in this way to marry him when they were grown up. Yet such a plan would no doubt be considered and approved by the Princess Catharine and her husband : to this doubtless refers the dangerous question which he put to the Regents, when he applied to them to direct him how his children should be educated; they answered that it was his own affair and not that of the State. Charles Gustavus, after travelling abroad for two years, returned to Sweden in 1640, and was viewed by the Regents, who were doubtless aware of his schemes, with great disfavour : it was apparent to Christina that he must go away again for a

time. She wrote to his father that everybody
was surprised "at the *tracasseries* which had
been shown to his son, and that whatever
may be his father's reasons for not wishing
him to come to. him, she, at least, perceives that
he cannot remain at Stockholm consistently with
his good fame, for fear lest they may push things
to a rude conclusion with him": and again, " Providence, which knows better than ourselves what
is good for us, will be able to set bounds to this
iniquitous affair, and turn it to our advantage."
Accordingly Charles Gustavus went to Germany,
and distinguished himself greatly in the war,
especially at Jankowitz, where he was almost
killed, being shot through the hair, hat, and
clothes.

That Christina had at this time a great
affection for him is proved by the following
letter, dated January 5th, 1644:—

"BELOVED KINSMAN,—I see by your letters that
you do not dare to commit your thoughts to the
pen. Yet we can write to one another with all
freedom, if you will send me the key to a cipher,
and compose your letters according to it, and put.
the initials C. R. on the address as well as inside,
sealing it at the same time with a different seal
expressly devised for that purpose, as I do with
mine. The letters can then be sent to your

sister, the Princess Maria. We must observe
every possible precaution, for people have never
been so much against us as now. But they
shall effect nothing, if only you will remain as
firm as I hope. People talk a great deal about
the Elector, but neither he nor anyone else in
the world, rich as he may be, shall ever turn
me from you. My love is so strong that it can
only be overcome by death; and if, which God
forbid, you should die before me, my heart shall
be dead for every other, but its memory and
affection shall follow you to eternity, and there
abide with you. It may be that some one will
advise you to demand my hand now and openly,
but I implore you by all that is sacred to have
patience for yet a year, till you have won more
experience in war, and I myself have got the
crown on my head. I beg you not to let yourself
think the time too long, but to remember the old
saying, ' He waits not too long who waits for
something good.' I hope, with God's help, that
it may be a good we both wait for."

These tender feelings, however, were destined
not to last: from this time a great change came
over Christina's mind. Her letters gradually
become colder, she assures the prince of her continued affection provided he keeps within bounds.
In proportion as she seemed inclined to draw
back, Charles grew even more eager. On his

return to Sweden he pressed her eagerly to declare herself. It was the common opinion that she would marry him ; it was moreover becoming a point of importance with the Estates in order to ensure the succession, now that Christina was of ripe age. In 1647 the clergy and the two lower Orders presented a petition recommending her to marry; the nobles, who were by no means so anxious, stipulating that no special person should be named : they would have been very well pleased to see things continue as they were, and were particularly unwilling to further the claims of Charles. The Queen, though she received the petition generously, said that at the moment she had no inclination to marry, yet inquired whether, should she make choice of the Prince, he would be acceptable to the Estates. They answered, Yes, and the matter remained there.

In the meantime, Charles felt himself in a very ambiguous position. The more he pressed her, the more she recoiled. In 1647, she signified to him her intention of appointing him Generalissimo of the Armies in Germany. But the Prince was determined not to go without gaining a definite declaration from her on the subject next his heart. This Christina would not give; when he thereupon informed her that in that case the earlier he left for the war the better, she replied that he must then remain satisfied with his ordinary rank. Nevertheless, she applied herself to his appointment with interest, and succeeded in carrying it against the opposition of the Chancellor and High Marshal. Charles Gustavus endeavoured to shake her resolution in a remarkable conversation which he had with her in the presence of Matthiæ and the Count Magnus de la Gardie. The Queen informed him that she could give him no promise to marry him; she would however promise not to marry any one else; and further, that if she finally determined never to marry, she would cause him to be appointed her successor to the throne; more she could not do. The Prince declared emphatically that if he did not marry her all was indifferent to him; he would never return to Sweden. The Queen angrily retorted, that all this was mere romance; he must recollect he was born for higher things than idling about on his paternal estate, and prepare to apply himself to his duty. When he referred to her childish promises, she told him that she did not consider herself bound by promises made at a time when she was incapable of recognising the seriousness of the position; he must be content with what she had said, and consider it an honour, should he die before gaining his hopes, that he had ever been considered worthy of such a fortune. Charles

ungenerously taunted her with the reports that
had been spread of her marriage with Eric
Oxenstiern, and said it did not apparently need
much honour to aspire to her hand.  This irritated the Queen, who declared he was unworthy of
what she had done for him.  The further expostulations of the Prince could not succeed in
drawing from her anything more definite than
what she had already told him ; to his demand that
he might be allowed to write to her, she replied
that he had her permission to correspond with
his father and Matthiæ.  They parted on these
terms ; yet when the Prince embarked for his
post, she followed him with her eyes as far as
possible from the terrace of her castle.

What now were the reasons which determined
Christina against marriage ?    They were not
merely personal.   Charles Gustavus was a man
of daring courage and ambition, and, if Christina
in jest used to call him "the little Burgomaster,"
she seems always to have preserved a respect and
affection for him.   It was said, indeed, with what
truth we cannot determine, that she had heard
rumours of his *liaisons* with other women, which
were not likely to impress her proud spirit in his
favour.  Further, Chanut tells us, that Christina,
before her resignation in 1654, sent to Charles
Gustavus to say that Count Magnus (then in
disgrace) was unworthy of his affection or com-

passion, inasmuch as he had been a false friend
to him while in favour. She wished him to know
that her not having married him was owing to
the Count, who had inspired her with a special
aversion to the Prince. This is by no means
impossible ; although Count Magnus was considered to be a great friend of the Prince, yet the
meanness of his character, which will amply
appear in the course of this narrative, and the
fact that his influence was destined to come to an
end should Christina marry Charles, give a
colour to the report.

However this may be, it is certain that the
determination of the Queen never to marry
lay much deeper down. The proud and
ineradicable independence of her mind and
character recoiled instinctively from the idea of
giving herself a master. " I will live and die
free," she said to the Jesuit Mannerschied ; in
later life she had a medal struck with the inscription, *libero io nacqui e vissi e morro sciolto.*
She told Chanut in 1651, that she would rather
choose death than a husband. The idea of
belonging to another, of being anyone's *chattel*,
disgusted her; she shrank from classing herself
in any respect with a sex she despised. From
an anecdote preserved to us, quite in keeping
with her character, but which will not bear
repeating, it seems that the merely physical

aspect of marriage was an insuperable obstacle to her.  With all this agrees what Duke Adolphus told Whitelocke, that the Queen's refusal to marry Charles came from her innate abhorrence of the tie.

Yet to this must be added what is, undoubtedly, the strongest motive of all.  At this time she was pondering a change of religion.  To the statement in a history of that time, assigning as a reason for her abdication in favour of Charles " that she wished to become a Catholic," Christina has added a note, " This is the sole foundation of Charles's fortune; all the rest is false."  Even when she was a child, when she heard that among Catholics the highest merit was assigned to the unmarried state: "Ah!" she had exclaimed, " how fine that is; it is of that religion that I will be."

We shall go more fully into the question of her conversion and its motives further on, when it will be seen that she had at this time already determined to become a Catholic; here it will be sufficient to point out how strongly the religious aspect of celibacy influenced her at this crisis.  In the very singular fragment entitled her Memoirs, which is addressed to the Deity, there are many passages which throw great light on this point of a single life.  " Thou hast been willing to let me know, from the cradle, the

advantage of this great independence; which I
have been able to maintain and will maintain till
death." "I was called to the glory of sacrificing
all to Thee, and I had to obey my vocation;" . . .
"my ardent and impetuous temperament has
given me no less inclination for love than for
ambition; into what misfortune might not so
terrible an inclination have hurled me, had not
Thy grace made use even of my defects to correct
me of it; my ambition, my pride, incapable of
submitting to anyone, my disdain, despising
all things, have served me as admirable pre-
servations; and by Thy grace Thou hast added
thereto so fine a delicacy, that Thou hast saved
me from an inclination so perilous for Thy glory
and my happiness; however near the precipice I
have been, Thy powerful hand has drawn me
back. . . . I should without doubt have married,
had I not been conscious of the strength Thou
hast given me to go without the pleasures of love.
I knew the world too well to be ignorant that a
girl who wishes to enjoy her life needs must have
a husband: above all, a girl of my rank, who
marries only to gain a subject, rather, a slave to
her will and caprice. I was born to such a
condition and walk in life that I might have
chosen among all men him who took my fancy,
for there was not one in the world who would not
have deemed himself lucky if I had been willing

to give him my hand, I knew my advantages too well not to have the mind to make use of them. Had I been conscious of any weakness, I should have known how, like so many others, to marry for pleasure's sake, and enjoy my good fortune; and I should not have had that insensible aversion for marriage, of which I have given so many striking marks, had it been necessary to me. But Thou hast given me a heart meet to be taken up with Thee alone; Thou hast formed it of so admirable and vast a capacity that nothing could fill it but Thyself."

To these extraordinary passages may be added the numerous places in her sentences and maxims which touch scornfully on marriage; and as a proof that this is not mere bravado, her conduct in later years, when, after the abdication of John Casimir, she endeavoured to gain the throne of Poland; at which time she would not yield to the condition necessary, and declared that for the empire of the whole world she would not marry, much less for the crown of Poland.

The motives which led Christina to remain unmarried, to resign the crown, and to go over to Rome, are so inextricably blended together that it is only after considering all three points that a complete judgment can be formed on any one of them. Enough has been said for the moment to throw a light on her love of celibacy, and let us partially understand her conduct to Charles Gustavus. Starting from the intention to become a Catholic, and, in close connection with this, to remain single, she found herself in a difficulty as regards the throne. The constitution of Sweden, and the national antipathy to Rome, would not allow her to retain the crown : this explains her exclamation to the Jesuit : "There is no help for it, I must resign." There were, indeed, further motives to assist her in her resignation, to which we shall return. This point gained, it was necessary for her to prepare the succession to the throne, and she now set herself to make smooth the way for Charles Gustavus. To do this was a task of no ordinary difficulty, but she showed in this as elsewhere her diplomatic skill and masterful strength of character.

Although all Christina's subjects were not equally desirous to see her married, a maiden queen and a disputed succession being thoroughly to the taste of the noble oligarchy, yet by the other Orders, and especially the clergy, to whom the celibate state was a stone of offence, representations and petitions continued to be addressed to her, recommending her to choose a consort. No suspicion of the actual state of her mind was at this time entertained, till in February 1649 the Queen herself opened the subject. She informed the Senate that for some years she had been continually solicited to marry; she could not disapprove of the foresight of those who loved their country and desired to prevent the evils that might arise, if God withdrew her from the world without leaving a fixed succession. . . . She could not, however, get over her repugnance to marriage; and accordingly, out of her anxiety and love for her country, she had determined to consult the safety of the State by a course which might finally be detrimental to herself, viz., to propose to the Estates a successor to the throne, whose nomination would deliver them from the fear of her death: for which office none were more suited than her cousin, Prince Charles Gustavus, upon whose qualities she proceeded to expatiate. She then laid before them for their consideration two questions:—1. Whether the marriage of the Queen was the only method of providing a successor to the throne. 2. Whether the good of the State would not better be consulted by naming Prince Charles heir to the throne in case of her own death. If the Senate would give its decision, she would propose it to the Committee of the Estates, and then bring it before the assembled Diet for confirmation.

After recovering themselves from their astonishment, they all spoke at once to try and dissuade her from the scheme, and assured her they would oppose it to the death. "I know well," said

Christina,. "that some of you are minded to establish an elective monarchy after my death; to these I must say that none of them are to be compared to Prince Charles; others wish for an aristocratic government, wherein they follow their own interests; such a constitution is by no means suitable for Sweden, otherwise I would myself at this moment try to establish it : everyone knows what the Chancellor and the High Steward are aiming at." Field-marshal Torstenson replied that except out of consideration for her Majesty, no one would ever have thought of Prince Charles; they must think twice before making themselves slaves; as to a Republican Government, no one had ever thought of it. . . . Finally, however, each senator severally answered for it that if the Queen died childless they would give their votes for Prince Charles. Christina answered that she could not trust to mere words, but must have this reduced to writing in due form. They endeavoured to point out the inconvenience arising from an heir-presumptive, especially for herself: they cited the evils caused by princes of the blood, and feared lest she might even after this marry some one else, the consequences leading possibly to civil war. Christina replied, she would answer for a good understanding between the Prince and herself; she solemnly engaged herself to marry none

but Prince Charles; in any case this remote
possibility was not to be compared to the danger
of her dying without heirs : and if there was to
be a civil war, it would be no worse that it
should arise out of the conflict between heirs of
the Prince and her own, than that of the Houses
of Oxenstiern and Brahé for the elective monarchy.
When one of the House of Oxenstiern begged
her not to cite his house in this invidious way,
she said that she had named it as she might have
named any other. The Senate still continued
obstinate not to entrust their promises to writing.
"If," said the Queen, "I marry Prince Charles,
you will doubtless recognise his children ; but
if I die without heirs, I will bet my two ears
he will never sit upon the throne." " Prince
Charles," said Torstenson, "will never marry, if
not your Majesty." "O, but he will," exclaimed
the Queen; "love burns not for one alone; the
crown is a pretty girl."

On resuming the discussion a few days later,
seeing them resolving to put the matter off to
the ensuing Diet, the Queen said that she saw
no reason for postponing the settlement, the
matter being one on which she had reflected
daily for three years. Should she determine to
marry, she could not give her hand to a mere
Palsgrave; he must first be nominated successor
to the throne. It was accordingly arranged that

I

next day the Committee of the Estates should be summoned to the Senate. After much discussion the Queen declared that they should get nothing out of her on the subject of marriage; it was, further, impossible for her to marry before she was crowned. Thereupon Matthiæ pointed out that her Majesty was bound by the laws of the realm to marry in order to ensure succession. Christina answered, no one could compel her to it; what more, besides, could they desire that the succession should be secured? Till the Prince was declared successor she could give no promise to marry; but at all events nothing should compel her thereto. Matthiæ assured her that it was noised throughout Europe that she was to marry Prince Charles. "When they have chattered enough about it," rejoined the Queen, "they will find something else to talk about." They could get nothing further from her than this: Charles must be declared successor before she could think of marrying him, and upon this she would not declare her mind till she was crowned.

The Committee retired after giving its consent. In the Diet, the three lower Orders agreed to accept Prince Charles; but the nobility still drew back, till the Queen exposed to them the danger they ran of getting a king in spite of themselves; adding, that the three other Orders had given their consent; she well knew that it was only a small part of them that set itself in opposition to her wishes ; she could distinguish between them, and mark those who consulted their own interests in preference to those of the State. They accordingly withdrew, amazed, and the bravest among them began to take another tone. The Senate, now left alone, saw itself obliged to give in.

One opponent only remained. "The Chancellor," says Christina in her Memoirs, " was one of the greatest obstacles I had to overcome in order to carry my design of sacrificing all to Thee." He had been absent from the Senate through illness ; Mr. Nicolas Tungel, Secretary to the Court, was despatched by Christina to take him the Act of Succession to sign, on March 11, 1650. Tungel drew up a report of the conversation. Oxenstiern answered, with a sinister air, that he had but little knowledge of the matter, and would not therefore have it said that he had ever a hand in it; had they taken his opinion on it, he might have given better counsel on so important a matter, which had been too much hurried on. "I assure you," he added, "that if at this moment I saw my grave open before me, and I had to choose either to get in or sign this act, devil fly off with me, if I would not rather lie down in it than sign this instrument, not that it

is not well drawn up, but that the future will
show when it is too late that the consequences
will be quite other than many persons suppose,
and bring repentance with them ; my consolation
lies chiefly in my old age, which will prevent me
from seeing that time. If I am mistaken, I will
allow that all my principles are false, and have
deceived me; and others may say that I am an
old fool, understanding nothing in these affairs."
The Secretary saying that the rest of the Senators
and the Estates had consented ; were their hearts
all tablets, said the Chancellor, and her Majesty
able to read them, she would see written there-
on quite other things : how few were those
who were sincere in the matter. As for himself,
he would stand out no longer, now that things
had gone so far, but go over to the majority;
but he wished to stand excused before God
and posterity, convinced as he was that the
affair would end badly for the weal of the State.
Never since the House of Vasa sat on the throne
had there come up for decision anything so
important.

Well might the old Chancellor feel disturbed.
He had seen three monarchs of his beloved house,
Charles IX., Gustavus Adolphus, and Christina,
and his long life had been devoted to their service; now at the close of his career came an act,
which seemed to herald the ruin of all his labours

and strivings, and hand over the national throne of the Vasas to a hated stranger.

Christina alluded to his opposition in the Senate, blaming him, yet without bitterness, for his antagonism to her wishes. She had gained her point, the first step and the most difficult, to the full accomplishment of her design. That she could so completely overcome all opposition, and successfully carry through so delicate a business, gives us a great idea of her power and influence in the government. Charles Gustavus had in truth great reason to be thankful to her; yet she did not content herself with this. In the following year, on his return, she caused him and his descendants to be declared heirs to the throne, in the event of her dying without issue. He was entitled "Prince of Sweden," and "Royal Highness," with a yearly pension of 50,000 thalers. Yet she would not permit him to hold any office, nor take any part in the government, nor would she endow him with any principality, calling this an *arcanum imperii*. The Prince on his side took an oath to recognise the Queen as his legitimate sovereign, and obey her, himself and his heirs; to do nothing of importance without her advice and that of the Senate; and to observe in every particular the constitutional rights and duties, should he ever come to the throne.

The year 1650 was closed by her coronation,

which took place on October 30; a long and
circumstantial account was published at Paris the
same year.

"Although the coronation of the Queen of
Sweden had been determined since 1648, it was
postponed again and again to allow time for the
extensive preparations, her Majesty wishing to
make it splendid and magnificent; but principally, too, owing to the delay in executing the
Peace of Germany, before which it was judged that
such a celebration would not be sufficiently joyous
or striking, while the most illustrious captains
and generals of the nation were still busied in
settling the long-desired Peace. At length,
in the beginning of this present year 1650,
there being every probability that the affairs of
war would finally be determined, and that all
would tend to a freer and more certain leisure
and repose, her Majesty, in conjunction with
the Senate, thought good to hold the Coronation.

"The day was fixed for the 20th October. Now,
according to ancient custom it appears that the
usual scene of this grand ceremony has been the
town of Upsala, the seat of the Archbishop of the
Realm; nevertheless, in order to avoid the inconvenience, in this coronation, more magnificent
than any that had preceded it, of conveying all
to Upsala, no less than that of causing so great a
multitude of people to betake themselves there,

it was considered more suitable to hold it at
Stockholm. . . . . As the day drew near, the
Queen left Stockholm on the 14th, and repaired
to Jacobstad, the house of the High Constable de
la Gardie, half a league away, in order to make
her entry into the town from that place two days
afterwards.   During her stay, this noble left
nothing undone to receive and entertain her with
the greatest magnificence ; the most striking
mark of his profusion was, that, on the first and
last day, to provide drink for all the world, he
caused four fountains of Spanish and French wines,
white and red, to run from noon till evening.

"The day of her Majesty's *entrée* into the town
having arrived, namely the 17th of October, all
the nobility came out to meet her in brilliant equi-
pages.   The *entrée* began between two and three
o'clock, and lasted till half-past five.   A regiment
of cavalry, armed with steel cuirasses and wearing
blue scarves, opened the procession.   They were
followed by five companies of the guards dressed
in yellow and blue. . . . (a long enumeration
follows of) the trains of the Senators, the nobility,
Foreign Envoys and Ambassadors, ladies of the
Court, with their several carriages, pages, trumpe-
ters, richly decorated horses and mules.   Specially
noticeable were the Princes Charles and Adolphus,
and the Queen-mother.   The Queen herself rode
in a carriage covered with black velvet richly

embroidered with gold, surrounded by pages, archers, halberdiers, and footmen. At the entry of the town had been erected by the Senators a triumphal arch ; "'twas the most superb thing that could be seen ; it cost sixteen thousand crowns, though it was only made of wood, yet it was covered with linen painted so curiously that it seemed to be built of stone ; all around it might be seen designs of the battles stricken during the last war in Germany, with emblems suited to their subject ; as, a crown, with the device, *Felix cum non dat honorem, sed recipit ;* a sun rising over fields and flowers : motto, *tot pulchra per unum ;* a lion, holding in one paw a thunderbolt, with the legend : *Nos etiam Jovis arma decent ;* a vine, from which various branches hung down : the device, *Juncti lætamur in uno !* Upon the arch itself was a long inscription, sounding the praises of Christina and her reign, with an epigram in Latin ; above hung a quantity of flags and standards, the prizes of war.' "

As soon as her Majesty had arrived at her room the signal was given throughout the Castle to fire salutes, as well of the cannon around Stockholm, as on the men-of-war. They lasted two hours ; there were two discharges ; each time might be counted nine hundred shots. The rest of the day was taken up with a banquet, to which the principal lords of the Court were invited.

The two next days were employed in preparations for the Coronation on the following Sunday, and the presentation of rich gifts from various States and towns to the Queen, such as Livonia, Pomerania, Riga, Stettin, Stralsund, Stockholm, and others.

On Sunday another splendid procession repaired to the Church; there, after a sermon by the Bishop of Strengnäs, the ceremony of the Coronation was performed. The Archbishop having made a short discourse, the oath of the Kings of Sweden was read by the Chancellor, the Queen repeating it word by word. Then the Archbishop anointed her Majesty with the sacred oil, and placed the crown on her head; the various grand officers approached and presented to her the Sword, the Sceptre, the Golden Apple, and Key; after which a herald came forward and shouted to the people, " *The most powerful Queen Christina is crowned, herself and none other!* " The Queen then took her seat on a throne opposite the altar, beneath a daïs, supported by the Generals of the Army, Königsmarck, Wittemberg and others, Prince Charles by her side; all the Senators and the Prince then took the oath of fidelity to her. On leaving the Church the Queen mounted a superb triumphal car, gilded all over, and drawn by four white horses. Before her went a treasurer, casting golden and silver

medals among the people.   Arrived at the Castle,
the cannon began, and in the evening a grand
feast was held in the great Hall.   This royal
feasting lasted three days; on the third the
Estates took the oaths to her Majesty; "on the
following Wednesday, people rested;" on the
Thursday there came a tournament, wherein
Prince Charles, the Landgrave of Hesse and others
did marvels; "what chiefly caused astonishment
was a fine triumphal car, which advanced by
itself along the course, without any one being
able to discern the secret means by which it
moved;" there was also "a mountain as high as
a house, on which persons dressed like goddesses,
representing the assembly of the Muses, dis-
coursed a pleasant music."

The Assembly of deputies of the Empire at
Nuremberg congratulated Christina, as well on
the conclusion of peace as on her coronation,
comparing her heroical virtues to a luminous
body spreading its rays throughout the Universe.
At Stockholm a great number of theatrical pieces
were given in her honour, amongst others, one
representing the superiority of women to men;
and as a memorial of the solemnities, a pyramid
was set up, as it were erected to Christina by
Antiope, Penthesilea, and Thalestris, the three
queens of the Amazons.

"After this Thursday," adds the report,

" attention was given to serious business, touching the conclusion of the Diet, which nevertheless did not prevent certain further rejoicings ; " the nobility, for instance, gave banquets and feasts one after another to honour the Queen and keep up the festivities.

One wonders indeed with what mingled feelings these gorgeous displays were viewed by the faithful commons, who were at this moment vainly endeavouring to get their wrongs redressed.

# CHAPTER IV.

To the well-known theory of Bolingbroke, and those attempted revivals of his principles in modern times which may be briefly described as the "monarch and multitude" constitutional ideal, hostile critics have objected that, apart from the abstract value of the remedy proposed, it did not fit the facts it sought to meet. But were it possible for such a patriot king as Bolingbroke dreamed of to exist in flesh and blood, of all times and places that which would have suited him best was Sweden in 1650, when a middle class did not practically exist, and only a close and oppressive Venetian oligarchy stood between the monarch and a down-trodden people.

As we have seen, Christina's confirmation, on her accession in 1644, of all the acts of the Regents, and her refusal to resume the alienated Crown lands, had aroused great discontent; this burst forth with violence, as soon as the termination of the war threw the Swedes back upon themselves. The centre of the question lay in this alienation of the Crown lands; with this is intimately connected the general social condition and the mutual relations of nobles and commons;

all evils being greatly enhanced by the extreme exhaustion of the country and the finances owing to the long war.

To appreciate the situation it is necessary to glance at the internal condition of Sweden, and the causes which led to the bad state of affairs. It must be carefully observed, however, that the prevailing aristocratic tendency was by no means peculiar to Sweden, but formed a part of that which was going on at the time throughout Europe. "There has never," says Ranke, "been a time more favourable to the aristocracy than the middle of the seventeenth century, when throughout the whole extent of the Spanish monarchy that power, which preceding kings had withdrawn from the high nobility, had again fallen into their hands; when the constitution of England acquired, amidst the most perilous conflicts and struggles, that aristocratic character which it retains even to our own times; when the French parliaments persuaded themselves that they could perform a part similar to that taken by the English Houses; when the nobility acquired a decided predominance through all the German territories—one here and there excepted, where some courageous prince overpowered all efforts for independence; when the Estates of Sweden attempted to impose insufferable restraints on the sovereign authority, and the Polish nobility attained to unfettered autonomy. The same spirit was now becoming prevalent in Rome."

This universal tendency was not unnoticed by the statesmen of that age; the troubles in France and England were marked with apprehension by Christina, who knew the state of her own country, and feared the influence of example. Already in February, 1647, she writes to Salvius: "I foresee there will be plenty for me to attend to here, so I pray for a peace." And it was especially on this account she distrusted the Chancellor, who was said to be so much in favour of the Republican form of government that he spoke of it and praised it openly. Chanut says of him that though he blamed the barbarity of the execution of Charles I., yet he admired and praised the designs and tendency of the Parliament. "I tell you," said Christina to Whitelocke in 1653, speaking of Oliver Cromwell, "under secrecy, that my Chancellor would formerly have been so in Sweden when I was young, but could not attain unto it; but if he was my enemy, yet I should say that he is a wise and gallant man."

In Sweden the nobility had always been strong. It was their temporary depression by the tyranny of Christian II. and his "blood bath of Stockholm" that enabled Gustavus Vasa to unite with the people and establish himself.

Charles IX. made it his especial aim to destroy their power, but Gustavus Adolphus, partly through his desire of conciliating them as a basis for his own power, partly by the combined influence of his continued absence in war, and the aristocratic tendency of his new system of nobility of office, greatly increased their preponderance. Under him and the Regency the nobles added to their enormous social influence that of political power; by the form of government, as already shown, the whole administration of the State was placed in their hands. Socially they were omnipotent. They could only be judged by their peers; their property could not pass, by sale or otherwise, into the hands of the Crown; they were untaxed; no taxes could even be imposed on the peasants in their domains without their consent; they had their own courts of justice; they might trade with their own wares free of toll. They stood shoulder to shoulder for their own interests against King and Commons, equally jealous of "new men" and the citizen class; by a marriage with a woman of this class a noble lost his rights. They alone benefited by the war, not only because its burdens did not fall on them, nor again because they acquired glory and huge sums in its conduct, but because they took advantage of the necessities of the State to purchase, often for merely nominal values, those Crown lands which the King had to sell to get money; for only the nobility might purchase these lands, and thus, having no competitors, they bought them frequently for next to nothing at all. All this power they abused and increased enormously by reckless neglect or open defiance of the law, and grinding of the peasants.

Upon this unfortunate class fell the whole weight of the war. Taxes, conscriptions, exactions of all kinds were not the worst; the impossibility of redress and the savage oppression of the nobles laid upon them the last straw. Things grew so bad that numbers left their homes; whole districts were evacuated, and the land lay untilled; agriculture was fast being ruined. Beyond all, they resented the alienation of the Crown lands; they complained that by the change of masters the free yeoman became a slave; for the nobles used their power to annihilate every vestige of personal right in their tenant. Instead of holding direct of the Crown, he now depended on the arbitrary will of the noble to whom he fell; even in cases where legally certain rights remained to him, his master used every means of persuasion or intimidation by force or fraud to reduce him to complete dependence. The nobles even made a boast of this altered relation. "We are all

subjects of the Crown," said the High Steward
Count Brahé, in the Diet of 1650, "we immediately, the peasants mediately." Not only the
Crown lands, but the Crown rents of the tax-
paying peasants were alienated; and "as there
were not wanting persons to maintain that all
liability to land tax had its origin in the Crown's
primary right of property in the soil, wherefore
the transfer of the rents must bring with it a
silent transfer of the soil itself," the one way was
as good as the other. The soil was rapidly
becoming vested in the nobility; the old complaint of Pliny, *Latifundia perdidere Italiam*, was
becoming applicable also to Sweden. In 1624,
the peasants even threatened in certain districts
to murder the nobles, and drive away the King.

The alienation of Crown lands arose out of the
financial difficulties. Gustavus Adolphus, always
pressed for money, could find none; the lower
orders were completely exhausted; no further
imposts could be laid upon them without danger
of a revolt : the occupation of certain monopolies,
such as salt, by the Crown, was insufficient and
temporary; no resource remained but the Crown
lands : these were mortgaged, sold, and given
away with reckless extravagance. Under the
Regency the practice was continued and greatly
increased. The ownership of large estates had
indeed something to be said on its side : a

K

greater capital could be employed upon the
land ; yet the entire want of consideration on
the part of the nobles rendered this advantage
trifling in comparison with the counterbalancing
evils. There can be no doubt that they aimed
at doing what had already taken place in
Denmark, and gaining a complete preponderance
in the State : they proved this well by their subsequent action during the minority of Charles XI.
We cannot acquit Oxenstiern of the blame, that
he made no thoroughgoing attempt to set
himself against the evil; but he seems to have
been of that school of statesmen who devote their
genius wholly to the welfare of the State as a
whole, in its foreign relations, rather than in its
domestic condition : and yet this was certainly
not for want of insight.*

Against the lack of income was to be set the
enormous expenditure of the State. The necessary outlay for the war was greatly increased by
the superfluous number of officers and the
enormous pay of the State officials. It is worth
while to particularise here. The five Regents
had each 18,000 thalers a year ; the Admiral
in addition, as he had to keep open table, 500 th.
a week ; every senator 6,000 th. a year, with
500 th. a month for table expenses. Further, most
of them had some governorship, which brought

* See page 29.

him in a large sum; any who had not, received instead 600 th. a year. And this only for the Senate! It was the same with ambassadors. John Oxenstiern received at the Congress 50 th. a day while alone, and 100 th. when the three plenipotentiaries were together. " What wonder," says Grauert, " that at Christina's accession the State chest was so empty that the ordinary necessaries could no longer be paid for, and credit was gone ! "

This, however, was not all. The higher officers in the army always received disproportionately huge sums; further, there was endless mismanagement and peculation among the officials. A certain councillor of the Exchequer, for instance, one Hanson, who had amassed great wealth, and was ennobled in 1641, was condemned to death in 1642 for great malversations, his patent of nobility being torn up. How powerful his accomplices were, and, let us add, how prevalent the crime, appears from this : that they induced the young Queen to beg for his life ; but the case was too glaring.

It must always be remembered in Christina's favour that she *found* the financial condition desperate and did not make *make* it so. Her thoughtless profusion certainly added to the difficulties, but was infinitely far from creating them. That the catastrophe occurred in 1650, during her reign, proves this absolutely; it was the discharge of the accumulated evils of fifty years. Hence the extreme necessity for peace, which yet, when it came, for the moment added to the distress. And she endeavoured to ameliorate the condition of the down-trodden peasants in various ways, before the outbreak in 1650. She provided by law that they should be paid for the lodging and horses which they had previously been obliged to supply to the nobles gratis, when they were travelling through the country. She endeavoured to promote emigration to America in her newly-established colony, by granting privileges to settlers. And she caused a committee to examine the laws and rectify as far as possible existing anomalies and abuses in accordance with the principles of equity. One of the complaints of the oppressed Fourth Estate referred specially to the abuse of justice, the private prisons and tortures, used against them by the nobility. The torture in trials, hitherto resorted to, was abolished by her.

In 1650, the wretched state of things described was enhanced by bad harvests and famine. The loud clamours of the peasantry against the nobles, and their angry demand that the Crown estates should be reclaimed, were accompanied by another complication which gave them a powerful support. Certain privileges of the nobles had given special offence to the clergy; in particular, the tithes, from which in respect of their manors the nobility was exempted, and the right of patronage in parishes; the nobles in a pastoral district could elect the minister, and, in spite of certain limiting conditions, " no priest could be forced upon a noble against his will : " the nobles had their own chapels, and their own chaplain, and " would not go to church." This caused the ecclesiastical order to unite with the people, by whom they were much esteemed, and over whom they had great influence. But within this order there was no cohesion ; the bishops, whose position in relation to the inferior clergy was analogous to that of the old nobility towards the " new men," were seen to abandon their class, and side with the aristocratic party.

Already, in 1649, there had been presages of that which was to come. While the peasants renewed their murmuring against the nobles, the clergy raised their complaints as to the abuse of patronage and the non-payment of tithes. The nobility treated these claims with insolent-arrogance. They " demanded the maintenance of their right of patronage unimpaired." The Queen replied that the nobility were bound, unless furnished with a legal excuse, to attend the churches; otherwise, from the number of chaplains, the land would be overstocked with clergy who were not wanted, so that they would be eventually compelled, to the

dishonour of the realm and degradation of the
order, to settle in farms and become peasants,
and be employed by the nobility like others of
their slaves.   In opposition to the prospect of the
civil service appointments being open to the sons
of priests, if capable, the nobles petitioned that
persons of their own order might be employed in
her Majesty's Chancery.   "They regarded the
first offices in the State as their patrimony."   The
Queen sharply answered, " Offices were no hereditary estates."   Things began to look very black :
seditious pamphlets and satirical pasquinades
were circulated.   " I see," wrote the Chancellor,
" that Europe and the whole world is disturbed ;
there seems to be at hand a great *conversio rerum.*"

The fulness of time and the stir caused by her
coronation brought things to a crisis in 1650.
On October 3rd the three lower orders presented
to her their "Protestation as to the restitution
of Crown Estates."   In this, after enumerating the
grounds of their discontent, they demand that all
Crown lands shall be resumed and that it shall be
declared illegal to sell such lands for the future.

The nobles endeavoured to excite the hostility
of the Queen against the Orders, by pleading that
this petition was an attack on the royal prerogat-
ive.   But although Christina was firmly determined not to resume any lands, either bought
with money or given away by herself, and

regarded such an act as mere confiscation, her
sympathies were entirely for the petitioners.
"She approved greatly of the protest of the
Orders, as being a salutary measure, recommending them most earnestly to be constant in their
purpose, and repeatedly ejaculating, 'Now or
never,'" says Terserus, the energetic and resolute
spokesman of the lower clergy, deserted by their
bishops.  It was entirely owing to her tact and
sympathetic mediation that some great social
convulsion was prevented, for "there was every
prospect of civil war, to which not only the
country people, but the burghers were much
inclined; some of the most wealthy nobles
thought of flight." There was fighting in the
streets of Stockholm; Oxenstiern is said to have
sat in his room, expecting every time the door
opened that some one would come in to assassi-
nate him.

How difficult a position Christina was in will
be realised if we recollect that at this moment
her Coronation was placing her in intimate
personal connection with those very men whom,
as nobles, she was politically opposed to; and
this made it almost impossible entirely to break
with them.  Still, it is to be remembered that,
throughout the danger, she was never unpopular
with the people; it was not her, but the nobles,
they hated.  One of the seditious pamphlets,

entitled 'Spectacles for Princes,' exemplifies their attitude; in it she is warned to open her eyes to the designs of the aristocracy, who are aiming at ruining her and enslaving the people. No intimidation on their part could induce her, however, to consent to resume the Crown lands; but she did what she could in their behalf. She promised both the clergy and the peasants her protection, and issued decrees confirming the privileges of the former, and directing that the nobles should abstain from oppressing their peasants. She found a certain support against the old aristocracy in those "new" men whom she raised in large numbers to the nobility during her reign, but she could not do much against them; they were too strong. The burgher class were appeased in some degree by a reduction of the salt tax; and the dexterous conciliation of the clergy by the Queen at length after a split of six weeks reunited them to their bishops. When the Estates had remained assembled for the unprecedented time of four months, they separated, their animosities allayed, not satisfied; and the temporary pacification was only effected by the clergy signing the protest, the nobles refusing to make the slightest concessions. How little they cared for expostulations is seen in their demand of the Queen that an example should be made of the boldest among their denunciators in the

Diet; when this was refused, they next asked her to address a sharp reprimand to the orders that had ventured to oppose them. No aristocracy has ever shown so sublime an unconsciousness that power has its duties, as the Swedish; they continued in their blind infatuation till retribution came under Charles XI. Christina scouted their request; she went further, and publicly declared, with regard to the contemptuous epithet "ill-born" they applied to the lower Orders, that no others should be understood by the word than those who had degenerated from their birth by the neglect of virtue, and stained their descent by sloth and baseness; and that all who were of legitimate birth and respectable ancestry, whether nobles or clergy, burghers or peasants, should neither be called "ill-born," nor excluded from any station of honour in their native country.

And here appears the only insoluble problem in Christina's career. How was it that, while she had the genius to appreciate the evil state of the people and the courage to take their part against the nobles, while in all other ways she laboured unwearyingly for the good of the State and neglected her own health in its service, she could yet indulge in such reckless extravagance, in the matter of Crown lands, as threw all her predecessors into the shade. For such is the fact. The budget of the Treasury in 1645 shows a deficit of nearly a million; that of 1654, one of nearly four millions: for, while the debts increased a million and a half, the Crown claims decreased by more than a million. The proportion between the alienation of Crown lands by Gustavus Adolphus, the Regents, and Christina is as 1, 2, and 4: "the registers of her reign are filled with deeds of sale, infeudations, letters of nobility, tokens of grace, and gifts of every sort. She had brilliant merits to reward, sometimes ancient wrongs to redress, and the care which she devoted to old or wounded soldiers deserves all praise." We shall presently see the lavish generosity with which she rewarded men of learning; and not only these; her donations to Magnus de la Gardie reach the incredible: he is said to have obtained from her landed estates alone to the value of 80,000 rix dollars *per annum.* We may, if we like, partly explain the deficit stated above by referring to the Coronation expenses; we may consider that the bulk of her gifts were to newly-created nobles, in order to support herself against the old aristocracy. But it remains after all not to be palliated. The fact remains that, though frugal herself to an extraordinary degree, she was possessed by a mania for squandering which is a great blot on her administration. It was the sole point in which she resembled her mother. She seems to have considered it only natural to give without stint to anybody at any moment; nay, more: she remained throughout her life completely unconscious that there was any reason why she should not: it never occurred to her that money came to an end. Even to Count Magnus, the gulf into which she threw so much, she complained, with obvious surprise, that she had not money enough to keep up her Court. She exactly illustrates the remark of the Roman satirist, that women never calculate accounts. But, on the other hand, the cause of the wretched condition of the country during her reign is by no means to be found in her lavishness, which was, after all, temporary; the evil lay deeper: in the misery produced by the war, and the oppression of the nobles. The popular instinct was truer. When Christina returned to Sweden in after years, it was not in the people, but in the governing classes, nobles and clergy, who feared for themselves and their religion, that she found her bitter enemies.

Thus then for the present the storm blew over. Christina now turned herself to the carrying out of her plan. In spite of all obstacles, she had continually increased her own power, and made two steps towards her design of substituting Charles upon the throne. She now prepared to advance still further.

The apparent calm of the Queen, and her continued expenditure, induced observers to suppose that she had some extraordinary means at her command of solving the difficulties : it was conjectured that she was nourishing the design of abdicating in favour of the Prince : it was noticed that she began to show more favour to the Chancellor and his party than heretofore, which augured a desire to stand well with everybody on quitting the helm of State : this suspicion was strengthened by her announced intention of making a voyage to the islands of Gothland and Oeland, places suited, it was thought, for her residence after her abdication. In the meantime Charles was in an ambiguous position. If he manifested any desire to take part in the government, it might easily be mis-interpreted; at the same time, what must have been his secret emotions at the thought of waiting so long for his accession as Christina's youth might give him to infer ! But, on the other hand, the state of the kingdom and her extravagant procedure must have dulled his desire to take charge of the State at such a moment, and given him fears for the future. Yet his present dexterity, when contrasted with the real ambition of his character as it was afterwards displayed, proved him to have at least one of the qualities of greatness : the power of

biding his time.  He lived retired on the island
of Oeland, spending his time in building, hunting,
and kindred pursuits ; paying at the same time
court to everybody ; occasionally writing to
remind the Queen of his marriage proposals,
though he began to see his hopes were herein
not destined to be realised.

The Queen's design was penetrated first by
Chanut, who hastened to try and dissuade her
from it.  The Court of France was by no means
anxious to see her replaced on the Swedish
throne by the warlike Charles, whom it distrusted.
In spite of his representations, however, Christina
remained inflexible, showing to Chanut good
reasons why to retreat was now impossible.  She
next communicated it to the Prince, who feared
she might be testing him, and thought it best
to endeavour to dissuade her from her intention.
Christina finally (in October) disclosed it to the
Grand Marshal and the Chancellor, telling them
to bid the Prince come and make his preparations for assuming the government.  In reply, he
bade them do all they could to turn her from
her purpose, and continue a reign so beneficial to
the country ; he never wished for himself to be
anything but her dutiful subject.  In spite of all
remonstrances, however, the Queen, on October
25, 1651, declared in full Senate her determination to resign the Crown in favour of the Prince,

and retire into private life. She told them that
after mature reflection on a point of such importance she could find no better means than
this of providing for the safety of the State and
the repose of the people, who wished to see the
succession secured by the birth of heirs to the
throne ; as she was firmly resolved never to
marry, the Prince being once declared king
would be obliged to take a wife, and the children
born to him would deliver the nation from the
fear it had of the evils usually accompanying
the elections of kings. The Senators vainly
endeavoured to bend her will by representing
to her that God had given them a queen, and
that as long as God preserved her life they
would acknowledge no one else ; they laid stress,
not unreasonably, on the exhausted state of the
finances, and the additional cost of another
coronation and the marriage of the Prince.
Finding her inflexible, however, it was determined
to postpone further consideration to the approaching Diet in February next.

In November, notwithstanding, the Senators
and the delegates of the Estates made a final
effort to overcome her resistance. They went
in a body to her, Oxenstiern himself acting as
spokesman. His eloquent appeal, directed to
touching her heart rather than changing her
mind, had a great effect upon her ; she agreed to

revoke her determination, upon the condition that nothing more was said to her on the subject of marriage. This was accepted; all, including Prince Charles, testifying their satisfaction at the change. Her birthday, on which she gave a feast, with games, tournaments, balls, and amusements, afforded an opportunity of giving vent to the general rejoicing (which was by no means feigned, for the nobles feared Charles becoming king); nevertheless she told Chanut, that, though she had not been able to refuse this satisfaction to her subjects, she had not so firmly renounced her plan as to leave it impossible that she should one day return to it.

Although Christina's attention was so much engaged during those years in the negotiations for the peace, the settlement of the succession, and the internal disturbances in her own kingdom; although at the same time she was devoting herself to hard study, and taking an eager interest in philosophical, literary, and scientific subjects, which will presently be examined, she found time to follow closely contemporary foreign events. "One would have imagined," says Whitelocke in 1653, "that England had been her native country, so well was she furnished with the character of most persons of consideration there, and with the story of the nation." She was no less interested in France and its domestic affairs. As we have seen, she laboured during the peace negotiations for a cordial understanding with that country : especially did she admire Condé ; after his victory at Nordlingen she wrote him a complimentary letter, which he answered in terms equally flattering.  She did not confine herself to compliments : when the French wished to engage the troops disbanded by Sweden for the Spanish war, which still continued, Christina, although the Senate was adverse, wrote to Prince Charles, then in Germany, bidding him oblige the King of France in this.  Again, still further to show her good will, she sent two men-of-war as presents, one to the Queen, and one to the Cardinal, the latter called Julius, in his honour, and valued at 40,000 crowns.  The view she took of the troubles of the Fronde was influenced by her esteem for Condé, who even wrote to demand her assistance, and a change is afterwards observable in her opinion of Mazarin.  With the view of mediating between the belligerent parties, she wrote to Condé twice, to the King of France, to the King of Spain, to the Duke of Orleans, to Mademoiselle de Montpensier, to the Parliament, as well as to Cardinal de Retz and Anne of Austria.

In that to the Duke of Orleans she alludes to Mazarin as a stranger, who wishes to dictate the law and not stop till he has ruined all. Mazarin was aware of her views and resented her interference; some incautious expressions of her resident in Paris, though she afterwards disavowed them, increased the bad feeling, and her attempts at pacifying differences led to nothing.

When we come to consider Christina's reign on what is perhaps its most brilliant side, we must beware of falling into the mistake of supposing that the sudden scientific and literary glitter which emanated from Sweden at this moment has anything in common with those periods in history, such as that of Pericles in Athens or Elizabeth in England, when the national activity in war is accompanied by a spontaneous impulse in intellectual creation. There was scarcely any native element in the specious, but factitious and imported mental energy of the Swedish court; it depended almost entirely upon Christina's personal interest and patronage. She found Sweden on her accession in a state of intellectual darkness, into which when she vacated the throne it sank back, or rather from which it had never risen; not that she did not make a great effort to promote a better condition of things, but the people were not able to respond to her attempts—in spite of here and there an isolated instance, which only show more plainly because of the general want of culture. The

L

position which Sweden then occupied in Europe was entirely based upon military relations, and far greater than its internal progress, whether commercial, intellectual, or social, entitled it to hold. A glance at this will materially assist us in estimating Christina's own influence.

The bad state of the finances, and the dangerous relation of the social strata to one another, as far as highest and lowest, nobles and peasantry, are concerned, have been already described. A middle class, manufacturing and commercial, was still in its infancy. The only good thing to be said for the war, that it brought Sweden into closer relation with the rest of Europe, and thus paved the way for commerce, must not be over-looked. Gustavus Adolphus endeavoured to improve it in various ways, especially in respect of handicrafts and manufactures; foreign artisans, refugees from Holland, France, Germany, and Spain, were encouraged to come and remain by special privileges and exemptions; by their instruction the fabrication of raw material, such as cotton and wool, weaving, metal and leather factories were improved; the working of the mines in which Sweden's chief wealth lay, silver, iron, and especially copper, received a great impulse from De Geer, who came from Holland, and the Walloon smiths he brought with him; this again acted beneficially on the manufacture of weapons

of all kinds, which formed a chief article of
export in exchange for, *e.g.*, salt from Portugal,
with which Sweden was ill supplied ; some Crown
monopolies, such as those of salt and corn, were
withdrawn. Axel Oxenstiern's large views on
trade have already been given, but monopolies
and the system of guilds were the basis of the
Swedish economical principles : " a man might
make himself king in Sweden," said Klas
Flemming, " but could not make himself a
tailor." This, and the doubtful political relations,
especially the jealousy of the Powers on the
Baltic, stood in the way of commercial progress ; though Sweden, in 1642, even extended
her trade to the Delaware, on the banks of
which was erected a Fort Christina. The trade,
principally tobacco, was held as a monopoly by
the State.

The educational provision in Sweden was very
poor. Gustavus Adolphus did what he could for
it ; he established the University of Upsala on a
new basis, endowed it with lands of his own,
furnished it with a library, and sent it books from
Germany : at Dorpat he founded a college. In
this respect even the nobles did something ;
during his governorship in Finland Brahé established various schools and a college at Åbo ;
Axel Oxenstiern, a college at Westerås ; John
Skytté, a chair of history and political philosophy

at Upsala; schools were also founded by Baner,
Bielke, and others. Little was taught, however,
but grammar, rhetoric, and logic, the most useless
of all subjects to begin on; history very scantily,
Latin badly. Whitelocke tells us that the
professors at Upsala were promised good salaries,
but complained that they were not well paid.
The library at Upsala was not as good as his own
private one; as he informed some of the scholars,
"who were not well pleased therewith." He
gave five pounds to Ravius, professor of Hebrew,
whose pension was supposed to be 500 rix dollars,
but he was never paid; he frequently refers to
the bad Latin of the students. Theology
flourished best, though there were few men of
liberal opinions such as Matthiæ. "The Swedes,"
an ecclesiastic told Whitelocke, "generally and
devoutly do adhere to the opinions of Luther and
to the practice of the churches allowed by him,
and whoever differs from them is not only looked
upon with an evil eye, but commonly driven
from the country." "In the seventeenth century
it was ordered in Sweden and confirmed by
Government, that if any Swedish subject change
his religion, he shall be banished the kingdom,
and lose all right of inheritance both for himself and his descendants. If any bring into the
country teachers of another religion, he shall be
fined and banished." Roman Catholics were not

allowed to exercise their religion in Sweden till 1781. Just as in Scotland, to which in this respect Sweden was very similar, long sermons were the special feature of the religious service. The people were very superstitious; even the leading clergymen believed in leagues with the devil and witchcraft. In Finland, where the inhabitants were not men, said Oxenstiern, but beasts, Brahé made it the necessary standard for a priest that he should know his catechism. The greatest intolerance prevailed, especially of Roman Catholics or Calvinists. In 1657 a peasant was condemned to death for railing against the minister of his parish. Science did not exist, although alchemy and astrology were generally practised, and the philosopher's stone hunted for; any man of a little knowledge was regarded as a magician and atheist; the celebrated Stiernhielm was accused of witchcraft for having burned a peasant's beard with a magnifying glass, and shown a clergyman a flea through it; he was in danger of his life, and was only saved by the interposition of Christina. The odium of his persecutors was further excited by his patriotic assertion that the Swedish was more ancient than the Hebrew tongue.

Especially deplorable was the condition of medicine: the nostrums of quacks and old wives' receipts were the only form of cure; no one

studied the subject, as a living could not be made
by it; such doctors as there were invariably
prescribed bleeding. The Regents endeavoured
to improve this by importing doctors from abroad,
who were not much better; they established a
school of anatomy, and tried to introduce surgery;
but the popular odium against dissection was so
great that they could hardly induce any one to
practise it. "There was in Sweden," said a
certain Mornichof, "one king, one religion, and
one doctor."

A passage in Whitelocke is well worthy
quoting. "He enquired how the Chancellor's
health was, and what physicians were about him.
Lagerfeldt said he was still sick of his ague, and
had no physician attending him but one who had
been a chirurgeon in the army, and who had
some good receipts, especially for the stone,
which agreed with the Chancellor's constitution,
which this chirurgeon only studied and attended."
And so it was generally in this great and large
country. Whitelocke met with no doctor of
physic or professed physician in any town or
country, nor any attending the person of the
Queen herself: but there are many good women,
and private persons, who use to help people that
are diseased by some ordinary known remedies."
The question of doctors will come before us again
with reference to Christina. In Philosophy an

Aristotelian scholasticism, or what was worse, the nonsense of Ramus, dominated the schools.

The private life was very rude; in Upsala, "not above nine or ten houses were built of brick." Whitelocke's own house, "a fair brick house," was the best in the town next to the Queen's own; most of them were built "of the bodies of great fir trees, covered with turf." The floors were generally not boarded, but paved with stone or brick; the walls were whitewashed, without any decoration, even in the best houses; the furniture was bad; at dinner a sort of canopy was ordinarily suspended over the table, to prevent spiders' webs from falling into the dishes. The cookery was very coarse, as also was the language; drinking and swearing were inseparable from a feast. " 'Thou hast preserved me," says Christina in her Memoirs, "from the vice of drunkenness, but suffered me to be infected with the vice of swearing by contagion; but by Thy grace, Lord, I have entirely cured myself of it; I am nevertheless in some sort excusable, because I was born in a country and an age where this defect reigned over both sexes alike, and people could not speak without swearing."

People were not generally well off. Whitelocke tells us of "a country minister's house, a very mean one, and his family in as mean a condition; his children in torn shirts, and no other clothes

upon them in that bitter cold weather, and his
wife little better furnished." During his journey
from Gothenburg to Upsala, he and his suite
were most miserably accommodated; "the gentlemen lay in fresh straw round about him, he
being frolic and cheering them, and it is no
small part of the art of government to know
when to be familiar;" "they could get no other
provision but the quarters of a beast which was
said to be found dead in the field; Whitelocke
commended the variety and dressing of this
meat, and it went down with good stomachs, and
made good meat afterwards to taste the sweeter,
besides the delight in remembrance of it." And
this is no isolated exception; the same thing
occurs throughout his journey.

We shall be forcibly struck with the contrast,
when we turn from this benighted condition of
things to examine Christina's relations with the
literary and scientific men of her time. The
Peace of 1648 left her at liberty to indulge her
many-sided intellectual interests: Stockholm
became a loadstone to draw together *savans*
from all parts of Europe.

Foremost among these was Descartes. She had
already heard much of him from Chanut, who was
a great friend of his, and a zealous Cartesian: in
1646 she sent to ask him, through Chanut, his
opinion on this question: When one makes a bad

use of love or hate, which of those abuses is the worst? Descartes, though we may suspect he knew as little as Bacon of the passion of love, concluded in his dissertation on the subject that when pushed to a vicious extreme, love was the most dangerous. She next asked him for his opinion on the *Summum bonum*, on which he sent her a treatise on the question; according to him, external blessings being precarious, there remain to us two points of special importance; to know, and to will, what is good: the sovereign good for us he places accordingly in always preserving a firm and constant resolution to do what according to our judgment is best, and endeavour with all our strength to discern it well. Shortly afterwards Christina wrote and invited him to come to Stockholm; after some hesitation he accepted, in a letter full of hyperbole; he wrote at the same time to Chanut, in which he says among other things (and the opinion of one who was so good a writer of French prose as Descartes is worth having), "I was surprised to see how easily and tersely she writes French; our whole nation is much obliged to her, therefore, and it seems to me that this Princess has been created far more in the image of God than other men have; the more so, as she can apply herself to so great a variety of business at once." Nevertheless, with characteristic caution, Descartes, to make sure of his ground, wrote to Freinsheim (whom Christina had made her librarian, the author of the 'Supplement to Livy'), and asked him whether, as he was the author of a new philosophy and a Roman Catholic, this might not be a snare of his enemies to do him harm. Freinsheim reassured him, and accordingly in October, 1649, he arrived at Stockholm, and was graciously received by Christina. The admiration was mutual : Descartes wrote soon after to his friend the Princess Elizabeth,*

" The generosity and majesty of the Queen in all her actions is combined with such sweetness and goodness, as to make all fall in love with her ; she is extremely given to study, though I cannot say whether she will approve of my own philosophy, as she knows nothing of it as yet." He adds, with a touch of his usual contempt for learning, that this keen ardour of hers in study incites her principally to the study of Greek and the collecting of ancient books, " but perhaps this will change."

The course of events furnishes an ironical commentary on this letter. Christina had so much to do that she was very avaricious of her time ; her ardour for study made it necessary for Descartes to come and see her at five o'clock

* On whom, see an essay in Courtenay's ' Studies, New and Old.'

every morning in her library ; her Greek studies
proved to be awkward, if it be true, as is said,
that she accused him of stealing his ideas from
Plato.   There seems to be a fatality in the
relations between philosophers and princes.  The
early rising in a very cold climate was fatal to
Descartes, who was fond of lying in bed in the
morning ; after about two months of these discussions before sunrise, he was attacked by fever
and inflammation of the lungs, and died on
February 1st, 1650.   But the concern Christina
showed at his death is a sufficient refutation of
ill-natured reports ; she was only dissuaded with
difficulty from giving him a funeral like that of
the ancient kings of Sweden ; although Baillet's
assertion, that she consulted him on political
questions, is no less foolish than the tittle-tattle
of Madame de Motteville, that he died because
Christina despised his philosophy.   He was
buried at Stockholm ; seventeen years afterwards
his remains were removed to Paris.   Though he
was viewed with jealousy by the ⌐pedants at the
Court, yet he left a few disciples in Sweden, who
formed the nucleus of a sect ; some time after, in
the reign of Charles XI., nearly all the professors
of philosophy at Upsala being Cartesians, the
adherents of Scholasticism complained to the
King, who decided in favour of the new method.
Christina always attributed to him a considerable

influence in her conversion; for this one of her biographers accuses her of superficiality, as, according to him, it is almost paradoxical that her Catholicism should have been induced by his sceptical principles. Why, certainly, there is here evidence of superficiality, but it is not Christina's.

A philosopher of a very different school was Gassendi, for whom, although she never met him, Christina always had a great admiration, but not greater than he deserved. In July, 1652, he wrote her a letter, telling her that he had heard of her from Bourdelot; he congratulated her on realising the ideal of Plato, who refused happiness to the human race till kings should be philosophers, and philosophers kings. Christina answered his flattery in a letter of which Malherbe declared that it was written in a style as pure as if it had been penned at the Court of France; and throughout her life she maintained a correspondence with him.

But the bulk of her admirers and protégés were men of learning rather than philosophy; of these Salmatius, or Saumaise, was the first; chiefly known now, just as Milton predicted, by his 'Defence of the People of England,' which was an answer to the 'Defence of the King,' by Saumaise. His great reputation for learning made Christina anxious to bring him to Sweden; she wrote him several letters to invite him;

finally he came in the summer of 1650, and was lodged in the royal palace. His University of Leyden, however, declared that they could no more do without him than without the sun, and he returned the next year. He was a man of an arrogant and overbearing temper, and thought that no one knew anything but himself; hence he had many enemies, especially at the Court of Sweden ; there during his stay he was at variance with Vossius, Nicolas Heinsius, and others. He treated other *savans*, even of the first order, as merely of the mob in comparison with himself. Being one day in the library of the King of France, in company with Gaulmin and Maussac, the former said, complacently, " I think we three could make head against all the learning in Europe." Saumaise promptly replied, "Add yourself and Maussac to all the *savans* in the world, I will make head against the lot of you, alone." Even Grotius he treated with contempt. " One would have thought," says Bayle, " he had placed his throne on a heap of stones, in order to throw them at all that passed by." Christina was perfectly able to distinguish between different sorts of ability, and mingled her esteem for his learning with a certain contempt for his pedantry, a thing she always abhorred, though there was plenty at Stockholm ; she used to call him " *omnium fatuorum doctissimum*," and said of him that he knew·the name for a chair in all languages, but did not know how to sit down on one. Nevertheless, she had a regard for his great acquirements, and when he died, wrote a letter of condolence to his widow, (a shrew before whom the imperious scholar quailed when alive, and who burned all his MSS. on his death), rebuking her "for the homicide she had committed on his writings." It was by Saumaise that Bourdelot was introduced to the Queen, and the *savans* put down her changed attitude to them after the arrival of the latter in part to the machinations of Saumaise. "*Constans hic est opinio,*" wrote Heinsius to Gronovius in 1655, "*Salmasii et Bourdelotii operâ Christinam periisse.*" This "*periisse,*" of course, represents the view taken of her conduct by the Swedish Lutherans and disappointed pedants.

In 1649, Isaac Vossius was invited to Sweden : celebrated especially for his knowledge of Greek, which Christina studied with him, he is also suspected of teaching her his own views on religion, or irreligion, for he was supposed to be an atheist, which did not prevent Charles II. from making him Canon of Windsor : the king's witticism on him, when Vossius was ventilating some wild theories about China, "This learned theologian is a strange man, he believes everything but the Bible," may have been partly the cause of his getting the canonry. He was certainly a man of lax principles as to *meum* and *tuum*, and made capital out of his commission to buy books for Christina's library : of which more anon. Nicholas Heinsius, a man of a simple honourable character, the editor of Ovid and Claudian, whose father had been much esteemed by Gustavus Adolphus, was also sent by Christina into Italy to collect MSS. and books : Herman Conring, the author of the refutation of the Papal Bull already mentioned : Naudæus, whom she made her librarian : John Amos Comenius, who was summoned by Christina to come and reform all the schools in the kingdom, in accordance with his *Janua Linguarum reservata*, dealing with a new method of teaching languages ; Loccenius, and Schoeffer, his son-in-law, who distinguished themselves in the study of Swedish antiquities ; John Henry Boecler, whom she made Professor of Eloquence at Upsala, and the year after, 1650, her historiographer, were a few among the host of *savans* who crowded her Court. "They came in flocks with their philology and antiquities, the fashionable learning of the age ; displayed their arts, wrote dedications and panegyrics, in which all the elegancies of the Latin tongue were brought to vie in praise of the Queen, presented books, were rewarded and dismissed."

Of Boecler the following story is told, which throws light on the university system. In his lecture one day, on Tacitus, he said, "*Plura adderem, si plumbea Suecorum capita ista capere possent!*" ("I would say more, if the leaden heads of Swedes could take it in!") One of the students answered immediately, "We have not only understood all you have said up to now, but we will understand all you can say in future." The lecture over, Boecler started to go through the antechamber of the lecture-room, when a number of students seized him and *whipped* him soundly; they furthermore broke all the windows of his house, and discharged guns into the windows of his sitting-room, where he sat with his family. Christina wrote in 1650, March 15, to order this matter to be sifted, and the authors severely punished. Boecler, however, fearing further outrages, applied for his *congé* and left; his pay while a professor had been 2500 crowns a year; the Queen gave him, by way of consoling him, a present of 4000 crowns, with a gold chain, and 200 ducats, besides making him perpetual historiographer with a yearly pension of 800 crowns a year. To Octavio Ferrario, an Italian *savant*, she gave a chain of gold worth a thousand crowns, though according to him "his joy at receiving it was nothing in comparison with that caused him by the addition of a letter in her own handwriting." She gave Grotius copper to the value of 12,000 crowns; to his widow she gave 3000 th. for an MS. history of the Goths found among his papers. Copper was a favourite present: she gave Chanut and Whitelocke amounts worth £2500; she presented Freinshein with 500 ducats for his speech on her birthday, and also remitted to his native town most of its contributions for the indemnification of the army during the war. Salmasius was "overwhelmed with benefits"; Conring had a pension of 1600 th. in virtue of his title of Councillor of Sweden. These are specimens of her open hand: small wonder if she was surrounded by an eager crowd, with mouths open to praise her, and catch as well anything that might be falling. It may be doubted whether any sovereign ever had so many complimentary odes, panegyrics, and addresses composed in his honour as this "tenth Muse" and "Pallas of the North." And yet Christina despised flattery, and like Charles II., was never deceived even by those to whom she carelessly gave; her *donandi cacoethes* was no respecter of persons. The parasitical crowd, when her abdication robbed them of their means of living, felt like the man deprived of his goose with the golden eggs.

Among other celebrated names connected with that of Christina may be mentioned that of

M

Huet, afterwards Bishop of Avranches, who came with Bochart to Sweden, and published years after a manuscript of Origen he had copied in her library.  He writes to a friend in 1653: "As to the Northern Queen, you must not trust the common portraits of her, which are libels.  She is rather plump, one shoulder higher than the other; below the middle height.  Her face is refined and pretty, her hair golden; her eyes flash so that she alone in Sweden might be said to have eyes at all.  There is nothing wrong with her morals; for I pay no attention to those rumours scattered, especially in Germany, to the contrary: they are all forged in Imperial workshops; she carries modesty written on her face, and shows it by the blushes which cover it at an immodest word or deed before her.  Her memory is not happy; her genius above her sex, her learning above her years; she is easy of access, genial, and courteous, yet tenacious of her majesty; still she has nothing of the German or Northern gloom, but you would think she was born at Rome or Paris.  She is very fond of French; this is hated by the envious Swedes.  What Cicero says of himself may be said with far more justice of her, that he was not a great eater but a great jester; for she is abstemious, though a Swede, and eats sparingly, but takes wonderful pleasure in merry jests."

Here we have another cause of her calumniators' abuse.  Her laughter-loving nature was viewed with jaundiced eyes by the morose Puritans of Sweden, to whom a long and sour face was a necessary element in religion.  A very good instance of her humour is a letter she wrote to Benserade.  He had sent her his poems, which pleased her, and was to have come to Stockholm on an embassy, but did not, for some reason or other; she wrote accordingly :—

" You may bless your fortunate star, which has prevented you from coming to Sweden.  A mind so delicate as yours would have caught a chill here, and you would have gone home with a spiritual cold in your head.  You would have been all the rage in Paris with a square beard, the coat of a Lapp, with shoes to match, just back from the country of hoar frost.  I can picture you winning the hearts of old women in such a costume.  No, I tell you you have nothing to regret.  What could you come to see in Sweden ?  Our ice is the same as yours, except that here it lasts six months longer.  And our summer, when it is violent, is so outrageous that it strikes terror into the poor flowers, which do their best to look like jasmine . . . . beware of deserving such an exile; yet I could wish that by some crime you might incur such a punish-ment, in order to let us poor folks in Sweden see

M 2

some of France's choicest and most refined wit. Your verses are much appreciated here, and she to whom you sent them is much in your debt."

Of a similar character is a letter to the Countess de Brégy :—

"I can't tell what keeps me from using hard words to you, after all you have done to deserve them. What! after keeping silence for two years do you think you can cry quits by simply 'kissing my hand' in your friend's letter. Really you ought at least to be scolded. Know that I am, so to speak, very angry with you, and that your silence has gone hard to wound me deeply. Still I pardon you, on condition you are dumb no longer. *A propos* of your silence, I am tempted to quote the Pythagoreans to you, but one must not speak of them to an ignoramus like you. So I refrain; neither will I mention all the fine things I have heard of those excellent Longbeards, for fear of being taken for a fairy. Speak, then, so as to escape the suspicion of belonging to their order. To tell you what I want, send me news of your excellent Mistress, and your young Prince; tell me of the conversations of your circle, and the playful ways of the little fellow. I will have no State secrets from you; when the fancy seizes me for them I will apply to some one else, for I believe you know nothing about them. In fact, were I King of France, I should consider you suited for quite other things than government, and employ you in a service quite distinct from that of the State. We women don't understand statecraft: your incomparable Mistress alone has shown herself an adept in it. This is the way to make up our quarrel, I commend it to you as I bid you adieu.

"CHRISTINA."

Other celebrities can but be cursorily alluded to ; Scarron, who sent her one of his comedies; Balzac, who was rewarded for the present of his works with a gold chain ; Desmarets ; Scudéry, who dedicated his 'Alaric' to her ; his sister, Mdlle. de Scudéry, enjoyed a pension from Christina ; Mézerai, the historian, to whom she assigned one of 3000 florins a year ; Ménage, who wrote an eclogue in her honour, called 'Christina,' and acquired a gold chain. It is from him we learn that in the dispute as to the relative merits of ancients and moderns, Christina was for the ancients ; speaking of philosophy, she declared that "*les sottises anciennes valaient bien les nouvelles.*" It was to him that she made one of her wittiest *mots.* She used to hold a literary assembly in her Academy every Thursday. " At that time," says Ménage, "my assemblies were on Wednesday. Learning this the Queen wrote to me, '*Ma Joviale est très humble serviteur de votre Mercuriale.*'

I have always thought," he adds, " this could not
have come from her, it is too French for a
stranger." But Huet avers that he had never
known any one like Christina for the "swiftness
of a keen and fiery wit." To these is to be added
Pascal, who sent her his " *Roulette* " machine, with
an explanatory letter; the English painter,
Cooper, who came to her Court; the learned
Manasseh Ben Israel, a Portuguese Jew, a wise
and excellent man, who offered to procure her
Hebrew books for her library, and dedicated to
her his work ' *Conciliador*.' He went to England
and was well received by Cromwell, and perhaps
may have had influence on that great man's
tolerance of Jews. Cromwell's secretary, Andrew
Marvell, wrote a panegyrical ode upon Christina,
and Milton's eulogy, in the ' Second Defence,' is
well known. Christina is said to have disgusted
Saumaise by praising Milton's ' Defence ' to him.
Milton declares her in the second part " fit to
govern not only Europe but the world."

These names and instances, many of them men
whose praise was worth having, are a sufficient
proof of Christina's wide-spread fame and various
scientific interests. Among those who adorned
her Court were but few natives of Sweden, yet
we must not omit Stiernhielm, a universal genius,
" at once philosopher, geometer, philologist and
poet," whom she protected from the bigots of the

day, and the two Rudbecks, father and son; the
latter, Olaus, celebrated especially for his
discovery of the lymphatic vessels, and his
'Atlantica,' a work of Northern antiquities, of
vast learning and great value for its time, though
its patriotic zeal was open to ridicule, as readers
of Gibbon will remember.   Other Swedish names
there are, but of little note; in point of fact the
national element was conspicuous mostly for its
absence; the splendour of the Court was a costly
exotic.

Christina took especial pains to collect books
and manuscripts for her libraries, as we have
noticed.   She writes to Sarrau in April, 1651,
who was negotiating to buy for her the celebrated
De Mesmes library (the only one, says Lacroix,
that could bear comparison with that of De Thou),
that she fears some one may have stolen a Varro
which ought to be there, but cannot find in the
catalogue, and bids him have an eye to it.   She
commissioned one Job Ludolphe, who knew
twenty-two languages, to go to Rome and buy
and bring to Sweden all MSS. relating to it
carried thither at the Reformation, though he
did not succeed, as they had already been
conveyed to Poland.   Nicolas Heinsius and
Isaac Vossius were also sent on the same mission;
the former to Italy, where he met with great
success: " the Italians began to complain that

ships were laden with the spoils of their libraries, and that all their best aids to learning were carried away from them to the remotest north." Heinsius, in a letter to the Queen, informs her that her name was venerated in Italy. Vossius went to Holland, France, and Germany, spending enormous sums in purchasing all the MSS. he could find. Her own library was much enriched by the sale of Mazarin's, as well as by spoils from various places taken in the war, as Wurzburg, Olmütz, Bremen, Prague. Vossius even sold her his own library for 20,000 florins, reserving to himself the superintendence and 5000 florins a year, besides lodging and board at Court. "The Royal Library," wrote Huet in 1653, "is stuffed full, four large rooms won't hold it." But the dishonesty of *savans* such as Vossius, who abused the confidence of the Queen, reduced it to a great extent. Heinsius says, in 1654, that the French had pillaged the library, and that Vossius had carried off rich but scandalous spoils to Holland with him; of the 762 MSS. which were sold after his death to the University of Leyden, doubtless most were Christina's. What became of her remaining library after her own death will be seen in the sequel.

The intellectual interests of the "Northern Pallas" are summed up in a letter which Naudé wrote to Gassendi in October, 1652: "Of the

Queen I can say without flattery, that in the
conversations which she often holds with MM.
Bochart, Bourdelot, Du Fresne, and myself, she
maintains her part better than any one of us:
I shall not lie if I tell you that her genius is
altogether extraordinary, for she has seen, read,
and knows all. . . . To say truth, I am sometimes afraid lest the common saying should be
verified in her, that short is the life, and rare
the old age of those who surpass the common
limits . . . . don't suppose she is only learned
in books, for she is so equally in painting,
architecture, sculpture, medals, antiquities, and
all curiosities : there is not a cunning workman
in these arts but she has him fetched : there are
as good workers in wax, enamel, engravers,
singers, players, dancers, here as will be found
anywhere. . . . She has a gallery of statues,
bronze and marble, medals of gold, silver, and
bronze, pieces of ivory, amber, coral, worked
crystal, steel mirrors, clocks and tables, bas-reliefs
and other things of the kind ; richer I have
never seen even in Italy ; finally a great quantity
of pictures ; in short her mind is open to all
impressions." This was not more than the truth ;
that her ardour in all these subjects was based on
a genuine artistic taste was shown in the eagerness to gain possession of her collections after
her death.

She has been very unfortunate, in that all her efforts could do little for Swedish culture, which did not meet her half-way. She laboured hard to promote the growth of learning and letters in Sweden. She took care to commit the various branches of study to the hands of learned professors who came from abroad. She frequently went to Upsala to encourage the speeches and dissertations; she went, for instance, to hear Terserus and Stiernhielm dispute on the Hebrew text of Scripture. At Dorpat she built a college, and gave it a library; at Abo in Finland* she increased the college founded by her father in 1627, and made it a University similar to that at Upsala, endowing it with money and books: during her reign six other colleges were established at other places. She sent books taken from Olmütz and Prague to the University of Upsala. She aided many students to go abroad and study at foreign universities, and even sent some to Arabia to study in the East. She would allow no one to be doctor in philosophy who had not twice held open disputation on definite theses. She ordered, that no theological professor should at the same time be professor in philosophy. She caused a certain Dutchman to come and establish a good printing press in Stockholm. She wrote to Forsius, enjoining him to

* She gave the Finns their first translation of the Bible.

publish his physical works in Swedish rather than Latin, in order to be understood of the people.

All this proves very sufficiently that Christina was genuinely anxious to do what in her lay to raise the standard of learning in Sweden, and worked hard to that end; was it her fault if she [effected but little? Her attempts, though productive of small results, have nothing whatever in common with the empty self-regarding patronage and posing of Louis XIV.; she never tried to display her learning, though it was said of her that she was the only learned man in Sweden : she never set any store by the flattery that was poured on her, and though the tendency of the age was to venerate learning too much in and for itself, she could despise pedantry without ceasing to respect knowledge. At a time when all the European states were engaged in revolutionary struggles or unprofitable wars, she was trying hard to improve her own in the arts of peace, which she not only gained, but preserved for Sweden, by her energy and persevering tact. And yet when she abdicated she was only twenty-eight! If we except Cromwell, what contemporary sovereign, or minister, is worthy to stand beside her? We may candidly allow her one great defect, her extravagance, but it would be well for the world if it had always had rulers like Christina.

## CHAPTER V.

WHILE the rumour of Christina's strange character and political genius, her profuse liberalities and patronage of learning and art, her power in the Senate, and her prospective resignation of her crown at so early an age, was turning the eyes of Europe curiously towards this " tenth Muse" and "Sibyl of the North," she was herself a prey to profound dissatisfaction. She began to find that her position involved too great a strain upon her. It is not wonderful that under such a weight of cares and occupations she should be on the point of breaking down. Frederick the Great was not more anxious to do everything in person than Christina ; she felt with her favourite historian that the necessities of empire demanded that all affairs should be referred to one head. But already in 1648 she had written to Salvius, reminding him " how arduous and subject to fortune was the burden of ruling all." The entire business of State passed through her hands ; ambassadors transacted their affairs with her personally ; internal discords and domestic affairs demanded her continual attention, and she would master all the smallest details ; yet for all this she studied hard in private, and kept up her intercourse with the philosophers and men of learning at her court; for this purpose she hardly allowed herself sufficient sleep. In addition to actual business the care of providing for the succession weighed upon her mind. The burden of affairs, in itself too great, was increased ten-fold by her growing dislike to them; she felt herself to be on a treadmill; she had nothing to satisfy the longings of her soul; only by the severest sense of duty could she bring herself to perform her task. "She found no pleasure in it, neither did she love her country: she had no sympathies with its customs, its pleasures, its constitution, whether civil or ecclesiastical, or even its past history. The ceremonies of State, the long harangues to which she was bound to listen, the official duties which compelled her to take personal share in some great ceremonial observance were abhorrent to her: the range of cultivation and learning within which her countrymen were content to confine themselves, appeared to her contemptible." Financial diffi-culties were pressing; her continuous study had begun to arouse a natural reaction; the vanity and petty disputes of some of the pedants who surrounded her awoke her disgust; she was heartily tired of the throne; like Severus, she felt that she "had been all things, and all was of no avail;" yet she could look no higher, she had nothing further to hope; and, finally, she stood alone. The only man to whom in any degree she opened herself, Chanut, had been replaced by another.

To the disquiet of her soul must be added the dangerous state of her health, at once its cause and its effect. Christina had always been delicate from a child; she was often dangerously ill, as in 1642, 1645; in 1648, the year of the peace, she was three times seized with fever; in 1650, she had a violent fever, twice, with symptoms of inflammation of the lungs; in 1651, being on a visit to her mother at Nycöping, she was seized with a syncope at supper, and remained an hour unconscious; these fainting fits became frequent; on one occasion she remained unconscious for some hours, her pulses stopped; on reviving she told the physician that she had never expected to hear his voice again. Overwork and mental worry, aided by the ignorance of her doctors, who knew no remedy but bleeding, would soon have been fatal. But just at this moment she made the acquaintance of Bourdelot.

The importance of this man's subsequent relations with Christina makes it necessary to dwell upon them, all the more as they have been completely misrepresented and distorted by

his enemies and Christina's biographers. His
real name was Michon, the son of a barber at
Sens, who became an apothecary. Young
Michon adopted the name of his uncle, Bourdelot,
as well as his profession, that of a doctor; he
went to Italy, and on his return asserted that he
had been physician to Urban VIII., who would
have made him a cardinal if he had stayed in
Italy. (We are not able to judge of the truth of
this story, but it must be recollected that in the
seventeenth century all things were possible to
adventurers at Rome; and it is not intrinsically
improbable, since Bourdelot was certainly a
better doctor than most of those of his age, and,
as will be seen, capable of gaining the good
graces of princes.) He was introduced to the
Queen by Salmasius, who, it is said, wished to
have a friend at Court after he had gone.
Bourdelot at once made many enemies the
moment he arrived by banishing the former
doctors and forbidding the Queen to have any
further intercourse with the *savans*: to these
beneficial preliminaries, he added a careful
regulation of her diet and regimen. But he was
not a mere curator of the body; he possessed
the most invaluable quality of a doctor, tact;
and he saw that Christina's temper and mind
had given way under the strain of work and dis-
tasteful associations, and required tonics no less

than her body; he accordingly applied himself to curing by amusing her, which he was well qualified to do, having a great command of the smaller social accomplishments; he had a very ready and satirical wit, could sing, play the guitar, was a connoisseur in perfumes (a neglected department of medicine); gifted, moreover, with a positive genius for inventing amusements; fertile in expedients to make the time go; in short, exactly the man suited for rescuing Christina from her gloomy situation. And he succeeded so well in his treatment that Christina was soon restored to health; she frequently says in her letters that next to God she owed her life to Bourdelot; and she preserved a lifelong gratitude towards him.

He speedily acquired a great influence at the Court, and at the same time a numerous band of enemies. Chief among these were the learned men. And it must certainly be admitted that he contributed not a little to this hatred by the tricks which he played to some of the fraternity. A certain Meibomius had written a treatise on the music of the ancients; and Naudé, one upon their art of dancing. Bourdelot persuaded the Queen to make them give practical illustrations of their theories: Naudé was to dance to the singing of Meibomius, who had no voice, and did not know a note of music; the scene was ludicrous in the extreme; those of the Court who were looking on were convulsed with laughter; so that Meibomius, losing his temper not unnaturally, struck Bourdelot in the face, for which he was banished from Court. Another time, when Bochart was to read his ' Phaleg,' a work on sacred geography, and expecting the applause of the Queen, Bourdelot would not allow her to be present, saying that she had been bled, and must keep her room; the mortified author had to read his treatise to an audience ungraced by the presence of Christina. Certainly such jests as these prove Bourdelot to have had no special reverence for some of the learned pedants who bore him malice. But for all that the heavy accusations which have been brought against him can all be traced to jealousy and spite, and will not stand examination. It was asserted by the doctors that Bourdelot knew nothing of medicine, and that all the senators he had treated died. But not to mention that no instances are given, and that this statement was refuted by the case of Christina—not to mention the incompetence of those who brought the charge, and their envy—there is still extant a statement by Bourdelot of the Queen's case, and a prescription for its treatment, which has been pronounced by modern physicians to be not without merit. It may be added that another assertion, adduced as

N

proof of his medical ignorance, namely, that he was of opinion that enthusiasts ought to be cured by exorcism, really establishes his insight into the nature of mental disease and its cure by the means of mental expectancy. It was asserted by the learned, that though he gave himself out for learned, he was very ignorant. This charge is completely refuted by the testimony of Naudé himself, who mentions Bourdelot with approval as taking part in studies with himself and other *savans;* by the fact that Salmasius had a high opinion of him ; and by the fact that he was the means of introducing to Christina Pascal and Gassendi, although it is quite possible that he had not the same claims to the title of learned as such men as Vossius, Heinsius, and others, which is no disgrace. He was, moreover, much of the mind of Lord Bolingbroke, and considered it no sign of a contempt for true learning to despise those who spend their whole life in collecting all the learned lumber that fills the head of an antiquary. They further asserted that, for instance in the case of Bochart and his ' Phaleg,' he tried to prevent Christina from showing favour to learned men. But so far was Bourdelot from cherishing a grudge against Bochart that he procured him some Arabic MSS. to assist him in composing the very book in question. And what would a modern doctor say if, when treating an analogous case of nervous exhaustion, he found his patient besieged by a crowd of pedants ready to bring on a relapse by plaguing her with inopportune treatises on sacred geography?

But these were not Bourdelot's only enemies. The Queen, having Chanut no longer by her, and not caring for the new resident, Picques, was now showing much favour to Pimentelli, the Spanish ambassador, a point to which we shall return; this aroused the keen jealousy of all the French at Court, who promptly accused her of deserting France and going over to Spain, a charge utterly without foundation; *hinc illæ lacrimæ* when they accused Bourdelot of intriguing against France. They further asserted that Bourdelot was the cause of the disgrace of Count Magnus de la Gardie; this is simply ridiculous, as will soon appear. The nobles, moreover, all hated him for his influence, as a foreigner and a Frenchman, and lent a ready ear to all accusations against him.

The source of most of these accusations against him is the letters of the discarded *savans*, and the last part of Chanut's 'Mémoires,' which are not to be ascribed to Chanut, but to the French, who were furious at being neglected, and caught at every scandal that might enable them to vent their malice. Certainly Bourdelot was not a man of solid character; on this point

Christina's own judgment is final; she calls him
a man consumed with vanity (a description
which would suit also most of the learned men);
though she never forgot he had saved her life,
she did not admire his character; if she considered him a marvellously clever man, that was
no more than the truth. But the baseless
assertion that he had great influence over her
mind—a thing quite absurd to any one who is
familiar with her astonishing independence of
spirit—renders it necessary to show the futility
of the attacks upon him. The last charge is
principally due to the worst of all his enemies,
the bigoted Lutheran clergy. He was supposed
to make a jest of all religion, and to have inspired Christina with his own sentiments. He
was called by some an atheist, by others a deist—
words in the mouth of a bigoted Protestant
applied to all beliefs somewhat higher than his
own. "They think a man believes not at all in
God because he believes little in Luther," said
a Catholic of that time. The chief authority for
calling Bourdelot an atheist is Vossius, who was
himself suspected of the very same thing; in a
letter to Heinsius he says, "*Ait enim nullos esse
Deos, cælum inane, et mera esse verba virtutem,
lucum ligna;*" a charge probably made in order
to enable Vossius to quote Horace. How much
the charge was worth is shown by this, that

Christina herself was accused of atheism ; and, finally, whatever Bourdelot's own religious views might be, it will be proved in a subsequent chapter that he had absolutely nothing to do with Christina's change of faith.

The true reason of the general hatred of Bourdelot is that, for the various reasons given above, he had enemies in all parties at the court : the doctors, the *savans*, the French, the nobles, and the clergy.   When after her abdication their doubts were changed to violent animosity by her conversion, they were only too eager to try and fasten on some one whom they could accuse of " perverting the mind of their Queen, and all the good dispositions she had for the Protestant religion," and Bourdelot became their scapegoat.   Among other things they abhorred were the festivals and masquerades, which Bourdelot was active in promoting, and it has been the traditional habit of biographers to frame their views of the sinful doings of her last years upon the accounts of the hostile French, the sour-visaged Swedes, and the Puritan Whitelocke, who though an admirable witness in all other matters, is not to be trusted here.   The simplest pleasures were a crime in their eyes, and evidence of a desperate downfall : Whitelocke expelled two young men from his suite, and would hardly be persuaded to take

them back, because they would go "forth to
take the air" on Sunday, instead of going to
church.

The jealousy and hatred of Bourdelot took
effect in repeated attempts to expel him. Count
Magnus accused him to the Queen of trying
to influence her against himself and other
nobles : Bourdelot denied this to his face, and
the affair dropped ; but a similar mean trick
against another honourable man ended, as will be
seen, in Count Magnus being disgraced. The
nobles laid their heads together with the French
resident Picques, to contrive some way of
getting rid of him. Meanwhile the clergy
determined to act. They had observed signs
on the part of the Queen, showing disapproval
of the national religion. For the clergy
Christina had always shown friendliness ; Oxenstiern accused her of favouring them too much.
But various circumstances had recently changed
their attitude. They were mortally offended
when the learned Jew before mentioned dedicated to her his work entitled "Conciliador,"
aimed at reconciling conflicting passages in the
Bible. Further, Matthiæ had published his
'Idea Boni Ordinis,' an exposition of his
favourite scheme of reconciling differences in
the churches, and Christina was not only very
intimate with him, but it was even rumoured

that she intended to establish a theological college in Germany to realize this ideal. " The bishops called on the Council of State to keep watch over the national religion ; the Grand Chancellor repaired to the Queen with representations which drew tears into her eyes." Such criticism was not likely to improve her temper. Moreover, " the prolixity of those discourses, to which she was compelled by the national ordinances to listen, had long been most wearisome to her ; they now became intolerable. She frequently betrayed her impatience by moving her chair, or playing with her little dog ; but the merciless preachers were but the more firmly resolved to continue their lectures, and detain her all the longer for these marks of weariness."

Hence the relations between Queen and Clergy became daily more strained. Not guessing what was passing in her mind, they ascribed all to the bad influence of Bourdelot. They therefore drew up a remonstrance against him ; but now the question arose, who was to present it ? None of them daring to approach the Queen with their instrument, the Queen-mother, Maria Eleanora, undertook to do so. Under cover of asking permission to retire to Nyköping, she intimated to her daughter her distress at the complaints made by clergy and people against

Bourdelot, and her apprehension of his bad influence on her; she took courage from Christina's silence, and was going on, when the Queen interrupted her by saying "she was much obliged for her good advice; but these matters were too hard for them, and must be left to the priests." Maria Eleanora attempting to reply, Christina answered sharply, that she knew well who had instigated her to this, and that she would teach them who she was, and cause them to repent their imprudence. She then quitted the room, and left her mother alone, who burst into tears as usual. Two hours afterwards Christina was informed that she would let no one come near her, and was still crying. "She brought this unpleasant satisfaction on herself," answered Christina, with a fine touch of criticism on Maria Eleanora's character. However, five or six hours afterwards, Christina went to see her, without talking of what had occurred: Maria Eleanora subsequently departed for Nyköping.

And this impertinent interference and small-minded criticism of her motives has often been quoted as an instance of Christina's want of filial respect!

Nevertheless the odium against Bourdelot was so great that Christina found herself soon afterwards obliged to dismiss him, though he gave out that it was not a dismissal, but that he was sent on an embassy to the Court of France, to treat for Christina on a subject of great importance. And it is indeed stated by Gualdo that she sent him, being privy to her design of going over to Rome, and abdicating, to see whether she could come to France after resigning the crown. However that may be, Bourdelot departed, retaining to the last the confidence of Christina, who gave him letters of recommendation to the Court of France, as well as 10,000 rix dollars, and a draft for 20,000 more, payable in six months. Prince Charles Gustavus gave him likewise a gold chain and his portrait in a box covered with diamonds; and Prince Adolphus did the same to please the Queen, " though they both had a mortal aversion for him." Cardinal Mazarin preferred him afterwards to the Abbey of Massay in Berry, where he did not get on well with the monks. The foolish story that the Queen, shortly afterwards receiving a letter from him, threw it aside, exclaiming, " Ha ! it smells of medicine," is sufficiently refuted by its authority, and by the fact that she continued to correspond with him for the rest of her life. But it is remarkable that Guy Patin, the scandal-monger to whom we are indebted for much that is said against him, makes the following statement about Bourdelot

towards the end of his life : " He says that everybody is ignorant, that there never was a philosopher equal to Descartes, that all the doctors of
to-day are pedants, with their Greek and Latin,
and that they have not the insight to try and discover any remedies other than the popular ones."
This is the secret of the abuse of Bourdelot ; it
is merely what Molière said in other words.

We have anticipated a little in order to clear
up Bourdelot's affairs. In the meantime the state
of Christina's health and her distaste of business,
arising from over-application, led her to employ
more of her time in relaxation than formerly, and
to vary the monotony by balls, masquerades, and
amusements of that kind. But the accusations
made against her, that in this last period she
completely neglected State affairs, wasted her time
in frivolous amusements, and showed a complete
change in her personal and political behaviour,
due to the influence of Bourdelot, Pimentelli, and
others, and still more scandalous charges than
these, are not only untrue, but in such glaring
contradiction with facts that it is hard to understand how they can ever have been made.
Though Christina did not study so hard, for her
health's sake, and avoided the gang of pedants,
she did not break off her intercourse with learned
men of real worth ; she was moreover engaged in
meditating over her change of faith, and the

necessary negotiations with Rome ; and the pages
of Chanut, Whitelocke, and the historical annals
of those years furnish ample evidence that so far
from neglecting business, she devoted long hours
daily to the careful ordering of affairs, both foreign
and domestic, and the consideration of necessary
political questions with ambassadors. And even
Whitelocke admits that her entertainments and
amusements were altogether seemly and decorous,
nor is there a particle of evidence to the contrary.

Among her more intimate associates in the
latter years of her reign was the Spanish ambassador, Don Antonio Pimentelli. On his arrival in
1652, Christina wrote to the Chancellor, bidding
him pay special attention to his reception and see
that nothing was wanting to make his lodging
comfortable. Pimentelli speedily became a very
great favourite with the Queen. It is said that at
his first audience he made her a profound bow, and
retired immediately, without a word. The next
day he presented himself again, and addressed
to her a studied and flattering discourse. Thereupon Christina asked him the meaning of his
withdrawing on the previous day : he replied,
that he had been so much struck with Her
Majesty's presence, that the interval had been
necessary to him in order to collect himself.
Whatever truth there may be in this story, the
Spanish ambassador was certainly a man of great

courtliness of demeanour and captivating address.
Whitelocke calls him "a man of great parts
and ingenuity, and of a very civil deportment."
When he came to see Whitelocke, "he fell into
a commendation of the Queen, her singular parts
and abilities for government and public affairs,
excelling all women, and scarce giving place
therein to any man he had ever met with; and
that she was of an admirable spirit and courage
beyond her sex, well skilled for military affairs,
and as fit as possibly a woman could be to lead
an army." He was a prominent figure at her
receptions, and possessed much of her confidence ;
being one of the few to whom she communicated
her design of becoming a Catholic.

Two other men are worthy of notice, both of
whom had influence at a later time on Swedish
politics. These were Count Corfiz Ulfeld, a
native of Denmark, and Radziejowski, a Pole,
both political refugees. The former, the favourite
of Christian IV., had married a daughter of that
king by a second marriage, had been Viceroy of
Norway, and Grand Master of the Danish Court;
after Christina's death his abilities and great
influence aroused the jealousy of Frederick III.,
who sought to ruin him by bringing various false
accusations against him ; in 1651 he fled with his
wife in the disguise of a page to Sweden, and claimed
the protection of Christina, which she afforded

him. To the remonstrances of Denmark she pleaded a clause in the Treaty of Stettin in 1570, by which political refugees of the various states concerned were allowed to claim shelter in the others; precedents were also adduced of Swedish refugees in Denmark in the time of Sigismund. Ulfeld was accused by Charles II., then in exile, of appropriating to his own use 24,000 dollars, which ought to have been paid to himself; it turned out, however, that so far from this being the case, Ulfeld had even increased that sum with half as much again of his own. He remained at Stockholm, and endeavoured to induce Christina to make war on his own country for the purpose of restoring him, giving her all the information he could about its resources; the war, however, did not come in her time.

Similar appeals were made to her by the other fugitive, Radziejowski, a resolute and daring intriguer, who had been Vice-Chancellor of Poland. Suspecting an intrigue between his wife and John Casimir, he had attempted to rouse ill-feeling against the king; his wife during his absence from home took refuge in a convent, whereupon Radziejowski collected a band of men and endeavoured to storm it; failing in this, and feeling himself in danger, he fled the country, going to the Courts of Transylvania, and the Emperor, and lastly to Sweden, in 1652. Here he busied himself

in trying to arouse the Cossacks against the King
of Poland, and also to excite a war between that
country and Sweden, for which purpose he betrayed to Denmark the designs of Ulfeld, to
prevent his plans from getting a start. He got
what he wanted as soon as Charles X. came to
the throne.

The national hatred of Roman Catholics and the
Imperialist and Spanish party, the distrust of
foreign influence, and the rancour of the envious
French have succeeded in presenting Christina's
relations with these four men in an entirely erroneous light. They are supposed to have corrupted
her morals and perverted her policy ; it was hinted
that Bourdelot and Pimentelli were strenuously
working to alienate her mind from her old allies, the
French, and substitute Spain in her good graces,
by working on her admiration of Condé (in whose
service Bourdelot had formerly been, and who
was at this time in the Spanish interests), by
commending the advantages of a commercial
treaty with Spain, and depreciating the salt trade
with Portugal. Pimentelli, we are told, was
inducing her to form an alliance with Spain and
England against Holland, and drawing her near
to the Emperor; rumours were whispered of a
marriage between her and the King of Hungary;
still darker "there-be-an-if-they-mights," "we-
would-an-if-we-coulds," were thrown out about

her and the fascinating Spanish ambassador. All these figments are, however, in flagrant contradiction with the facts.

. To begin with, Christina was at no time more closely allied with Pimentelli than other ambassadors whom she thought it necessary to conciliate for political reasons. The insinuations against him are due to his country and his religion, and were never directed against another ambassador to whom she showed equal if not greater favour, Sir Bulstrode Whitelocke, who was sent by Cromwell to Sweden in 1653 to negotiate a commercial treaty with England and establish friendly relations between the two countries. His first interview with Christina took place on December 23, 1653:

" He perceived the Queen sitting, at the upper end of the room, upon her chair of state of crimson velvet . . . he put off his cap, and then the Queen put off her cap, after the fashion of men, and came two or three steps forward upon the foot carpet. This, and her being covered and rising from her seat, caused Whitelocke to know her to be the Queen, which otherwise had not been easy to be discerned, her habit being of plain grey stuff, her petticoat reaching to the ground, over that a jacket such as men wear, of the same stuff, reaching to her knees; on her left side, tied with crimson ribbon, she wore the jewel of the order of Amaranta; her cuffs ruffled *à la mode*, no gorget or band, but a black scarf about her neck, tied before with a black ribbon as soldiers and marines sometimes use to wear; her hair was braided and hung loose upon her head: she wore a black velvet cap lined with sables and turned up after the fashion of the country, which she used to put on and off as men do their hats. Her countenance was sprightly, but somewhat pale; she has much of majesty in her demeanour, and though her person were of the smaller size, yet her mien and carriage were very noble."

Christina took great delight in Whitelocke's company and humour; she would frequently have him to her palace, and after " calling for stools " in deference to his lameness, she would sit hours at a time discussing English and foreign affairs, not unmixed with what he calls " drollery." The accounts he has left us show what tact she would bring to bear on her negotiations with foreign powers. To oblige him, she ceased to hold balls on Sunday, as was customary in Sweden, which he considered a profanation of the Sabbath. She always expressed a great admiration of Cromwell, whom she compared to Gustavus Vasa. She would sometimes ride with him, and on one such occasion tried his pistols and her own to see which were the best. On February 20th, Valentine's Eve according to the old style, she gave him leave to be her Valentine, and wear her name in his hat; he sent her as a present "a great looking-glass." It was just such instances of graceful humour that in cases other than Whitelocke's were twisted into scandals by malevolent calumniators.

He describes for us the balls and festivals given by the Queen: "The Queen and her ladies would first dance the brawls, then French dances; . . . she took great delight in English country dances, and herself danced with more life and spirit than the rest of the ladies, or any he had seen:" as well as masquerades and ballets, such as that in January, 1651, called the "triumphant Parnassus;" sometimes the national costumes of Europe, past and present, would be represented, Christina appearing now as a Dutch maidservant, now a Moorish lady, or citizen's wife. At a "Banquet of the Gods" in 1651, in which Ulfeld, Radziejowski, Pimentelli, and Count Magnus appeared as Jupiter, Bacchus, Mars, and Apollo, she instituted her "Order of Amaranta." The origin of the name is obscure; perhaps from the Greek "never fading;" or a pastoral in which Christina was a shepherdess, Amarantha. The badge was a gold medal on

o

which was engraved a double A, interlaced,
with the motto " *Dolce nella memoria.*"  There
were thirty members in addition to the Queen;
they swore to follow Virtue and Honour, and
had the privilege of feasting with her on
Saturdays at a country house near Stockholm.
One condition was that the candidate must be
unmarried; this must have been abrogated in
the case of Whitelocke, who was made a
member; he had been married three times.
" *Pardieu, vous êtes incorrigible!* " said the Queen,
when he told her.

Her enemies fastened on this " Order," trying
to connect it scandalously with Pimentelli,
whose Christian name was Antonio; a thing
refuted by the date, when he had not as yet
come to Sweden. They saw further evidence
in the diamond ring she gave him, at one of
these masques, to hold for her till she asked
for it, when she went to change her dress; when
he offered it back to her, she said she had not
asked for it yet, nor would; he was to keep
it in memory of her. But Whitelocke, who
relates it, speaks of the whole thing as taking
place " genteelly, and without the least offence
or scandal."

Not only are charges of this pitiful kind absolutely without foundation, but neither is there
anything in the assertion that at this time she

abandoned politics for frivolous amusements. A typical illustration is furnished by the innumerable discussions between Whitelocke and herself respecting his mission, in which her careful consideration of all details is obvious. Certainly, there was considerable delay in settling and concluding it, of which Whitelocke complains. But he does not notice the reason for this delay ; his own pages furnish continual evidence that Christina and the Chancellor were waiting to see whether Cromwell could establish his power on a sure basis. In the meantime Balandine, Charles II.'s envoy, came to Sweden to ask assistance. Christina wrote an answer with her own hand, " regretting her inability to provide any remedy for the incurable evils of the age, and hoping that time which cures all things might put an end to his evil fortune, and furnish her with opportunities to assist him without detriment to her own interests and obligations." But after Cromwell became Protector, in December, 1653, the treaty of commerce progressed better : it was finally signed in April, 1654. On his departure, Christina made Whitelocke a present of raw copper worth £2500.

There is no more truth in the allegations respecting her neglect of affairs with Spain, or the dark surmisings of her enemies as to

this power. There are no signs of any inclination on her part to a treaty between Spain,
England, and Sweden ; Pimentelli indeed spoke
to Whitelocke on the subject, but such a treaty
was to the taste of neither Christina nor
Cromwell, and the idea was not entertained.
The Queen confined herself to sending an
ambassador to Spain, to make overtures as to a
commercial treaty with Sweden ; this was the
*status quo* when she abdicated. She showed no
appearance of hostility to France, but assured
Picques of her continued good will to that
country.

It is the same when we examine her dealings
with the Imperial Court. Christina showed
favour to its ambassador Montecuculi, and
endeavoured, indeed, to conciliate Frederick III.
by supporting the claims of his son to be elected
King of Rome, writing for that purpose to the
electors in April, 1653. But the motive of this
was purely political, and had nothing to do
with Pimentelli or Montecuculi. She aimed
at settling the difficulties that had arisen
about Bremen. Sweden had, it will be remembered, acquired the bishopric of Bremen by the
treaty of Westphalia ; the present disputes
turned upon the respective rights of the town
and those Sweden had gained over it. There
were also differences with Brandenburg and

Pomerania. It is not necessary here to examine details; the settlement of both questions took place in the next reign, but the point to be noticed is that in order to a settlement it was necessary to gain the goodwill of the Emperor, to which accordingly Christina applied herself, as usual, with diplomatic skill. She had not time to accomplish it, but she prepared the way.

With Holland, in spite of certain vexatious actions tending to injure and interfere with Swedish commerce, she confined herself to sharp remonstrances, which had their effect; she took no part in the war of 1652–3, in which the Dutch were beaten by Cromwell, and here maintained her usual peace policy. As to the old enemies, Denmark and Poland, the prospect looked darker; the jealousy and fear of the former country, and the irritating claims of the latter, were respectively complicated by Ulfeld and Radziejowski, each anxious to forestall the other in attacking his own country and enforcing his rights by the help of Sweden. A war with these countries was merely a question of time; Christina pointed to this, when, in answer to the protestation of Poland against the election of Charles Gustavus, she replied that her cousin would " prove which had the best right to the throne by the testimony of thirty thousand men : " a prediction verified by the

" New Pyrrhus," as soon as he came the throne. For the wars of Sweden with Poland and Denmark, however, not Christina was responsible, but the old national animosities and the fiery character of Charles X.

The opposition between Christina and the Chancellor had arisen from, and depended upon, their antagonistic views of the proper policy to be followed in settling the affairs of Germany. Having gained her object in the Peace of Westphalia, this cause of difference ceased to exist, especially as she had now long since established her independent position. In view, too, of her resignation, she was desirous of standing well with all parties in the State; and hence, as the factitious party formed by her for a special end, to oppose that of the Chancellor, began to fall to pieces, being no longer required, the influence of Oxenstiern and the aristocracy began now once more to regain its old position. This was agreeable to the nobles, who therefore strongly opposed any scheme of abdication in favour of Prince Charles, carefully though he paid his court to all; he himself, on the other hand, and the generals of the army, who looked forward to a war, were prepared to support it. To these belonged Count Magnus, who depended either on the Queen or the Prince, and was hated by the nobles for his connection with France. His position was now becoming ambiguous. Christina's new relations with Pimentelli, and the comparative shelving of himself and the French, as he thought, gave him cause for great uneasiness. He began to suspect his favour was declining, and sought to remedy this by expostulating with her, accusing her of allowing herself to be influenced against him by backbiters. His petulant suspicions irritated her to an extreme degree, partly because they assumed her capable of such meanness, partly because they seemed to imply he had claims upon her. In spite of all that has been said to her disadvantage, there is not the shadow of a proof that she ever regarded him from any other point of view than that of a patron, and the summary way she dismissed him, as one of her biographers has said, is clear evidence that she never was anything else to him. The base character of De la Gardie, who never lost a chance of damaging her afterwards, would have caught at any straw in his power to blacken her reputation in order to save his own. During the whole time he was in favour, he was not two years in all at Court; and the facts now to be related will show that Christina saw through him long before the crash came, through his own folly.

Already, as has been noticed, the Count fixed his suspicions on Bourdelot as the author of his

declining influence; he complained to the
Queen of him, who told him she did not believe
him; and Bourdelot himself happening to come
by, " told her Majesty that he knew well he had
many enemies at Court, who endeavoured to
ruin him in the opinion of the great, but that no
one would ever be able to prove that he had
spoken to any one's detriment." The Count
produced two witnesses; but in the presence of
the Queen they did not dare to charge Bourdelot
to his face with their accusations, and the Queen
declared they were impostors. She forbade them
to appear again in her sight, saying " they were
all French, and creatures of the Count."

Finding that he had only done himself harm
by this attempt, De la Gardie demanded permission to retire from Stockholm to his country
house, which the Queen refused, telling him that
his presence was necessary on business (he was
Grand Treasurer at the time). Soon after this
the Count finally ruined himself by a somewhat
similar endeavour.

Having to speak to the Queen, on matters
connected with the state of the finances, one
day after a meeting of the Senate she retained him alone with her. The Count immediately began to harangue her on her present
misinterpretation of his sentiments, and regretted that she should have complained of

him, saying "that he had acted treacherously towards her, but that she would not punish him for his bad faith herself, but leave it to the Prince to do so; yet would not be displeased should others affront him;" this he said he had learned from some one very near her Majesty's person, who told him he had it from her Majesty's own mouth. The Queen, much surprised, told him he ought to know her better than to suppose her capable of such a thing, . . . and she bade him tell her who was his informant. He said it was Steinberg, her chief Equerry. " I cannot believe it," said the Queen, " he is a man of too much honour to tell such lies." She averred that if Steinberg allowed he had said it, she would admit having made the complaint. Accordingly, Steinberg and some senators were summoned from the antechamber by the Queen herself, who told him what the Count had said, and bade him say whether he acknowledged it. Steinberg replied he was astonished that Count Magnus, for whom he had always had respect and affection, should calumniate him to the Queen and seek his ruin in this way; he solemnly swore he had never heard her Majesty say any such thing. . . . The Queen, satisfied with Steinberg's disavowal, and feeling pity for the Count, did not wish to proceed any further in the matter; but Steinberg considered it concerned his own honour to know who had told this to the Count, and the Queen approved his judgment, not sorry to see that he wished to sift the matter, as she was beginning to get tired of the Count's repeated attempts to prejudice her against others. Accordingly Steinberg went to the Count's house, and begged him to give him the name of the person who had slandered him; the Count, with profuse apologies, said he was quite willing to take his word for it, that his informant was a rascal. This did not satisfy Steinberg, but as he could not induce De la Gardie to disclose his authority, he went to the Queen to beg her to interfere. Christina sent Prince Adolphus to require the Count to give his informant's name; but the latter begged to decline to do so, as he had promised to keep his name a secret. The Queen sent the Prince to him again, telling him that he must; she had taken upon her to defend Steinberg's honour. Count Magnus thereupon declared, after deprecating any disgrace for him, that it was Schlippenbach, Colonel and Grand Seneschal at Stockholm. The Queen bade him write to him, as she would herself, to come to Upsala. "The Count wrote him a rigmarole which no one could understand." Schlippenbach came immediately; the day after the Count sent him four friends to ask him whether he would not maintain that Steinberg had said the thing.

He said positively, "No; he saw well that they were trying to ruin him; but he would speak the truth to her Majesty, and show himself a man of honour." On December 18, the Queen summoned Schlippenbach, Count Magnus, Steinberg, the senators, and the other chief men in the Court, who had been present before. She made a speech on the whole question, and told the Count to restate the matter alleged to have come from Schlippenbach; she then took the latter by the button of his doublet, and said to him, "Understand that I am prepared to own it, if Steinberg says I said it." Slippenbach answered, that he did not know what Count Magnus meant; that he had never told him what he alleged; that Steinberg had never spoken to him of it, nor he himself to the Count, of Steinberg: except that once, dining with the Count, he had said to him, that it was obvious the Queen no longer had the same esteem for him as formerly, and that Steinberg was in great favour; on which point the Count had often spoken to him, as a thing he could not bear. The Count thereupon told him he was a rascal, and lied like a Schelm. Schlippenbach answered he was himself a man of honour, but as to the Count, he was not acting like an honourable man. The Count said it was true there were no witnesses, because the affair had taken place in private : Schlippenbach protested he had never spoken to him *tête-à-tête*, on which the Count fell into great confusion. The Queen, taking pity on him, said this was a matter which did not concern her, and withdrew. The Count sent to beg permission to bring Schlippenbach to justice : the Queen replied, such a course would only end in his own confusion. After dinner on the same day, the Count, through Prince Adolphus, begged her to let him go into the country to settle his domestic affairs, not to suffer Schlippenbach at the Court, and not to speak of the matter to his disadvantage. The Queen, astonished at these demands, sent to him to say, she not only permitted but ordered him to leave town, and go wherever he chose, except to her Court, to which he was not to return till he had cleared himself to his honour ; as for Schlippenbach, she could not think of it ; as to his third demand, he might console himself in his disgrace by the thought that, had she not retained some goodwill towards him, severer measures would have been used ; all she could do for him was to pity his self-inflicted misfortune. The Count, though he ought to have gone that evening, waited till the next day, in hopes she might relent ; finding she did not, he sent her a letter by Prince Adolphus, which she read twice, saying each time, *" Poor Count ! "*

She sent no answer, and the Count departed on the following day to a country house ten leagues from Stockholm. He was dissuaded from challenging Schlippenbach by the representations of the nobles, that being the fifth man in the Senate, the inequality of rank forbade it. Subsequently he wrote to the Queen, and received the following crushing reply :—

" SIR,

"As you express a wish to see me again after your disgrace, I am obliged to tell you how opposed this wish is to your advantage; and I write this letter to remind you of the reasons which prevent me from listening to it, and which ought to convince you, too, that the interview is useless to your repose. It is not for me to bring remedies for your misfortune : it is to yourself you must look for the reparation of your honour. What can you hope from me ? or what can I do, except pity you and blame you ? The friendship I had for you compels me to do both; and whatever indulgence I have had for you, I cannot, without giving myself the lie, pardon you the crime you have committed against yourself. Do not imagine I am angry with you—I assure you I am not. I am henceforth incapable of feeling any other sentiment for you than that of pity, which can do

you no good, since you have yourself rendered
useless the sentiments of goodwill I had for
you. You are unworthy by your own confession,
and you have yourself pronounced the decree
of your banishment in the sight of several
persons of rank who were present. I have
confirmed this decree because I found it just,
and I am not ready to undo it, as you are given
to suppose. After what you have done and
suffered, dare you show yourself to me? You
make me feel ashamed when I think how many
base actions you have stooped to, how often you
have submitted to those whom you have so
grievously injured. In this unfortunate affair,
no spark of magnanimity or generosity has
appeared in your conduct. Were I capable of
repenting, I should regret having ever con-
tracted a friendship with a soul so feeble as
yours; but this weakness is unworthy of me,
and, having always acted as reason dictated, I
ought not to blame the veil I have thrown
over the course of events. I would have preserved this all my life had not your imprudence
compelled me to declare myself against you.
Honour compels me to do it openly, and justice
forces it upon me. I have done too much for
you these nine years, in that I have always
blindly taken your part against all. But now
that you abandon your dearest interests, I am

released from all further care of them. *You have yourself betrayed a secret which I had resolved to keep all my life, by showing that you were unworthy of the fortune I built for you.** If you are determined to hear my reproaches, you can come to me; I consent on this condition. But do not hope that tears or submission will ever force me to yield a hair's-breadth. The only favour I can do for you is to remember you but little, and speak of you less; being determined never to mention you except to blame you. For I ought to show you that you are unworthy of my esteem after a fault like yours. That is all I had to do for you. Remember, however, that you are yourself to blame for what has occurred to your disgrace, and that I am just towards you as I always will be for all the world.

" CHRISTINA.

" *Upsala,* Dec. 5, 1653."

Throughout the whole of this narration the native baseness of the Count is clearly seen. And when we remember that the Count's household were nearly all French, and that he was especially connected with the French interests, we have the solution of many a slander directed against the Queen in later years. Even he did not venture to apply again to Christina directly,

* The Italics are ours.

but great efforts were made by his friends to revoke her decision. Prince Charles wrote in his behalf, but Christina sent him an account of the transaction, and remained inflexible. Count Magnus actually applied to his old enemy the Chancellor, to get him to use his reviving influence with Christina; to which appeal Oxenstiern retorted, it is said, by quoting the words De la Gardie had in his sunny days used of the Chancellor, "that he doted, being already in his second childhood, and no longer capable of giving counsel," at the same time bidding him observe that he could now do nothing for him but bewail his misfortune. To the Queen, who wrote to appeal to his judgment, Oxenstiern replied that he approved her action, yet was inclined to mercy; to his son Eric he described the Count as having brought it on himself, and as little capable of supporting bad as good fortune. Although the Senate interceded for him, Christina refused to alter her resolution; saying that on his accession the Prince might do what he liked, but that she did not wish to hear of him again. Count Magnus took the mean revenge of testifying his joy when he heard of her resolution to resign, and expected that Charles would restore him to favour as soon as he came to the throne; but the latter declared that his gratitude to Christina would never permit him to let any person approach him who had been in her bad graces. Notwithstanding, the Count did return, and was foremost in thwarting all Christina's wishes and projects in later years, as will be seen. He lived to display his baseness on a grander stage by taking bribes from Louis XIV., as Chancellor of Sweden, and contributing largely to the downfall and degradation of his country; but Nemesis overtook him under Charles XI. The state in which he closed his contemptible and consistent career is an ironical commentary on its brilliant outset, and furnishes an edifying instance of retributive justice such as history does not often afford.

On more than one occasion Christina's life was in danger, and in every case she displayed the same cool courage and presence of mind. In 1647, in the Castle Church, a lunatic seized the moment when the congregation was kneeling after the sermon was over, to rush into the elevated gallery where she was, and got within two steps of her; quite unmoved, she rose, and pushed her Captain of the Guards, who seized him by the hair. It was doubtful what the man's intentions were; two knives were found on him; however that may be, the incident showed the steadiness of the Queen's nerves. In June,

P

1652, she went at four in the morning to inspect
the fleet which was being fitted up at Stockholm.
While Admiral Herman Fleming was showing
her a new ship, they were standing together on a
plank; it suddenly tilted up, and the Admiral
fell into the sea, in very deep water, dragging
the Queen after him; fortunately her Equerry,
Steinberg, being close by, jumped in just in time
to seize her by the skirt of her dress, only just
visible, as the Admiral, who had sunk, was
clutching hold of her petticoats. Several people
hurried up, and succeeded in getting her on
board. Though she had fallen in head first and
swallowed a lot of water, she was no sooner pulled
out than she bade them save the Admiral, who was
still grasping her clothes. So far from blaming
him for this, she praised him, as he would certainly have been drowned if he had not. She
was moreover, she said, used to drinking cold
water, only not salt and dirty; but the Admiral,
she maliciously added, must have found the
change from beer and wine unpleasant. She
made no fuss about it, and dined in public as if
nothing had happened.

An equally great danger of a different kind
threatened her in the conspiracy of the Messenii.
The discontent, suppressed in 1650, continued to
burn the keener on that account in certain
democratic breasts. One of these was Arnold

Messenius, son of the old John Messenius, who after an imprisonment of twenty years in the icy Uleaborg, during which time he still worked unweariedly at his 'Scandia illustrata,' died in 1636. Of him Oxenstiern said, that natures such as his should be treated like fire, which we must furnish with material to feed upon, to prevent it from turning to do evil. His son Arnold, fourteen years in prison with his father, had been released by Christina, who made him her historiographer and raised him to the nobility with a pension. The loss of a lawsuit against his sister, in which Christina compelled him to make restitution, turned him into an enemy, and he swore to plot the ruin of the Queen ; building upon the popular discontent and the ambition of Charles Gustavus. The imprudence of his son, a youth of twenty, who had been page to the Prince, caused the design to be discovered in the following manner: In December, 1651, Charles, who continued to reside at Oeland, received an anonymous seditious pamphlet, afterwards traced to the young Messenius, in which the Queen was accused of ruining the kingdom by her extravagant expenses, feasts, and donations to foreigners ; of being wholly under the influence of the Chancellor, the High Constable, and Count Magnus, who aimed at excluding the Prince from the government, and wishing to poison him. He was summoned to take arms, murder the Queen and her advisers, and possess himself of the throne; the people of Stockholm, of the country, and the lesser nobility would rise in his favour. The Prince sent the pamphlet to the Queen, with a letter expressing his uneasiness. In the meantime news of the conspiracy had reached her from other sources. " She heard of it in the evening just as she was about to go to bed. Shortly after appeared Governor Fleming, bringing the intelligence she had already heard, through some one who had betrayed the conspirators. The Queen, who was a very fearless and discreet princess, stood and looked very quietly at Fleming, and after considering a short time, replied, 'What you say, Lord Herman, is well judged, but what say you of the hereditary prince? For I know maybe more than you, I know that they have communicated their damnatory projects to the Prince. You who are in his confidence, what think you of it?' Lord Herman answered, 'It is very possible: but what I know for certain is, that his Royal Highness does not bite the hook.' Then the Queen said to Lord Herman, 'In order to get exact knowledge of all the conspirators, we must let the matter come to a rising, and have them all together on the stage, before we drop the curtain, and have them all in the trap. We may well see a fray of it, but I with my people fear the issue not a jot.' Lord Herman had enough to do to draw the Queen from this daring and bloody idea, assuring her that all would yet come to her knowledge, and the matter be quashed without noise. The most notable circumstance was that just so much time as an express takes to go to Oeland and return at the utmost speed, elapsed between the Queen's conversation with Governor Fleming and the arrival of the Prince's letter to the Queen informing her of the audacious designs of the Messenii." It is perhaps still more notable that " subsequently the Queen changed her mind and did not wish to know all." The Messenii were executed. Their confessions implicated many other persons, but it was found unadvisable to push things too far, as the revelations pointed to things that it was better not to know, and persons whose punishment would not have been easy. Among others, Terserus, Nils Nilson, Burgomaster of Stockholm, Benedict Skytté, senator, son of the John Skytté, the leader of the democratic party in the preceding reign, and the great enemy of Oxenstiern, were accused, but acquitted. The records of the trial were destroyed by the Queen's orders.

## CHAPTER VI

On January 21, 1653, Christina sent for White-locke, and drawing her stool nearer to him, said, "I shall surprise you with something I intend to communicate to you, but it must be under secrecy."

Whitelocke: "Madam, we that have been versed in the affairs of England, do not use to be surprised with the discourse of a young lady."

The Queen: "Sir, this it is. I have it in my thoughts and resolution to quit the Crown of Sweden."

Whitelocke: "I suppose your Majesty is pleased only to droll with your humble servant?"

The Queen: "It is my love to the people which causeth me to think of providing a better governor for them than a poor woman can be. And it is somewhat of love to myself, to please my own fancy by private retirement."

Whitelocke: "With your Majesty's leave, 1 shall tell you a story of an old English gentleman" [who was persuaded to hand over his estate during his lifetime to his son: all things being prepared for signing the agreement]. "The father, as is much used, was taking tobacco in the better room, the parlour, where his rheum caused him to spit much, which offended the son; and because there was much company, he desired his father to take the tobacco in the kitchen, and to spit there, which he obeyed. All things being ready, the son calls his father to come and seal the writings. The father said his mind was changed. . . . because he was resolved to spit in the parlour as long as he lived. And so I hope will a wise young lady."

The Queen: "Your story is very apt to our purpose, and the application proper to keep the crown upon my head as long as I live; but to be quit of it, rather than to keep it, I shall think to be to spit in the parlour."

Christina's determination to abdicate was so closely connected with her change of faith, that a full examination of her motives has been postponed till now, although in strictness it was necessary for the proper understanding of her previous conduct. At the time of the conversation with Whitelocke the rumour of her intended abdication had got about, and was causing much disquiet in Swedish political circles. She did not tell Whitelocke, however, her real reason, and few people had any knowledge of what was passing in her mind; of these few, one was Chanut. In January, 1654, being at that time ambassador at the Hague, he wrote to her endeavouring to dissuade her. Christina sent him the following reply :—

"*Westeras*, Feb. 28, 1654.

"I have told you before the reasons which have obliged me to persist in my design of abdicating. You know that this fancy has lasted long with me, and it is only after having pondered on it for eight years that I have determined to carry it out. It is at least five since I informed you of my purpose, and I then saw that it was only your sincere regard and the interest you took in my fortunes that compelled you to oppose me, in spite of the reasons you could not condemn, however keenly you set yourself to dissuade me. It pleased me to see that you found nothing in the thought that was unworthy of me. You know what I told you on this matter, the last time I had the satisfaction of conversing with you about it. In so long a course of time nothing has happened to alter me. I have determined all my actions with reference to this end, and have brought them to this final point, without hesitating now that I am ready to finish my part, and go behind the curtain. I care not as to the *Plaudite*. I know that the scenes I have played in could not have been composed according to the ordinary dramatic laws. With difficulty will any strong, masculine, or vigorous touches therein please. I leave it to every man to judge it according to his lights: I can deprive no one of his liberty herein, nor would I even if I could. I know that there are few who will pass a favourable criticism on it, and I am convinced that you will be of those few. The rest are ignorant of my reasons and my humour, since I have never declared myself to any one except you, and one other friend, whose soul is great and elevated enough to judge it as you do. *Sufficit unus, sufficit nullus.* I despise the rest, and should do honour to any one of the herd whom I should find ridiculous enough to amuse myself with. Those who consider this action in the light of common every-day maxims, will doubtless condemn it, but I will never take the trouble to make my apology to them. And in the fulness of the leisure which I am preparing for myself, I shall never be idle enough to remember them. I shall pass it in examining my past life and correcting my errors without either astonishment or repentance. What pleasure shall I not find in recollecting that I have joyfully done good to humanity, and punished those that deserved punishment. I shall find consolation in never having made any person guilty who was not so already, and even in having spared those who were. I have placed the welfare of the

State above all other considerations, I have sacrificed all cheerfully to its interests, and have nothing to reproach myself with in its administration. I have possessed without pride, and resign without difficulty. After all this, do not fear for me. I am in safety, and my good is not in Fortune's power: I am happy, whatever occurs:

> Sum tamen, O superi, felix: nullique potestas
> Hoc auferre Deo.

"Aye, I am so, more than any one, and will always be : I have no fear of that Providence of which you speak to me. *Omnia sunt propitia.* Let Providence take it upon itself to settle my fortunes, and I will submit with that respect and resignation which I owe to its decrees: let it leave the direction of my conduct to myself, and I will employ any such faculties as have been granted to me in making myself happy. And I shall be so as long as I am persuaded that I have nothing to fear from God or man. I shall employ all the rest of my life in familiarising myself with these thoughts, in fortifying my soul, and observing from the haven the troubles of those who are tossed about in life by the storms that one suffers therein, for want of having applied their minds to these meditations. Am I not to be envied in my present condition?

Beyond doubt I should find many enviers if my happiness were known. You love me, however, well enough not to envy me, and I deserve it, since I am honest enough to admit that I have got some of these sentiments from you : I learned them in conversations with you, and I hope to cultivate them some day with you during my leisure. I am certain that you cannot break your word, and will not cease in these altered circumstances to remain my friend, since I am abandoning nothing that is worthy of your regard. I will, in whatever condition I may be found, preserve my friendship for you; and you will see that no changes will ever be able to alter the views in which I glory. You know all this, and you are doubtless of opinion that the best pledge I can give you of myself is to tell you that I will always be

"CHRISTINA."

In answer to this Chanut wrote expressing his approval of her resolve, yet reminding her that the world holds as defects those virtues it is incapable of noticing: he promises always to bear her witness that her first and strongest motive has been the good of her subjects and the safety of the State; yet the stroke is so bold that it will astonish all those who do not know that the retreat which her Majesty is preparing

for herself is greater than all the kingdoms of
the earth.

This 'retreat' is not merely an allusion to her
intention of becoming a Catholic; it has a deeper
meaning, which will become clear as we proceed.
Some passages in Christina's 'Life' of herself
will furnish the best starting-point. This strange
fragment of autobiography is a kind of confession :
it is addressed to the Deity, and reminds us of
nothing so much as the ' Confessions ' of S. Augustine. " This heart was Thine since it first beat
in my breast; . . . . nothing can content me,
nothing satisfy me, but Thou alone." Throughout, its spirit is analogous to that of a mystic
quietism, and subjection of the individuality to
the Divine will, which recalls Madame de Guion.
" After the grace Thou hast shown me in introducing me to that admirable and mysterious
solitude, where we neither seek nor find anything
but Thee; " . . . " Thou art all, and I am
nothing; " . . . " Make me worthy to possess
Thee by that blind and entire resignation, which
is Thy due." With this is combined a dislike
to forms and common notions of religion. " All
the respect, admiration, and love which I have
had all my life for Thee, O Lord, never hindered
me from being incredulous and little inclined to
devotions; I believed nothing of the religion in
which I was brought up. All that they told me

seemed to me unworthy of You. I thought that
men made You speak after their fashion, and
that they wished to deceive me, and frighten me,
so as to govern me in their own way. I hated
mortally the long and frequent sermons of the
Lutherans; but I knew that I must let them
speak, and have patience, and conceal my secret
thoughts. But when I was grown up a little, I
formed a sort of religion in my fashion, whilst
waiting for that Thou hast inspired me with,
towards which I had naturally so strong an
inclination. Thou knowest how often, in a language unknown to common persons, I have
prayed to be lightened by Thy grace; how I
made Thee a vow to obey Thee at the expense of
my life and my fortune."

The peculiarity of her religious views finds its
explanation in her character and the influences
brought to bear on it during her education.
She was naturally very reflective, and very
secret; having lost her father, and being deprived of her mother very early, she was thrown
back upon herself. Conversations preserved by
Chanut show, too, that there was never any
sympathy on religious subjects between her and
Maria Eleanora, who could see no point of view
but her own. The peculiar isolation of her
position increased her natural bent to secrecy,
and she early framed a sort of religion of her

own. The influence of Matthiæ, whose great idea was a neglect of non-essential distinctions, prevented her from imbibing Lutheranism, to which she had, besides, an instinctive dislike : " I was never a Lutheran," she says herself. Between the general Lutheranism, the Calvinism of her uncle's house, and Matthiæ's syncretism, she became impressed with liberal opinions as to dogma, and all through her life she showed a toleration and a strong aversion to persecution, whether of Catholics at the beginning or of Protestants at the end, rare in that age. The point of contact between her own private, and as yet undefined, opinions, and Roman Catholicism, was almost certainly the idea of self-abnegation, especially as illustrated in abstaining from marriage. We have already mentioned her delight at hearing of the celibacy of the Catholics, when a child. The independence of her character made this " dedication of herself to Heaven " irresistible. Thus the attraction of the Church of Rome found a powerful support in her mind at the very outset.

But she did not arrive at her later half-Catholic, half-mystical doctrines all at once. The tendency of her early associations was increased by her studies, and the influence of the two most remarkable men with whom she came in contact, Chanut and Descartes. As to the first, she combined a strong taste for ancient philosophy with a fondness for the Fathers of the Church ; while the former led her away from Lutheranism, the latter brought her nearer Rome. On the one hand, Cicero's remark that all religions might be false, while only one could be true, struck her forcibly, and as she is said to have been fond of Lucian, his ' Hermotimus,' a practical commentary on Cicero's text, would be to her all that ' Bossuet's History of Protestant Variations ' was to Gibbon. On the other hand, this sceptical tendency was corrected by the study of the Fathers and Christian antiquity ; how could the mushroom sects of a day compare with the venerable Catholic Church, with all its great men, its martyrs, and, above all, its admirable virgins ? Over and over again, in her collection of 'Maxims,' does Christina emphasise this point of view.

Thus, while the cold and insufficient appeal of Protestantism to her intellect was undermined by her scepticism, in the traditions and æsthetic attractions of Rome she found something that met her emotional needs half-way. The contact between her own aspirations and the spirit of Catholicism, as she read its history, was like the junction of the electric coil, producing a spark ; she felt that the truth must, if anywhere, be found here. And this line of argument was confirmed by her intercourse with Chanut and Descartes. Here were two men, at once the best and wisest she had ever seen, both Roman Catholics. We have no record of any conversations which she held with them; but even if Christina had not expressly stated that she owed her conversion to a great extent to Descartes, we do not need to look far for proofs of the close connection between his sceptical principles and Catholicism; an illustrious apologist has placed that position on a casuistical basis in his 'Grammar of Assent.'

The foolish and short-sighted assertions, due principally to the irritated Swedes, that Bourdelot and Pimentelli were mainly instrumental in her change of faith, which was either altogether insincere, or a refuge from frivolity and atheism, are entirely without foundation, and have been partly refuted in what has been said of Bourdelot. Christina was neither frivolous nor an atheist; further, any one who supposes that a man like Bourdelot would ever have influenced her anyhow, is infinitely far from a knowledge of her character. But fortunately, there is another and final disproof: " A lie about dates," said Bentley, " is the easiest of all lies to disclose." Her mind was made up long before she ever saw either of them. In 1648 she fell dangerously ill of a fever, and " it was in this sickness," she says, " I

made a vow to quit all and become a Catholic,
should God preserve my life." With this agrees
what she says in her letter to Channut, that it was
eight years since she thought of her design, and
five since she spoke to him about it. And as to
the charge that her change of faith was insincere
or indifferent, the story of the rest of her life will
render that assertion simply ridiculous. The
virulent and never-ending calumny and slander
to which she was subjected all her life long have
done her great injustice in this way, that they
necessarily raised her anger and disdain, and
caused her to assume an antagonistic and, as it
were, self-conscious attitude in her religious
views; there is a sort of "*virtute me involvo*" air
very often in her letters, which springs really
from her keen sense of wrong; it gives her an
artificial and unnatural appearance which belies
her greatly, for she was really full of *bonhomie*
and kindly humour. But the mud thrown by
her detractors has left its mark.

The determination to change her religion im-
plied her abdication, for she could not become a
Catholic and remain upon the throne of Sweden;
legally and morally it was impossible. In
working out her plans, the two points from which
she started were, that she must become a Catholic, and that nothing should induce her to marry.
The former was, she said at a later time, the

unique foundation of the fortune of Charles. These two premisses being given, the conclusion was inevitable. Yet it was not without a hard struggle that she brought herself to resign ; just before she did so, her usual serenity left her, and she appeared pale, silent, and disturbed. Certainly there were compensating advantages which lent a support to her design : she would escape from her cold climate and inappreciative Swedes, and gain in exchange the congenial atmosphere of Rome, Italy, and the sunny South—the prospect of wandering in new lands, and the glorious uncertainty of an adventurous step, were not for nothing to a character like hers. But the eternal statement of her enemies that her domestic difficulties drove her away, is not only entirely gratuitous, but betrays a lamentable want of insight into her nature. Christina was, like all her race, one who was rather attracted than repelled by danger and difficulty, and we might safely assert, without other evidence, that a motive of this kind would rather have kept her on the throne than forced her to leave it. But there is other positive evidence against it. Mr. Daniel Whistler, one of Whitelocke's assistants on the Swedish embassy, wrote to Cromwell in February, 1654, saying that Christina's proposed abdication is a puzzle to politicians, because her crown is not too heavy for her, and she is not reduced to any disagreeable extremity, except that want of money nearly always customary with generous princes; she has no declared enemy, and is universally esteemed among her people for her liberality, her wisdom, her moderation, and her temperance. Her action, he goes on to say, is as difficult to penetrate as the meaning of Parker's prophecies—they must wait for the event. This sober statement by an unprejudiced observer is worth all the idle declamation of her enemies, who must besides have read history to very little purpose, if they think that want of money is a sufficient reason for resigning a crown.

The steps Christina took in preparing the execution of her plan, her refusal to marry, her substitution of Charles Gustavus, have been already related; she now made another advance.

The Portuguese ambassador, Don Joseph Pinto Pereira, who came to Sweden in 1650, could talk no language but his own; his secretary, who served him as interpreter with the Queen, fell ill, and Pereira, in the interval, made use of his confessor, Macedo,* for the same purpose. Chris-

* The honour of converting her has been disputed between Macedo and a certain Francken. Dates give the preference to the former; but it is to be observed, that the Jesuits were merely the instruments called in by Christina to complete her design, determined upon long before. This is apparent, not only from what has been said, but from the

tina seized the opportunity one day to inform Macedo that she would like to discourse with some one of his persuasion on private matters, if he could manage to bring them to Stockholm without writing for them, as she did not wish to entrust so dangerous a business to paper.  The delighted Jesuit entered heartily into the scheme : they held frequent conversations in the presence of the unsuspecting Pereira, and it was arranged that Macedo should go to Rome and communicate with Piccolomini, General of the Order.   He accordingly applied for leave of absence, on the ground that the climate did not suit him ; this, however, being refused, he took French leave, and suddenly disappeared.   The ambassador prevailed on the Queen to send after him : but she took good care that he should not be caught. On his arrival at Rome, he found Piccolomini dead ; the new General, however, immediately selected two men suitable for the task : Francesco Malines, Professor of Theology at Turin, and Paolo Cassati, Professor of Mathematics at Rome. They arrived at Stockholm in March, 1652, so well disguised that Rosenhane, a senator, and Wachtmeister, Grand Equerry, with whom they

---

narration of Cassati.  The Queen amused them with casuistical questions, quite other than they expected, played with them a little, and then suddenly gave in just when they thought themselves furthest from their object.

fell in, took them for two Italian gentlemen
travelling to view the country, and told the
Queen so. Christina swiftly divined their errand
and summoned them to Court. Seizing a favourable moment, when all were leaving the dining-
hall, she whispered to Cassati, " Perhaps you
have letters for me ? " and he, without turning
round, answered " Yes." She rejoined : " Do
not mention them to any one." They now held
·frequent interviews with her, and were very much
astonished at the questions she put them—as to
whether there was any real distinction between
good and evil other than utility ; of the existence
of Providence, and the immortality of the soul ;
in short, philosophical lemmas rather than religious points of dispute between the churches.
In the whole course of their efforts it is perfectly
obvious that Christina was merely delaying a
foregone conclusion. " What should you think,"
she suddenly asked them at a moment when they
were inclined to despair, " if I were nearer
becoming a Catholic than you suppose ? "   " Hearing this," says Cassati, " we felt like men raised
from the dead." She then asked whether the
Pope could grant permission to receive the
Lord's Supper once in the year, according to the
Lutheran rites. He replied that he could not.
" Then," she exclaimed, " there is no help for
it—I must resign the crown."

She now sent Cassati back to Rome to prepare
for her subsequent arrival and find out what her
expenses might come to should she reside there;
just as it is probable Bourdelot had some such
commission in France. She wrote letters to the
Pope, Innocent X., and Cardinal Chigi by means
of Malines. In the meantime she carefully
preserved silence; the only man in Sweden who
was privy to her design was Pimentelli, who
kept the secret. She had indeed great reason to
be cautious. In a country like Sweden it would
have gone hard with her had her intention of
becoming a Catholic been commonly known. To
reject Lutheranism was to desert the traditions
of her house, and a kind of national insult, for
for which her countrymen have never forgiven
her. She wrote ambiguously to Godeau, Bishop
of Grasse, who had written to her expressing his
wish that she might put the coping stone on her
virtues by being converted, to say that what he
wishes cannot be; she has long been persuaded
that what she believes is that which she ought to
believe. And in the very month in which the
Jesuits arrived in Sweden, she wrote to Prince
Frederick, Landgrave of Hesse, to dissuade him
from taking the very step she was meditating
herself, wherein she confines herself to purely
political grounds:

"March 10, 1652.

" MY COUSIN,

" My reason for not breaking silence
before was that I might not bother you with a
letter which will not please you, since you will
learn from it the rumour that is flying about here
of the change you are meditating after the
example of my cousin your brother, who has
just declared himself a Roman Catholic. But
our friendship of so many years' standing forbids
me to keep you in ignorance of the unfavourable
criticism all your friends are making of you in
this matter. I think you cannot fail to notice it
if you give it your attention, and you will easily
judge that it is by reason of their instant request
that I am speaking to you on the subject. They
suppose that the influence arising from your
friendship for me gives me sufficient power over
your mind to enable me to restore it to its original
sentiments. And therefore they have begged
me to make this last effort, hoping that it may
be not without effect. It is then in compliance
with their wishes and to perform the duty which
friendship imposes on me that I write you this
letter, begging you to reflect upon it. It is not
for me to deal with this matter after the fashion
of Colleges or the Chairs of Theologians. I
leave it to those whose business it is to discuss
controversial points to cut their throats over the

case at their good pleasure: it would sit ill upon
me to preach to you on a subject so foreign to
my profession. On this account I set aside the
points of dispute between your Doctors and those
of the Church of Rome. And since I am of a
third religion, which, having discovered the
truth, has cast away their views as false, it
behoves me to speak to you as a neutral party,
who will attack you on only one point, on which
you ought to be sensitive; and it is that of
honour. Can you be ignorant how much converts
are hated by those whose views they quit? and
do you not know, from so many illustrious
examples, how they are despised by those whose
side they adopt? Consider, I beg of you, how
necessary to the reputation of a Prince is the
belief in his constancy, and be assured that you
are doing great wrong to your own, in making
such a mistake. If you take all this into consideration, I feel sure you will readily disapprove
of your design. And I do not believe you would
wish to do that, which, in my opinion, is so likely
to cause you to repent, a thing that would be
irretrievable, and would leave you for the rest of
your life an eternal remorse. . . . You see that
I keep my word, and avoid burying myself in
religious matters. . . . We are born for the
Sceptre and Arms; . . . after making our profession so loud, it would be to profane the sanctuary

to enter and handle the sacred objects: I must take care not to play the theologian."

In Feb. 1654 she wrote her letter to Chanut: on the eleventh of the same month she had already communicated her intentions to the Senate; she told them that she had summoned them to hear what she was going to lay before the Diet at the next meeting, namely, her abdication. Though three years ago she had yielded to their dissuasions, she had now determined to carry it out: for her successor they had Charles Gustavus, already nominated, and well able to supply her place. She did not fear criticism, her resolution was taken: she did not apply to them now for advice, but assistance in furthering the matter. The Senate, astonished and dismayed, made every effort to alter her mind, but unsuccessfully; she said her purpose was fixed, and left them. On a subsequent meeting, four days later, she placed it before them again. Count Brahé opposed her with great vehemence, asserting it to be a desertion of duty, and that they who counselled her in the matter were rascals. Christina said he was going too far; there were many who would see her abdicate with great pleasure: she was not able to discover to them the true reason for the course she took, which, however, they would learn ere

long. The matter was adjourned to the meeting
of the Diet in the following May. In the
interval Christina treated with Charles respecting
the revenues she wished to retain in her private
condition. The ambitious Prince saw the dawn
of his reign with secret joy, nevertheless he made
decent but ineffectual attempts to turn her from
her purpose. Christina at first demanded the
absolute sovereignty and revenues of many important towns and districts; this, however, she
had to forego, and content herself with a fixed
revenue, to be submitted to the Diet. She also
endeavoured to make further regulations for the
succession, seeing Charles Gustavus was as yet
unmarried, and might die without heirs; but
here, too, she had to give way. She is said to
have cast her eyes for that purpose on the young
Count Tott, whom she viewed with favour at the
time, a descendant of Eric XIV.; she wished to
make him a duke, along with Brahé and Oxenstiern; but by the representations of the two
latter she relinquished her design.

On May 12 the Diet was held at Upsala.
Among others, Whitelocke has left us an account
of it, "being in an upper room or gallery, where
he sat privately, not taken notice of by any, yet
had the full view of the great hall where the
*Ricksdag* met, and heard what was said." He
describes the splendid appearance of this great

hall and the entry of the four Orders. "About
nine o'clock there entered at the lower end a
plain lusty man in his boor's habit, with a staff in
his hand, followed by about eighty boors;" after
them the citizen Order, then the nobility, and
clergy. "All being sat," came in the Queen's
guard, the senators, the Court, and the Queen
herself, who walked up the lane they made for
her and took her seat "in the chair of state, all
of massy silver, a rich cushion in it, and a
canopy of crimson velvet richly embroidered over
it." The Chancellor should have made the
opening speech, but he remained silent. The
Queen beckoned to him, and after a little speaking
together he returned to his place; he would take
no part in removing the crown from the head of
a descendant of the house of Vasa. "The Queen
sat down again a little time; then rising up with
mettle, she came forward, and with a good grace
and confidence spake to the assembly." She told
them that they would doubtless be astonished at
the reason why they had been summoned, being a
thing without precedent: but if they reflected
upon it, they would see that it was no new resolve,
but a thing of long premeditation. She reminded
them of the succession assured to her cousin, and
his eminent qualities, whom they would doubtless
joyfully welcome to the throne; she recalled her
unwearied diligence and service of the state

during the ten years of her reign, demanding
nothing in return but that they would consent
to her resolution, which was firm and ineradicable :
and concluded with her wishes for the future
good of the country. Her speech was answered
by others from the Archbishop and the Grand
Marshal, setting forth their gratitude and approbation of her reign, and praying her to give up
her determination to abdicate. "In the last
place stepped forward the Marshal of the Boors, a
plain country fellow, in his clouted shoon, and all
other habits answerable ; " " without any *congées*
or ceremony at all, he spake to her Majesty :

"'O Lord God, Madam, what do you mean to
do? It troubles us to hear you speak of
forsaking those that love you so well as we do.
Can you be better than you are? You are
Queen of all these countries, and if you leave
this large kingdom, where will you get such
another? . . . Continue in your gears, good
Madam, and be the forehorse as long as you live,
and we will help you the best we can to bear
your burden.' . . . When the boor had ended
his speech, he waddled up to the Queen without
any ceremony, took her by the hand and shook
it heartily, and kissed it two or three times ;
then turning his back to her, he pulled out of
his pocket a foul handkerchief, and wiped the
tears from his eyes."

Schering Rosenhane then read a paper in which the Queen reviewed her political and domestic relations, and invited the Estates to consider the allowances to be paid her. And then the Estates left the hall as they had come in.

After attempting to shake her resolution once again, the Diet agreed to her abdication; yet would not, as has been said, grant the lands demanded, but only the revenues accruing from them: namely, from the isles of Œland, Gothland, and Œsel, Wollin, Usedom, the town and castle of Wolgast, and some lands in Pomerania. There were some who wished to compel her to live in Sweden, and not spend these revenues out of the country. But Charles Gustavus opposed himself to this, not only to oblige Christina, but because he had no wish to see her remain in the kingdom on his own account.

Some weeks before her resignation, Christina went to Nycöping to bid farewell to her mother. Before the Prince, whom she summoned for this purpose, and the Count, she asked her pardon if she had not at all times shown all the respect and care towards her that she ought; this was not owing to a want of goodwill, but the result of certain circumstances which had tied her hands. She was now going to resign the crown and would be still less able to do anything for her than before; but if her mother was going to lose

a daughter, she would find a son: and she presented to her Charles Gustavus, and committed
her to his care. They bade each other farewell,
Christina firmly, but Maria Eleanora burst into
tears. She cried all night. Christina got up
and went to her to endeavour to console her; at
five in the morning she returned to Upsala.

A day or two before she abdicated, she disconcerted the Senate and Charles Gustavus by
a strange and apparently unaccountable action.
She sent to the Portuguese resident to say it was
useless for him to remain in Sweden, since she
was determined no longer to recognise the Duke
of Braganza as king, and should always look upon
him as a usurper. There seems to be something
underneath this which we do not know; but
taking the facts as we have them, we can only
explain the proceeding as a sort of friendly
signal to the Spanish party, in view of her forthcoming abdication; for it neither had, nor could
have, any meaning in itself, nor any consequences.
The Portuguese ambassador continued at Stockholm on the same footing as before.

At length the day came. On June 6, Christina and the king-elect entered the Senate, and
the Act of abdication was read, by which she
resigned the crown for ever, herself and her
posterity, and recognized Charles as her successor,
provided that he maintained her rights to her

revenues. She was tied by no conditions except that of doing nothing injurious to the State ; she was to be subject and accountable to no one, and was to reserve supreme power and jurisdiction over her domestics and the members of her household. This, and another Act, in which the Prince promised to observe these conditions, being signed, the grand officers clothed the Queen in her royal robes and placed the crown on her head; she took in her right hand the Sceptre, and in her left the Golden Ball ; two Senators, representing the Grand Marshal and the Treasurer, went before her, carrying the Sword and the Key. In this state she entered the grand hall of the Castle, where all the Estates of the realm, the foreign ambassadors, and the ladies of the Court were assembled. She mounted the daïs, and sat for the last time in the silver throne : behind her were her Grand Chamberlain and her Captain of the Guard ; on her left, the Prince.

Schering Rosenhane then read in a loud voice the two Acts, which he handed respectively to the Queen and the Prince. Then, at a given signal, the grand officers came forward to receive the royal insignia. But Count Brahé would not take the crown off her head, and she had to do it herself. Then she removed the royal mantle, which was seized by the nearest spectators, and torn into a thousand pieces : each one wishing to carry away a memorial of the Queen they were never again to see. Divested of her royal trappings, Christina, no longer the Queen, stepped forward in a dress of plain white silk, and spoke to the assembly, bidding them farewell in an affecting speech :—" I thank Almighty God, who caused me to be born of a royal stock, and raised me to be Queen over so large and mighty a kingdom : and for that he has granted me so uncommon a measure of success and blessing. I thank, too, those nobles who preserved the State when I was in tender years, and likewise the Senate and the Estates for the fidelity and attachment they have shown me." She then recounted all that had been done in Sweden during the ten years of her reign, and solemnly affirmed that in a difficult position she had done nothing for which she had to reproach herself; she had sacrificed her own time and repose to the welfare of her people. She spoke of her father, Gustavus Adolphus, and what he had done for Sweden ; then turning to the Prince, she praised his fine qualities, and predicted that he would increase the national glory. She bade them transfer to him the fidelity they had shown to her, and renew to him the oaths, from which she now released them, that they had taken to herself.

Her speech was received with profound emotion;

few could restrain their tears. Schering Rosenhane made answer for the Estates, for the Chancellor would take no part in the ceremony. They
were obliged to consent to a measure they disliked against their will; yet they thanked her
for the trouble she had taken in their behalf.
Then addressing Charles Gustavus, the Queen
bade him keep his eye fixed upon the great
examples of his ancestors, protesting that his
worth, and not his kinship, had caused her to
choose him for her successor. She wished for no
other recompense than that he would be kind and
attentive to her mother, and those of her friends
whom she had recommended to him. The Prince
begged her to re-ascend the throne; but finding
this of no avail, he thanked her for her goodness
to him, and promised to observe all her wishes.
He next addressed the Senate and the Estates,
who, through the mouth of Rosenhane, assured
him of their love and obedience. Then taking
Christina by the hand he led her back to her room.

The same afternoon his own coronation was
performed, very simply, owing to the exhausted
state of the finances. He caused a medal to be
struck, to commemorate his gratitude. On the
obverse was himself, as king—CAROLUS GUSTAVUS
REX; on the reverse, a picture of Christina crowning him, with the motto: A DEO ET CHRISTINA.

The reign of Christina had come to an end.

R

# CHAPTER VII.

PAGES might be filled with the opinions expressed in Europe upon the extraordinary spectacle of a young woman in her twenty-eighth year voluntarily throwing away a crown; but they would add nothing to our knowledge. The onlookers of the time had less means of getting at the truth than we have, and the various judgments, ranging from the most extravagant panegyric to equally extravagant invective, were only dictated by personal feeling or party interests; very few were there who considered it impartially. The King of Spain, dubious at first, afterwards gave it his warmest approval. "Where," exclaimed Condé, "is this Queen who has cast off what we are all hunting for?" "It is well," wrote Bochart, "to despise the world, but with the crown she has lost the power of doing good." "You have cast away your shield," wrote Heinsius to Christina; "of your flatterers but few praised Christina, most the Queen." Here and there she found an isolated admirer, such as Gassendi or Milton, in those who could take a philosophic view. The suddenness

of so startling a course at first took the world by
surprise and merely perplexed it ; but no sooner
had Christina capped her abdication by her
profession of her new faith than all doubt
vanished. From that hour the Catholics extolled
her to the skies, and the Protestants, especially
in Sweden, with the large contingent of disappointed French and learned parasites, became
her bitter enemies. Calumny and abuse, however, are always stronger than praise, and her
vilipenders have won the day up to the present
time. A sound historical criticism will dismiss
both these special pleaders. The politician and
the man of the world will perhaps side with the
Swedes, and pronounce it to be a desertion of
duty, if not an act of complete folly ; but in
that case he must accept the logical consequences
of his position, and regard it as *reductio ad
absurdum* of religion, for there is not the shadow
of a doubt that she herself considered she was
sacrificing her crown to her convictions. The
religious motive was her starting-point, nor
would the attraction of brighter skies and more
congenial surroundings, even aided by her
native restlessness, even have been strong
enough to draw her away from the throne
without it. The more plausible assertion that
she was driven away by her difficulties is completely refuted by a fact admitted even by those

who make it, that she had determined to resign as early as, and even earlier than, 1648.

Those who have of their own free will abandoned the supreme power—Sulla, Diocletian, Charles V.—had not long to live after it; their private life has added to, instead of damaging, the general effect of the whole. But Christina lived thirty-five years after she abdicated, and hence there is a sort of dramatic impropriety in the second and longer half of her career, which in itself has detracted from her fame. There is a great drop from a public to a private stage; the brilliancy of her ten years' reign—ten years of absolute rule—during which the young Queen, as she said herself, *donnait tout et pourvoyait à tout*, is sadly dulled against the subsequent period nearly four times as long, when she had only her own peculiar character to depend on. From the point of view of art and her own fame, it is a very great pity she did not die immediately after her abdication. The remainder of her life produces the same effect as the third rhyme in a heroic couplet; intrinsically good though it be, it mars the general effect.

Her first anxiety after becoming a private person was to get out of Sweden as fast as she could; she would not even stay the night at Upsala, though it was raining hard. To Count Brahé, who begged her not to be in such a hurry, she replied, "How do you suppose I can stay in a place over which I was but now sovereign, to see another wielding my power?" There were, besides, good reasons for making haste. The peasants were openly talking of compelling her to stay in the country and spend her revenues in Sweden; and what was worse, rumours were beginning to spread of her design to become a Catholic. Delay might have fatal effects: accordingly, she remained only five days at Stockholm. To lull suspicion she gave out that she was going to drink the waters at Spa, and would soon return. She had before this packed up and sent to Gothenburg the bulk of her furniture, statues, pictures, medals, and personal possessions. Charles Gustavus presented her with 50,000 crowns for her journey and a fine diamond and pearl pin as a souvenir. Before starting she wrote to her hero, Condé, assuring him of her continued admiration, and declaring that her resignation of the crown should never be lowered by any vain regrets. She also, as if to initiate her new career, wrote to the French Academy, thanking them for the praise with which they had received her portrait, which they had asked for, and telling them of her intention to devote herself to the *belles lettres*. Partly, too, to assure herself of what she was not wholly convinced, she had medals struck; one showing Pegasus on a high rock with the inscription, *sedes hæc solio potior;* another, displaying a crown, with the motto, *et sine te;* a third showed a labyrinth, with the words *fata viam invenient.* The world was, indeed, all before her; it required courage to take the fatal step.

She set out from Stockholm at nightfall, escorted by many of the principal persons in the kingdom, and observed by a large crowd, amidst the salutes of cannon from the fort and the men-of-war. Travelling all night and the whole of the next day, she arrived in the evening at Nyköping, where she bade farewell to Maria Eleanora, and continued her journey without resting till she came to Norköping. She remained there a day, not having slept since she left Stockholm. A little farther on she was seized with pleurisy, and had to stop for a week at a private house. Here, although twelve ships of the line had been ordered to Calmar to escort her, she wrote to Charles X. to say she would not go by sea, but by land to Denmark. Passing through Halmstadt she wrote to Gassendi, fixing on him an annual salary, together with a present of a chain of gold. She now disguised herself as a man, giving herself out to be the son of Count Dohna, for the sake of security on her travels. At the last moment, before crossing the frontier, Baron Linde once more made her the offer of

Charles' hand; she answered calmly, that if she had been inclined to marry, she would have done so with better grace while she was still on the throne, adding that the king was prudent enough not to need counsel of her.

We need not dwell on her journey through Denmark. On July 10, she arrived at Hamburgh, and resumed her own sex and personality. She stayed at the house of a Jew, named Texeira; this scandalized the Lutheran ministers, who inveighed against her in the pulpit for it. From subsequent letters it appears that she had bought or engaged this house from Texeira, who acted as her agent in various money matters. A story is told of her here, which may or may not be true. Being at the church of St. Peter's with the Landgrave of Hesse, the Rector pronounced a panegyric upon her, on the text of the Queen of Sheba, and was rewarded by the present of a gold chain, "though possibly she had not heard much of it"; for after she left the church, a book richly bound was found in her pew, which turned out to be a Virgil; it was taken to Christina, who received it with a smile.

She wrote to Charles X., reminding him to look after her revenues; and there was no harm in having a friend at Court, for a rumour that she was meditating a change of religion had got about, and the Swedish clergy were talking of cutting down her revenues. The Senate determined to send a remonstrance, adjuring her to remain steadfast in the faith of her fathers, as being the best.

Meanwhile, she was visited by numerous German princes, among others, the already mentioned Landgrave of Hesse, who gave her "a stately feast without the city," on July 30. After supper she returned home, resumed male attire, because the roads were dangerous by reason of the dispute with the city of Bremen, and accompanied only by Steinberg and four others, departed at midnight, bidding the rest of her retinue meet her by a certain date at Amsterdam. On August 6, she came to Munster, and went next day to visit the Jesuits' college there. A letter written by one of the Reverend Fathers gives an account of it. She was shown over the church, library, and precincts, jesting with the Father on the morals of the Order, in that they were all things to all men. Just before going, being offered a cup of wine, she accepted it, and poured it away on the ground, saying, " I am no great wine-bibber," and departed, much pleased with her entertainment: next morning she sent them 100 ducats. One of the Jesuits, who had her portrait, discovered her, in spite of the big hat, large boots, black wig, and sword on thigh, which announced the young man, but said nothing at the time. Thence passing through Holland *incognita*, in spite of the wish of the States to receive her magnificently, she arrived at Antwerp on August 12, and assumed her own dress.

Among those who came to see her here was the Archduke Leopold ; " the Queen received him at the foot of the stairs, conducted him to her lodgings, made him sit down over against her, in such another chair, gave him always the title of Highness, and accompanied him to the bottom of the same stairs, with reciprocal satisfaction, still speaking in Italian." But her hero Condé sending to demand the same ceremony as that shown to the Archduke, she was annoyed and refused it; whereupon he would not come at all. *It is said* that he did come *incognito* in the crowd one day, and on Christina's recognising him, withdrew, remarking only, when she would have detained him, " All or nothing ! " Meeting him one day as if by accident, Christina exclaimed, " Cousin, who would have believed, ten years ago, that we were destined to meet like this ? " From the Hague came secretly the Queen of Bohemia, Elizabeth, the friend of Descartes, with her daughter, "only to see her, as they did, at a comedy," as well as other notables ; she passed her time in receiving visits, frequenting the theatres, and making tours to neighbouring

colleges and libraries. To the admonition of the
Senate she wrote back, refusing politely to be
guided by their well-meant advice.

While she was at Antwerp, circumstances not
fully known to us brought about an awkward
misunderstanding between her and her old friend
Chanut. She had wished to see him; accordingly,
he came from the Hague, where he was ambassador, and was well received. After he returned,
the report spread that this visit had not been one
of mere courtesy, but that its object was to
invite Christina to try and make peace between
Spain and France. Chanut wrote to her, to ask
her to deny this rumour publicly. Whether it
was that there really had been some such talk,
(Chanut, for instance, wrote to a friend, to say
that the Queen was by no means such a Spaniard
as was given out,) or whether she suspected the
rumours were designed to injure her with Spain;
or finally, wished to conciliate the Spaniards, she
refused; telling him " that for all answer to his
letter, which he was trying to give weight to by
publishing copies, she would say only that all it
contained was baseless; . . . the French were
well known to be hindering the peace; the
Spaniards were waiting patiently, even though
they might have to wait till the French grew
more modest; and neither the cunning, nor the
boasting of France would terrify them; the King

of France would one day find that peace was his truest policy." Chanut wrote back a letter of surprise and remonstrant apology for his country; and laid the correspondence before the Court of Sweden, to which France had complained. King Charles contented himself with announcing he had taken no part in the business, and did not understand it, as, indeed, neither can we.

Shortly afterwards, Christina made a magnificent journey to Brussels, on December 23; being conveyed thither in a barge, richly decorated and gilded, armed with twelve pieces of cannon, and drawn by twelve horses; the banks were lined with gazers, and soldiers drawn up to receive her, who fired volleys in her honour; night fell before she arrived at the gate of the city, which was adorned with an artificial firework, representing two angels holding the name of Christina, crowned with laurel. As she passed through the town, she was welcomed with bonfires, illuminations, bell-ringing, and discharges of cannon, and the plaudits of the all-eager multitude. On Christmas Eve, she made her private abjuration of Lutheranism in the presence of the Archduke, Montecuculi, Pimentelli, and others; at the moment she was absolved, the ordnance of the town, by a special providence, according to Gualdo, by a previous arrangement, according to Arckenholtz, were simultaneously discharged.

Although her public reception into the bosom of the Church was deferred till she came to Innsbrück, the news of her conversion was bruited through Europe, and from that hour, among the Protestants, her doom was sealed.

In the meantime, she gave herself up to the amusements which were liberally provided for her; balls, plays, tournaments, hunting parties, rapidly succeeded one another; Mazarin even sent a company of actors, who acted plays alternately in Spanish, French, and Italian. She writes a playful letter at this time to her only female friend, Ebba Sparre (a letter which the thickheaded Arckenholtz, and others after him, interpret seriously):

" How supreme my happiness would be, could I share it with you," she says ; then, after assuring her of her affection for her: "Adieu, *belle*, remember your Christina.   P.S.—Give my compliments to all my friends, male and female, even to those who have no wish to be friendly : I forgive them with all my heart, all the more that I am none the worse for them.   I forgot to tell you that I am perfectly well, and receive untold honours ; I get along well with everybody, except the Prince de Condé, whom I never see except at the play, or on the field.   My occupations are to eat well, and sleep well, study a little, talk, laugh, and go to the French, Italian and Spanish plays, and pass the time pleasantly. In short, I listen to no more sermons; I despise all orators, in accordance with Solomon's 'All is vanity,' for we ought all to be content with eating, drinking and sleeping."

She stayed in the palace of the Archduke, who vacated his own apartments for her; afterwards she moved to that of the Duke of Egmont. A few *savants*, such as Vossius, came to pay their respects: she wrote to Bourdelot she had no more need of a doctor. She sent to invite Ménage, who would not come, judging she would be at Paris before long. But with the exception of worthy men such as Heinsius, Bochart, and Gassendi, the bulk of the learned combined with the French to defame her, and a plentiful crop of libellous anecdote sprang up, on which we may listen to Bayle: "I have heard multitudes of people retail all kinds of scandals about her, but as soon as I looked into them, I never found anything to make them credible; I take this opportunity of warning others to put no faith in such stuff." It may very well be, indeed, that on some Jesuits promising her a place in the calendar beside St. Bridget of Sweden, she replied, "I would rather have a place among the wise." Like most people who feel deeply, Christina studiously avoided betraying it externally; her lively and satirical humour in such instances

as these was misrepresented by her enemies, and
eagerly improved upon to her disadvantage.
The Swedish ecclesiastics were by this time furious
with her; she judged it advisable to write to the
king and Brahé, recommending to them the care
of her interests on the matter of her revenues;
her forebodings that all might not always be
well with them were justified afterwards, as time
will show.

In Sweden, things were altering quickly from
what they were in her time.   Charles X., among
other things, was a most devout Lutheran, and
gave entire satisfaction to the clergy.   The old
Chancellor, Axel Oxenstiern, did not long sur-
vive her departure from Sweden: in August,
1654, he died.   His last thoughts were of the
daughter of Gustavus Adolphus :—" What news,"
he enquired, " of Christina ? " and on receiving
an answer, " I predicted," he said, " she would
repent of what she had done, but "—with a deep
sigh—" she is none the less the daughter of the
great Gustavus."   They were his last words.
His whole life had been devoted to the service of
the House of Vasa; Christina's abdication was,
as it were, the ironical shattering of all his schemes.
Eight months afterwards, Maria Eleanora followed
him; on receiving news of her death, Christina
retired into the country, and remained for three
weeks inaccessible to visitors.

While she remained in Flanders, awaiting the completion of the arrangements for her journey to Rome, Pope Innocent X. died, on January 7, 1655. After a protracted conclave, the " flying squadron " carried the election of Cardinal Chigi, who became Pope in April, taking the name of Alexander VII. He was enormously delighted with Christina's conversion, and took all the pains in the world, says De Retz, to convince us all that he had himself been the unique instrument of which God had made use to bring it about, whereas everybody knew very well he had had nothing to do with it. He immediately wrote to Christina, advising her to let her light, which was at present under a bushel, shine out before the world by making public profession of her faith before entering Rome, and sent to her for that purpose his legate Holsteinius, canon of St. Peter's, and librarian of the Vatican, himself a convert. She accordingly took leave of the Archduke, presenting him with a Swedish horse whose harness and trappings were worth 30,000 crowns ; another, not quite so magnificent, she gave to Count Fyensaldagne, as well as jewels to various officers worth 10,000 pistoles, and left Brussels in September, 1655, with a large retinue, among which was Pimentelli. On the way Charles II. came to see her from Frankfort ; the conversation was unfortunately not reported : doubtless he bore her no malice for not lending him assistance.

At Innsbrück her public profession was solemnized on November 3. At ten in the morning she was conducted to the cathedral church by the Archduke and a procession of nobles and ecclesiastics. She was dressed in black silk, her only ornament being a cross of five magnificent diamonds on her breast. Holsteinius read his commission from the pope: she then made her profession, reading the form presented to her in a firm and composed voice—declaring her belief in the doctrines contained in the Nicene creed, which she recited, the ecclesiastical traditions, the interpretation of Scripture placed upon it by the Church and the Fathers; the seven sacraments; the doctrines of original sin, and justification, according to the Council of Trent; transubstantiation; purgatory; the invocation of Saints; the worship of images; indulgences; the supreme power of the Pope; condemning and anathematizing the opposite heresies. Holsteinius then gave her absolution, and pronounced the benediction. A Jesuit then preached a sermon on the text: "Hearken, O daughter, and incline thine ear: forget also thine own people and thy father's house." Four copies of this profession, one for Christina, Innsbrück, the Vatican, and the Pope, respectively, were prepared and signed by Christina, the Archduke, the Archbishop, Pimentelli, and Holsteinius.

The ceremony over, it was celebrated with great rejoicings, bonfires, the firing of cannon, plays, and spectacles : a musical tragi-comedy was performed by the best musicians in Italy. As a specimen of the sort of thing invented about Christina, Chevreau, a fertile source, declares that on this occasion she said to the circle surrounding her, " 'Tis but right, gentlemen, you should treat me to a comedy, since I have just treated you to a farce." Impudence could go no farther ; as if at such a moment she would have trampled on the Catholic proprieties on the point of going to Rome.

During the week she remained at Innsbrück, she wrote to the King of Sweden, informing him that if her faith was changed, so was not her regard for Sweden. She wrote also to the Pope, professing her complete submission to him, and hoping speedily to present herself for his benediction in Rome. With Holsteinius, a man of learning and culture, she had many a conversation on the eternal city: doubtless he lost no opportunity of increasing her already eager desire to see it. " Where indeed," exclaims Ranke, " could she have lived except in Rome ? With any of the temporal sovereigns, whose claims were similar to her own, she would have

S

fallen into ceaseless strife and collision." "Rome
still continued to be the metropolis of intellectual culture, unequalled in the variety of its
learning and in the practice of art; it was still
productive as regards music. . . . 'A man must
have been ill-treated by nature,' exclaims Spon,
who visited Rome in 1674, 'who does not find his
full contentment in one or other of the branches
to be studied here;' the libraries, where the
rarest works were open to the student; the concerts in churches and palaces, where the finest
voices were daily to be heard; the many collections of ancient and modern sculpture and
painting; the numberless stately buildings of
every age. Villas wholly covered with bas-
reliefs and inscriptions; . . . the presence of so
many strangers of all lands and tongues; the
beauties of nature to be enjoyed in gardens
worthy to make part of paradise; and for him
who delights in the practice of piety, a treasure
of churches, relics, and processioning, that shall
occupy him his whole life long."

In such an element Christina felt she would
be entirely at home. The necessary preliminary
over, she left Innsbrück on December 8th. Her
progress to Rome resembled the triumphant
procession of a Roman Dictator, or a scene in the
Arabian Nights; at every stage gorgeous spectacles, fêtes, decorated arches, illuminations were

strewn upon her path. The Venetians not allowing her to pass through their territory for fear of the pest in the countries through which she had come, she turned aside to Mantua, and was royally entertained by the Duke. On entering the Papal States she was met by four Nuncios, with a letter of welcome from the Pope. His legate escorted her into Ferrara, and did the honours of that town. During a splendid banquet there she astonished him by her intimate acquaintance with the principal musicians of Italy, and its painting and architecture. The three first cathedrals in Europe, she said, were St. Peter's of Rome, the Duomo at Milan, and St. Paul's in London; but the last, she added with a sigh, is now become a stable.

It would only be tedious to recount in detail the vain repetition of her reception at all the towns through which her route lay, Bologna, Faenza, Rimini, Pesaro, Ancona; at the last place, beneath a building representing the seven hills of Rome, was the Tiber, which "instead of water did actually cast wine." Sometimes she would enter the town in the garb of an Amazon on horseback. At Loretto she dedicated a crown and sceptre adorned with diamonds and pearls to the Virgin. She arrived at Rome on December 19th, entering the city incognita, amidst a blaze of illuminations, at seven o'clock in the evening.

s 2

Observing the multitude assembled to look at her, she jestingly inquired if this was the received fashion of stealing privately into Rome. On being introduced to the Pope, she made him three profound courtesies, and respectfully kissed his toe ; he raised her, and led her to a throne of crimson velvet embroidered with gold. The interval of three days before she made her public entry was filled up with visits to the Vatican and concerts.

"The Happy and Joyous Entry of Queen Christina of Sweden into Rome," as an inscription on the arch of the Porta del Popolo, through which she entered, declared, took place on December 23rd, 1655. Riding on a white horse in the manner and garb of an Amazon, she passed with her train through lines of troops drawn up on each side, through crowds of spectators in festive attire, and entered St. Peter's, where being received by the clergy, and conducted to the Pope's chapel, she was confirmed by his Holiness ; taking the name of Alexandra in addition to her own, with a double complimentary allusion, it was thought, to the Pope and the historical character she most admired.

These costly but wearisome ceremonies over, she employed her time in visiting the buildings and antiquities, the museums and galleries. At the College *de Propagandâ Fide*, where printing in twenty-two languages was carried on, the scholars complimented her in each ; " Let Christina live for ever," was printed in eight different tongues ; and the whole was subsequently published in a book to commemorate her visit. As she stood one day before a statue of Truth by Bernini, she exclaimed in admiration, " How beautiful ! " " God be praised," said a Cardinal who stood near, " that your Majesty loves truth, a thing rare in those of your station." " I believe you," answered Christina, " but all truths are not of marble." She frequently showed herself equal to her surroundings not only in learning and culture, but in satirical repartee. She used to laugh and talk to the Cardinals during mass, an enormity which we must beware of criticising from a modern point of view ; in that age people were very lax in their behaviour in church. The Pope sent her a rosary and exhorted her to use it in her prayers, to which Christina forcibly replied, " *Non miga voglio essere Catholica da bacchettone*," (" I did not become a Catholic to tell beads "). This is not, as perverse malignity will have it, a confession of indifference, but a refusal to tie herself up in the foolish symbolisms designed for fixing the attention of common minds : she was all her life, as she says, little of a devotee. She soon became a leading figure in the literary society of Rome, and founded an academy, which met for the first time on January 21st, 1656: we shall examine this side of her life more fully further on.

The approach of the Carnaval was a signal for new concerts, plays, moralities, and amusements. The principal families of Rome and the Cardinals vied with one another in fêting her. Prince Pamphili and his wife gave a magnificent series of shows and banquets in her honour; the Barberini exhibited tournaments, and an extraordinary opera, entitled 'Human Life,' varied with elephants, bulls, streams of real water, and the like, such as had never been seen in Rome. Cardinal Colonna actually fell violently in love with her, though he was fifty years old; as his passion led him into ridiculous and unseemly positions—he used to serenade her—the Pope banished him from Rome, in order that Christina might not be scandalised. Of this he was very careful, and it was even said that his aim in welcoming her thus honourably was to "compel others to come in." An epigram was made by some anonymous wit on his rejoicings over Christina, alluding to the conquests of Charles X. in Poland going on at the same time, to the effect that the Pope in gaining one sheep had lost a whole fold.

In one country at least his chances were gone for ever; the news of Christina's final reception into the bosom of the Church had been the last straw to the Swedish clergy. The feeling of their helplessness increased their malevolence: in this condition, they vented their malice upon Matthiæ. He was considered to have directly contributed to Christina's lapse, by inspiring her with sentiments hostile to Lutheranism. (In 1662, his books advocating conciliation, the 'Idea of a Better State' and his 'Branches of a Northern Olive,' were proscribed in Sweden, and he anticipated his deposition from the bishopric of Strengnås by resigning.) In 1655 he wrote Christina a letter, deploring that the daughter of Gustavus should have belied her race by going over to Rome, and hoping that it might be her secret aim to work for a reunion of all churches, in which case she would merit eternal gratitude; otherwise he prays her to return to her ancient faith. Christina, though she did not take his advice, retained her affection for him, writing to him and sending him money. "Have patience," she says, "I share your misfortune, and will never abandon you; you shall never want as long as I am alive."

During this first period, Christina yielded herself to the fascinating enjoyment of her new existence, with a delicious feeling of relief after the restraint and false position of the last few years in Sweden. This careless easiness was not destined to last long. Already in her reign the jealousy of French and Spaniards had drawn her into their miserable animosities; how much more was this likely to happen in a centre like Rome—Rome, where politics were based entirely upon a balance between those two Powers? No sooner had she begun to form a part of the life of the capital, than between the two parties she found herself involved in their political intrigues and squabbles. Her bat-eyed biographers lay the complications that ensued to the door of her own "fickleness," rather than the varying relations between the parties; it is so much easier. But what are the facts?

As she was now meditating a journey to Paris, she engaged some French people in her service; she also engaged some Italians, dismissing some Spaniards to make room for them; in both cases, consulting merely her own convenience. But the Spaniards, who had got into the habit of considering her their private property, and quite erroneously supposed she had till now been a particular partisan of their interests, were furious at this manifest predilection for France, and began to abuse her; they even went so far, according to an author by no means favourable to Christina, as to publish some defamatory lives of her in Spanish. This was not calculated to win her back again, and she is said to have

complained to Madrid about it.  But however
that may be, it was the Spaniards themselves who
by their arrogance brought about the very thing
they accused her of doing, namely, viewing them
with less favour than before.  Their method
of action is fully described in a manifesto
Christina published on the subject, which gives
so thorough an insight into the genesis of the
accusations against her that it is worth while to
quote it at length :

"The Queen having entered the Papal States,
and met, from Ferrara to Rome, with certain
Cardinals, of the 'flying squadron,' with whose
conversation she was pleased, the Spaniards in
her suite were seized with jealousy as usual, and
claiming to be the only ones enjoying her favour,
did not abstain from time to time from saying all
they could to prevent her from establishing any
relations with them.   But her Majesty gave them
to understand that their advice was thrown away.
Having coming to Rome, M. de Lionne, the
French ambassador, holding frequent and long
interviews with her, the Spaniards complained,
and told her that apparently she was wishing to
damage the friendship she had promised to the
King their master, by forming a still closer one
with France.   To which her Majesty answered
that she would cultivate the friendship of whomsoever she chose, and that they ought not to be

surprised at her wishing to entertain a correspondence with France, with whom she had been
on good terms at all times; this was not to make
new friendships, but to continue an old one ; and
finally, she was not the King of Spain's subject,
that she should blindly second their counsels and
conform to their designs.

"The Spaniards, entertaining further suspicions
of the frequent visits of the Cardinals Barberini,
Borromeo, and Azzolini, went and complained to
the Pope, thinking thereby to put a stop to these
visits.   But finding that this did not produce the
desired effect, they formed plots among themselves,
sometimes in the house of Cardinal de Medicis,
sometimes in that of the Duke de Terranuova, at
which assisted Cardinal Landgravio, Don Antonio
Pimentelli, Don Antonio de Cueva, and others of
the Spanish faction ; in which were held discourses
showing very scant respect to her Majesty, which
were made public throughout Rome.   Cueva was
the principal instrument of the Spaniards in
carrying from house to house these calumnies on
the Queen, who being informed of them, judged
it at first best to despise all such reports.   She
dissembled for more than three months, treating
Cueva as usual.   But finally, seeing that things
went on, and that further disguise would only
have the effect of making him still more insolent,
she began to treat him with greater coldness than

before, and give him to understand that it would
give her much pleasure if he asked leave to
return to Flanders; he said he hoped to start in
a week. Next day her Majesty made Sentinelli
her chamberlain; Cueva, taking this as a mark
of contempt for himself, demanded leave to return
the same evening. Don Antonio Pimentelli also
took umbrage at the matter, and though accustomed to come every day to the Farnese to visit
the Queen, he let pass five days without presenting
himself; on the sixth he came to try and settle
the Cueva affair."

When Cueva came to take leave some days
afterwards, Christina summoned her principal
domestics as witnesses, and told him that it was
for his conscience to determine whether he had
served her well or ill; but he might be certain
she would always know how to reward the man
of honour, and punish the scoundrel; and if she
ever heard that he had spoken disrespectfully of
her in future she would take care to reward him
according to his deserts, wherever he might be.
The same day she sent Count Fiene to tell
Cardinal de Medicis, as in the Spanish interest,
what had occurred; and bade him tell the King
of Spain that if Cueva had not been one of his
generals she would have had him horse-whipped;
signifying further to the Cardinal that her respect
for his rank and cloth would cause her to over-

look all he had himself done or might do.  Next morning she sent to warn the Duke de Terranuova to behave himself like a gentleman, as, now that Cueva was dismissed, she had only gentlemen in her service, who were ready to give him proof of it, unless he remembered his character as ambassador of Spain.  She subsequently told the Pope what she had done, who gave her his entire approval, and sent to the Duke to warn him that his Holiness viewed his behaviour to the Queen as very strange, and would take any further insult as made to himself.

This affords an explanation of these dark intrigues, and completely exonerates Christina from the blame.  Of Cueva we are further told that he refused to go through a room in her house, because it contained a portrait of Louis XIV.  Small wonder if she felt a strong desire to have him soundly thrashed !

In the April of that same year, 1656, she fell dangerously ill again, but recovered by the aid of her own strength of mind and the doctors of the Pope, who was much concerned.  About this time she wrote to Ebba Sparre :

"How happy I should be, could I see you, *Belle* ; but I am condemned to the hard fate of loving you from a distance; the envy the stars have of human happiness prevents me from being myself entirely happy, as I cannot be so absent from you. . . . Is it possible, *Belle*, that you remember me? am I as dear as I always used to be to you? was I not rather mistaken when I persuaded myself I was the person you loved best in the world? Ah! if so, leave me my illusion, do not undeceive me, then neither time nor absence shall deprive me of it. Adieu, *Belle*, adieu; I embrace you a million times.

"CHRISTINA ALEXANDRA."

In the case of the beautiful Ebba Christina, she made an exception to her general contempt of women. She wrote to her again after her return from France, pressing her to come and stay with her in Italy; but this never took place: five years afterwards Ebba died of a fever.

The need of change, and her disgust at the Spanish disagreeables, increased Christina's desire to go to France, and the prevalence of an epidemic afforded an excuse. Nevertheless it was not without difficulty that she could raise the necessary funds; the war between Poland and Sweden caused difficulties and arrears in her revenues; she was obliged to pawn her jewels for 10,000 ducats and accept besides a loan of 20,000 crowns from the Pope. Embarking at Civita Vecchia in one of his galleys, she arrived at Marseilles on July 24th. The Duc de Guise was sent to meet her, and on her journey through France she was received everywhere with great ceremony. At Lyons an ecclesiastic complimented her with more wit than reason : " I will not bore your Majesty with a long discourse, but content myself with saying, ' *Suecia te Christinam fecit ; Roma Christianam ; faciet te Gallia Christianissimam.*' "

At Fontainebleau, where she arrived on September 4th, she was met by Mademoiselle de Montpensier, who describes the scene and the impression made upon her :

" I had so often heard of her strange way of dressing that I was dying with fear lest I should laugh when I caught sight of her ; but when I perceived her she surprised me indeed, but not in a way to make me laugh. She wore a grey petticoat, laced with gold and silver ; a close-fitting jacket of camelot, of the colour of fire, with lace to match that of her petticoat ; a point lace handkerchief round her neck, tied with a fire-coloured ribbon ; a fair wig, with a knot behind, such as women wear, and a hat with black feathers which she carried in her hand. She is very fair, with blue eyes, which are sometimes very soft, but at others very bold, a pleasing though large mouth, fine teeth, large and aquiline nose ; she is very small, her bad figure is hidden by her jacket; her general effect is that of a pretty little boy. When I presented Count Bethune to her she spoke to him of his manuscripts. She likes to show that she knows every one, and is *au fait* on all points.

"After the ballet we went to the Comedy; there she astonished me. In her praise of places that pleased her, she would swear by God, throw herself back in her chair, tossing her legs about, and assuming postures scarcely decent. She spoke on all sorts of subjects, and said what she did say very agreeably; sometimes she would fall into a profound reverie, sighing deeply; then all of a sudden come to herself like one waking from a dream; she is altogether extraordinary. Then we went to see some sham firing on the water. She held me by the hand during the performance; several shots came close by us; I was afraid. She laughed at me, saying, 'What! a young lady who has seen so much, and done so many fine things, afraid?' I told her I was only brave at special moments, and it was enough for me. She said something aside to Mademoiselle de Guise, who told her she must tell me. She then said that the desire of her life was to be present at a battle, and she would never be happy till she had been; she was jealous of the Prince de Condé for all he had done.

We must make allowance here for the eyes and ears of a prim Louis XIV. dame, which were easily scandalised by a little unconventionality; with regard to her swearing, the account of another lady says that she had never heard her swear, and was persuaded it was an invention of her enemies. Christina herself says it was a vice she had caught from her countrymen, but she had entirely cured herself of it. She seemed herself conscious that her dress "smacked of the masculine;" on many of the ladies in waiting advancing to kiss her, she patiently accepted their salutes, with the comment, "What makes all these ladies so anxious to kiss me; is it because I'm like a man?"

On September 8th she made her entry into Paris, in a very magnificent style, the city troops being drawn up to receive her, and welcomed by an enormous crowd. She rode a white horse, splendidly adorned; her dress was of scarlet, with a black hat and feathers; a thousand cavaliers escorted her. At the Porte Ste. Antoine she was met by the Governor of Paris, De l'Hôpital, who was to have addressed her in a set speech; the plaudits of the crowd, however, made this impossible, and he gracefully substituted the compliment, that there was no need for him to express welcome on behalf of the good citizens of Paris, whose own voices and demonstrations were a more original testimony of their joy and good-will. She proceeded first to the Cathedral of Notre Dame, where she heard a *Te Deum*, and then drove in a carriage to the apartments prepared for her in the Louvre. There she found De l'Hôpital waiting for her with a numerous company of ladies; the same evening the Rector of the University of Paris conveyed her the compliments of his college; next morning the clergy paid her their respects. She was visited by many people of note, amongst others, Queen Henrietta of England; and Patru pronounced upon her in the Academy a eulogistic harangue. A day or two later she left Paris for Compiègne.

"We saw the Queen of Sweden arrive at Compiègne; she was perfectly well acquainted with the whole Court, and completely *au fait* with all matters great and small. She said on one occasion, that she was well aware that people had spoken much good and evil of her, and would find out when they saw her that there was neither one nor the other in her. She did not speak the truth herein: for in point of fact she is a mixture of great virtues and great defects.

"At this first meeting she seemed attractive to all good people. Her clothes, which sound so extravagant when described, were not excessively so to look at, or at any rate one soon gets accus-

T

tomed to them.   Her face seems good-looking
enough, and all admired the vivacity of her wit,
and her intimate acquaintance with France and
French matters.   She was familiar not only with
the families and their arms, but the various
intrigues and affairs of gallantry, and the names
of all who loved painting or music.   She told the
Marquis of Sourdis all the valuable pictures in
his own gallery, and knew that the Duc de
Liancourt had some very fine ones; she went so
far as to instruct the French as to what they
possessed in their own country ; she maintained,
against certain opponents, that there was in the
Ste. Chapelle a very valuable agate, which she
wanted to see ; and it was in fact discovered at
St. Denis.   She seemed courteous, particularly
to men, but brusque and violent, giving no
grounds for putting faith in the evil stories
circulated about her.

" Our Swedish Amazon gained all hearts at
Paris, which she might soon have lost, if she had
stayed a little longer.   After having seen all
which she thought worthy of her curiosity, she
quitted the town, where she had always been
hemmed round by an eager crowd, to go and see
their majesties at Compiègne.   She was received
not only as a Queen, but as a Queen in high
favour with the Minister.   Cardinal Mazarin left
Compiègne the same day to be at Chantilly when

she arrived for dinner. Two hours after, arrived the King and his brother; they came in as private gentlemen among the crowd; as soon as he saw them, Mazarin presented them to her, saying they were two of the best born young men in France. She recognized them by their portraits in the Louvre, and said, 'I believe you, they seem born to wear crowns.' The Cardinal answered that it was difficult to deceive her, and it was true; they were the King and Monsieur. The King apologized for her bad reception; although he was shy at that time, and had every reason to be more so to Christina, her manner soon succeeded in placing him at his ease.

"The next day the King, his mother, and their suite came out three leagues from Compiègne to meet Christina and escort her back. Only the Cardinal and the Duke of Guise were with her, for the only women in her suite were 'very miserable looking creatures' and did not appear. As soon as she saw Anne of Austria, she got out of her carriage, and they saluted one another cordially. The young King gave Christina his hand to lead her into the house, and she took precedence of the Queen of France; this had not apparently been Louis' intention; in after years, when he had grown punctilious in such small matters, he used to upbraid his mother with having forgotten her dignity.

T 2

"Anne of Austria used to say that she was never so much surprised as when she saw the Queen of Sweden ; and that however much she had been told that she was not like other people, she could not have imagined her to be as she actually was. 'I was among those nearest to her,' says Madame de Motteville, 'and she surprised me very much. The hair of her wig had not been curled that day, and the wind, as she got down from her carriage, lifted it ; her carelessness as to her complexion has made it lose its whiteness, and she seemed to me, at the first glance, a sort of dusky gipsy, who chanced to be rather less brown than she ought to have been. While I looked at her, she struck me as terrible rather than pleasing. . . . When I began to grow accustomed to her dress, manner of dressing her hair, and face, I found she had fine lively eyes with a mixture of haughtiness and sweetness in her look. I soon observed with astonishment that she attracted me, and at every moment I found myself completely changing towards her.' "

The Duke of Guise pointed out Mademoiselle de Mancini to her ; Christina leaned over to pay her a compliment. At this time Louis was desperately in love with this young woman, and Christina, in jest or earnest, took his part. She told them they must marry, and she would be their confidante. "If I were you," she said to

Louis, " I would marry whom I chose." This is said to have been one reason why Mazarin and the Queen of France were not anxious for her to prolong her stay.

" The Queen-Mother told us that Christina, under pretence of wishing to see the portrait of the King and his brother, which the Queen carried on her arm, had made her take off her glove, and paid her extravagant compliments on the beauty of her arm. As soon as she had taken a little rest in her room, she came to us, and was taken to the Italian Comedy. She thought it very bad, and said so frankly. She was assured that they usually acted much better. I don't doubt it, she replied coldly, as otherwise you would scarcely keep them. . . . On returning to her rooms, she had to be provided with valets, for she was quite alone, without either ladies-in-waiting, officers, equipage, or money ; she alone composed her whole Court. Chanut, who used to be her Resident, when on the throne, was with her, and two or three ill-looking men, whom she had honoured with the title of Count ; one might truly say she had none, for, besides these moderate gentlemen, we saw only two women, who looked more like old clothes dealers than ladies of any condition.

" The first day she spoke but little, which seemed to show her discretion. The Count de

Nogent, according to his custom, eagerly relating some old stories, she told him gravely, she congratulated him on his capacious memory. Some of our rude jesters had designed to make her ridiculous, and thereby annihilate those who had so lightly offered her incense; but they could not manage it: whether owing to her merit, or the haughty way she treated them, or the support given her by her favourable reception. On September 18th she went to a tragedy enacted by Jesuits, and laughed at it unmercifully. Next day Father Arnaut, the King's confessor, went to see her, on some complaints she had about their Order . . . after the excuses of the Reverend Father, she told him, in the brusque, mocking manner natural to her, that she would be sorry to have them for enemies, knowing their strength, and equally sorry to have them either as confessors or actors. She professes to despise all women, and chooses rather to converse with men. She says she does not like men because they are men, but because they are not women. She was compared by some wit to Fontainebleau, whose buildings were grand and beautiful, but wanted symmetry. When she went to communicate at Notre Dame, those who saw her were scandalized at her devotion, convert as she was, who ought to be in her first zeal; she spoke the whole time Mass was going on, with the Bishops, standing

up the while. The Abbé Camus, the King's
Almoner, asked her, whom she would like to
confess to; she replied, ' Choose some one for me.'
He chose the Bishop of Amiens.   When she went
in to confess to him, she looked him full in the
face, 'which is extraordinary enough.'   The
Bishop professed himself much more edified with
her sentiments, which were devout, than her
manner."

Christina left Compiègne on September 23rd.
At Senlis she paid a visit to Ninon de l'Enclos,
for whom she is said to have had great admiration.
" Thence," says Motteville, " she departed in the
hired carriages which the King gave her as well
as the money to pay for them; followed by her
miserable troop, without a suite, with grandeur,
without a bed, without silver plate, or any royal
mark."

This ludicrous climax makes it sufficiently
plain that a small-minded common-place woman
may look as hard as she likes, but will never
make anything out of a great one.   In addition
to the insufficiency of the point of view, that of
trim conventionality, looking for royal externals,
and finding only originality, there is a delicious
dash of feminine spite and jealousy, which is
explained by Christina's contempt of the sex,
and perhaps of Motteville, and the admiration of
the men.   The Duke of Guise draws a **very**

different portrait. "The Queen of Sweden is about as tall as Madame de Cominges, but her figure is fuller, and broader; her arm is handsome, her hand white and well made, but more like that of a man than a woman; one shoulder a little higher than the other, which defect she conceals by the turn of her dress, her walk, and her gestures, so that one might make a bet about it. Her face is large without being faulty: all her features cast in the same mould, and strongly marked; her nose aquiline, her mouth large, but not unpleasing; her teeth pretty well, her eyes very fine and full of fire: her complexion, notwithstanding somewhat marked with small-pox, bright and pretty; the face as a whole pretty good, aided by a bizarre method of dressing the hair; a man's wig, very broad and high over the forehead, and very thick at the sides; her dress is much like that of a man, she hardly ever wears gloves; boots like a man's, and she resembles one in the tone of her voice, and all her actions. She affects the Amazon; has as much ambition and pride as ever her father Gustavus could have. She is very civil and caressing, speaks eight languages, especially French, as if she had been born in France. She knows more than all the Academy and Sorbonne put together; is an admirable critic in painting, as in everything else; knows the Court intrigues

better than the courtiers; in short, an extraordinary person."

Another account describes her as always careful to avoid saying things that give offence, and
anxious not to appear *savante*, in spite of her learning.  Some one having mentioned Homer and
Virgil, she began to gibe at their heroes, Achilles,
for consoling himself for the loss of his mistress
by playing the flute, Æneas, for being as inseparable from his nurse at forty years of age as if he
were a baby.  " I have not heard her swear, and I
am certain that the reports that she does so are
merely inventions of her enemies, her mind is
too large to submit to the grimaces necessary to
play the feminine farce."

She returned to Italy by way of Turin, and
was entertained by the Duke of Savoy, on
November 17th.  But hearing that the plague
was at Rome, she decided to go to Venice; the
Senate however begged her not to, as owing to
the war with the Turks they could not receive
her as they wished.  She accordingly remained
principally at Pesaro, though she is said to have
gone to Venice *incognita*.

## CHAPTER VIII

In September, 1657, Christina paid a second visit to France. The French Court, to whom she was rather a white elephant, being too important a personage to be neglected, yet too expensive to be received with ceremony, were not very anxious to see her again so soon; Mazarin, it is said, was suspicious that she might have political designs; it was intimated to her that they were not prepared to receive her at Paris, and it would be as well if she remained at Lyons or Avignon; but as this hint was ineffectual, they assigned her apartments at Fontainebleau, where she arrived in October. About a fortnight afterwards, she did an act of justice, whose autocratic character has laid her open to darker insinuations than any other part of her career.

Of the numerous accounts, two only are entitled to credit, which are given here *ipsissimis verbis:* the first is that published by her own Court; the second, the relation of Father Le Bel, an eye-witness.

" Since the month of October, as nearly as may be fixed, the Queen of Sweden had conceived some suspicion of the Marquis Monaldeschi, her

Grand Equerry, and this was confirmed daily by various proofs she had of his treachery. Watching all his actions, and the letters written to him, she discovered that he was betraying her interests, and by a double perfidy was scheming to fix upon an innocent man, also an officer of the Queen's, the crime of which he alone was guilty. The Queen made pretence of believing that the treachery came from that other, and assured the Marquis she had no doubts of himself, in order the better to discover all. The Marquis thinking he had succeeded in his object, said one day to the Queen : 'Madam, Your Majesty is betrayed, and the betrayer is the absent one known to Your Majesty and me ; it can be no other. Your Majesty will soon find out who it is ; I beg her not to pardon him.' The Queen said, 'What does the man deserve who betrays me so ? ' The Marquis said : ' Your Majesty should put him to death at once, and I offer myself to be executioner or victim, for 'tis an act of justice.' 'Good,' replied the Queen, 'remember your words ; as for me, I promise you I will not pardon him.' Meanwhile she had sealed up the intercepted letters, which she placed in the hands of the Prior of the Maturins at Fontainebleau, in order to present them to the Marquis, when it should be time. He on his side, considering that several posts had passed without his receiving any letters,

began to feel some distrust, and endeavoured to
find at Lyons another surer correspondent;
showing further by different actions that he was
thinking of flight. Therefore the Queen, wishing
to forestall him, on the 10th November had him
summoned to the *Galerie des Cerfs* according to
custom. The Marquis was long in coming; he
did so at length trembling, pale, out of countenance, and quite another man, just as the Court
had remarked him for the last few days with
surprise. The Queen addressed to him at first
some indifferent observations. Meanwhile she
had ordered the Prior to come to the Gallery,
into which he entered by a door that was immediately closed, and the Captain of her Guards came
in by another. The Queen then changed her
talk, and having caused the Prior to give back
the letters, she showed them to the Marquis,
and reproached him with his enormous crime
and his horrible treachery; she caused also all
the papers he had on him to be taken from
his pockets, among which she found two coun-
terfeit letters, one addressed to the Queen, the
other to the Marquis himself, whereby she discovered a new treason against her, still blacker
than the preceding, of which he wished to
make use in order to confirm the bad impression he had attempted to give her against his
enemy ? "

[The remainder of this first account is a somewhat more
succinct version of that which follows : the innocent
person against whom the Marquis was plotting was
Sentinelli.   The Prior was Father le Bel, whose testimony is as below.]

" On November 6, at a quarter past nine in the
morning, the Queen being at Fontainebleau,
lodging in the *Conciergerie* of the Castle, sent for
Father le Bel, by a Groom of the Chambers, who
was ordered to bring the Prior of the Community.
He arrived accordingly alone, for fear of keeping
the Queen waiting, and waited some time in the
anteroom.   After a while he was introduced into
the room where the Queen was, alone ; she told
him, that for greater freedom of speech, he must
follow her, which he accordingly did, as far as the
*Galerie des Cerfs*.   There she asked him if she
had ever spoken to him.   He answered that her
Majesty had done him that honour.   She said,
' Your cloth assures me that I may speak to you
in confidence,' and she made him promise, under
the seal of the confessional, to keep the secret of
what she was going to tell him.   He answered
that in matters of this kind he was blind and
dumb.   She accordingly placed in his hands
a paper packet sealed in three places, without
address : bidding him give it back to her, in
presence of whomsoever she might choose ;
warning him to mark well the day, hour, and

place at which she gave him this packet; which he carried away with him.

"On Saturday, at one o'clock in the afternoon, the Queen sent again for him by a Groom of the Chambers. The Prior, thinking it would be for her packet, took it with him : and following the Groom by the door of the donjon, came to the *Galerie des Cerfs.* Scarcely had he come in, when the Groom shut the door so hard that it alarmed the Prior a little, and seeing the Queen in the middle of the *Galerie* speaking to one of her suite, he advanced towards her. Her Majesty, in a rather loud voice, asked him for the packet, in presence of the Marquis and three other persons, of whom two were about four paces from the Queen, and the third beside her. 'Father,' she said, 'give me the packet I entrusted to you, as I wish to read it.' The Prior gave it to her, and the Queen having considered it a little, opened it, and drew out some letters and papers, which she made the Marquis look at and read, asking him in a loud and angry voice if he recognised them. The Marquis, trembling, said they were nothing but copies made by herself. 'You have,' she said to him, 'no knowledge of these letters and papers then?' and after letting him think a little, she drew out the originals and showed them to him, exclaiming, 'O, the traitor.' As soon as he avowed his writing and hand, she

put several questions to him. The Marquis
excused himself as well as he could, casting the
blame on various persons. Finally he threw
himself at the Queen's feet, imploring her pardon,
and at the same instant the three persons
mentioned above drew their swords from the
scabbards, whither they did not return them
till they had executed the Marquis. But before
this consummation he got up, and drawing the
Queen now into one corner of the Gallery, now
into another, begged her unceasingly to listen to
his justification. This she did not refuse, but
listened to him with great patience and moderation, without showing by the slightest sign that
his importunity was displeasing to her. At
length she drew close to him, leaning on an
ebony stick with a round handle, and turning
towards the Prior, said to him, 'Father, see, be
witness that I hurry nothing, but that I give
this traitor more time than he could ask from an
injured person, to set himself right, were that
possible.' The Marquis, pressed by the Queen,
gave her certain papers, and two or three little
keys which he drew from his pocket. This
conference having lasted for more than an hour,
and the Marquis not satisfying the Queen, she
approached the Prior, and said to him, in a loud
but solemn and measured voice, ' Father, I leave
this man in your hands; prepare him for death,

and have care for his soul.' At these words the
Prior, as terrified as if the sentence was against
himself, threw himself at her feet, as well as the
Marquis, to ask his pardon. She said she could
not grant it, adding that the traitor was more
criminal than those who were broken on the
wheel : he knew well she had confided to him
the most important affairs, and her own most
private thoughts, as to a faithful subject, without
wishing to reproach him, in addition, with the
benefits she had loaded him with, beyond even
what she would have done for a brother, having
always considered him as such, and that his own
conscience must be his executioner.

"She then went away, leaving the Prior with
the three men with their swords bared, ready to
kill him. When she had left them, the Marquis
cast himself at the feet of the Prior, whom he
implored to go and beg for his pardon : but the
three men pressed him to confess himself, holding
their swords against his body, though without
wounding him. The Prior, with tears in his
eyes, exhorted him to ask pardon of God. The
chief of the three went to find the Queen, to
implore her mercy for the poor Marquis : but he
came back again very sad, and said, weeping,
' Marquis, think upon God and your soul, you
must die.' The Marquis, beside himself, threw
himself for the second time at the Prior's feet,

pressing him to go yet again and ask his pardon from the Queen. He did so, and finding the Queen in her room, her countenance calm and unmoved, he prostrated himself at her feet; his eyes bathed with tears, his voice choked with sobs, he adjured her, by the passion and wounds of the Saviour, to have mercy upon the Marquis. She told him how sorry she was not to be able to grant his request, and represented to him the blackness of the treachery and cruelty this wretch had wished to commit in her regard: that accordingly he had neither pardon nor mercy to expect; many were broken on the wheel for less crimes than that of this traitor.

"The Prior, seeing he could accomplish nothing by prayers, took the liberty of representing to her that she was in the palace of a king, and that she could not reflect too much on what she was about to do, and whether the king would approve it. She answered that she had the right to do justice, and took God to witness that she had no personal grudge against the Marquis: that she had put away all hatred against him: that she confined her wrath to the enormity of his crime and his treachery, which were without parallel, and affected all the world: further, the king was not lodging her as a prisoner, or an exile; she was mistress of her own will, and could do justice on her officers,

everywhere and always ; that she had to answer
for her action to God alone, adding, that the deed
was not without precedent. The Prior answered
that there was a distinction ; that if queens had
done something similar, it had been in their
kingdom and not elsewhere. But fearing to
irritate her, he went on : 'Madam, it is by the
honour and reputation that your Majesty has
acquired in this kingdom, and by the hope that
the nation has conceived in her negotiations, that
I beg you humbly to consider that this action,
entirely just though it be from your Majesty's
point of view, may be regarded from others as
violent and precipitate. Let your Majesty do
rather an act of generosity and mercy towards
this poor Marquis, or at any rate place him in
the hands of the king's justice, and cause his
trial to take place according to form. Your
Majesty will get complete satisfaction, and
preserve by this means the title of Admirable,
which all your actions have acquired.' 'How,
my father,' she replied. 'I, who ought to have
sovereign and absolute justice over all my
subjects, should I be reduced to beg it against a
domestic traitor, for the crime and the perfidy of
which I hold the proofs, written and signed with
his own hand ?' 'It is true,' said the Prior,
'but your Majesty is the interested party.' 'No,
no, father,' she said, 'I will let the king know of

it; return and have a care of his soul, I cannot in conscience do what you ask;' and so sent him away. The Prior remarked by the change of tone with which she pronounced the last words, that if she could have gone back and changed the state of affairs she undoubtedly would have done so; but having gone too far, she could no longer draw back without placing herself in peril of her life, had the Marquis escaped.

"In this extremity the Prior knew not what to do; he could not go away, and even though he could, the duty of charity and his own conscience compelled him to prepare the Marquis for an edifying death. Accordingly he went back to the Gallery, and embracing the poor wretch, whom he bathed with his tears, he exhorted him in the most energetic and pathetic terms with which God inspired him to compose himself for death, and bethink himself of his conscience, since there was no further hope of life for him, and that offering and suffering his death through justice, he ought to cast upon God alone his hopes for eternity, where he would find consolation. At this sorrowful news, after two or three loud shrieks, he knelt at the feet of the Confessor, who had seated himself upon one of the benches in the Gallery, and began his confession; but after getting well through it, he

got up twice, crying out at the same time; the
Confessor caused him to make his acts of faith;
renouncing all adverse thoughts he finished his
confession in Latin, French, and Italian, as he
could best express himself, in his agony. The
Almoner of the Queen arrived just as the Confessor was asking him a question to clear up a
doubt. The Marquis perceiving him, without
waiting for absolution, went to him, hoping for
pardon by his influence; they spoke together for
a long time in a low voice, holding each other's
hands, in a corner; their conversation ended, the
Almoner went out, and took with him the chief
of the three commissioned to execute him.
Shortly afterwards, the chief returned alone, the
Almoner remaining away, and said to him, 'Marquis, ask pardon of God, for without any further
delay you must die; have you confessed?' And
so saying, he forced him against the wall at the
end of the Gallery, where the picture *St. Germain*
is. The Confessor could not turn away so well
as not to see that he gave him a stab in the
stomach, towards the right. The Marquis,
wishing to guard it, seized the sword in his
right hand; the other, in drawing it back, cut
off three fingers of his hand, and finding
his sword blunted, he said to a companion that
the Marquis was armed underneath, and in fact
he had a coat of mail weighing nine or ten

pounds on. He then gave him another stroke in the face, at which the Marquis cried out 'Father;' the Confessor drew near him, and the others stood aside. Kneeling on one knee he asked pardon of God, and added a few words, when the Prior gave him absolution, with the penance of suffering death patiently for his sins, pardoning all who were causing his death; this received, he threw himself on the floor, and as he fell one of them gave him a blow on the top of the head, carrying away some bone; as he lay on his stomach he made signs for them to cut his head off. [They finally kill him after several unsuccessful attempts.] Thus the Marquis ended his life at a quarter to four in the afternoon. . . . The Queen, assured of the Marquis' death, expressed her regret at having been obliged to order this execution of the Marquis, but that it concerned justice to punish him for his crime and treachery, which she prayed God to forgive him. She bade the Confessor to be careful and take him away and bury him; she sent 200 livres to the convent, to pray God for the repose of the said Marquis' soul."

From these accounts it is easy to see that at any rate the Marquis thoroughly deserved his death; the dastardly traitor was judged out of his own mouth. But it is not so easy to settle how far Christina was justified in taking this

method of punishing him. Precedents might
indeed be quoted, but it is not a case to be
settled by precedents, or to form one, and requires to be carefully viewed in its own special
circumstances. We must, first of all, pay no
attention to the abuse of her enemies, or the
sentimentality of women, such as Mademoiselle
de Montpensier and Madame de Motteville, who
branded her with brutality, cruelty, and similar
qualities; such charges are merely foolish when
brought against Christina, who was humanity
and compassion itself, as many instances to be
related will show; in the present case, her attitude was entirely free from anything of the kind,
and marked by a purely judicial tone befitting
the occasion.

The whole point turns on the legal aspect of the
case; how far had she a right to exercise the power
she claimed of life and death over the culprit?

In this respect it is to be observed: 1. That
by a special clause in the Act of Abdication,
Christina retained the absolute and sovereign
jurisdiction over her servants of all kinds, just
as though she still sat on the throne; that she
appointed and removed at her pleasure her own
governors, intendants, judges and officers, in her
domains; that she received accredited ministers
and ambassadors from foreign Courts; and that
these also recognised hers; and that in general

she was after her abdication everywhere treated as a Sovereign. 2. That, therefore, leaving to the lawyers the question whether or no this absolute right *could* be retained after her abdication, and starting merely from the premise that it *was*, it is an undoubted fact that Christina considered herself to possess this right, and is so far morally justified, and that she was considered also to possess it by other powers; the French Court raised no objection on this head, confining themselves merely to complaining that she ought not to have permitted it to take place at Fontainebleau.

We must accordingly decide in favour of Christina, with Leibniz, who adds, "That all that we can reproach the Queen of Sweden with is, that she had not sufficient respect to the place where she caused the execution to be performed; yet that even here she might be excused, by the necessity she was in of speedy despatch.  Christina found Monaldeschi deserving of death; it is not hard to judge that his crime was of a nature to prevent it from being submitted to a third person; and it would have been ridiculous to demand that the Queen should leave such a matter to some third person, which must necessarily have derogated from her dignity.  If the Court of France took it ill, it was because it no longer had the same regard for her, and because the execution took place in the king's palace."

Christina had, in fact, exactly the same right as any court of law has—a right provided for by statute, and, in addition, the moral right that lies behind the legal one, a stern regard for the interests of justice. Yet the only appropriate summing up of so unique a case must be, in the words of Tacitus, applied to it in her own day by a celebrated author : "*habet aliquid ex iniquo omne magnum exemplum.*"

Although the French Court took no exception to Monaldeschi's execution on the legal score, yet it added to their disinclination to see Christina at Paris. She remained some time at Fontainebleau, during which she sent an ambassador to London, to compliment Oliver Cromwell and sound the territory for a visit to England. It was said with very little probability that Mazarin wished to make use of her diplomatic skill to engage the Protector in his interests, and get him to repudiate his wife and marry one of his nieces. But Cromwell, for obvious reasons, had no wish to see Christina in England, and contented himself with returning her compliments.

At length, on February 24, 1658, she went to Paris, and found herself *de trop*. The apartments of Mazarin in the Louvre were assigned to her,

as a hint, says Madame de Motteville, that she
was not to stay long; according to Guy Patin,
she was not a little displeased at hearing that
the Queen of France had said, that if Christina
did not go, she would.   The same authority adds
that she got 200,000 livres from Mazarin, a
miracle which is explained by him in another
place as being a loan on some of her jewels; but
it is to be remembered that these writers love
scandal more than truth.   It was during this
stay at Paris that she went to the French
Academy, of which visit the following well-
known story is told.   Wishing to show her a
specimen of the dictionary then in preparation,
the secretary opened at a page containing the
word *Jeu*, in which connection occurred the
phrase: "*Jeux de Prince, qui ne plaisent qu'à
ceux qui les font.*"   Christina coloured, conceiving
at first some insult might be intended; but
speedily recovered herself, and turned the matter
off with a smile.

Perceiving, however, that her stay in Paris
was not agreeable, Christina shortly afterwards
left for Toulon, and arrived in Rome on May 4.
Here she inhabited Mazarin's palace, which,
taken in conjunction with her recent visit, awoke
the greatest jealousy and suspicion in the Spaniards; they spread plentiful reports of her intended machinations in behalf of France and

England. Thus, by dint of favouring neither party, Christina was regarded by each as in the interests of the other. To all this she paid, as usual, no attention, and applied herself to forming her establishment, a matter of no small difficulty. She was at all times too regardless of accounts, but her straits were extreme at the present moment by reason of events in the North. The wars of Charles X. with Denmark and Poland not only demanded all the money he could get, but made it impossible for Pomerania, continually occupied by troops, to pay Christina her fixed stipend ; her revenues were at once curtailed and in arrear. She was obliged to pawn her plate and jewels. Finding that letters to her agent, Senator Bååt, produced no effect, she sent her secretary, Davison, to remonstrate with Charles. He was by no means unwilling to do what he could for her, but insisted on political grounds, before he saw Davison, that he should declare himself to be no Roman Catholic, since the rumour was going about in Sweden that Christina had designs of converting the Swedes. Davison, who was, in fact, one of those of her servants whom she had persuaded to change his faith, wrote to consult her as to what he should do. She replied :—

" I believe you so little suited to be a martyr that I will not advise you to expose yourself to the danger of doing anything mean to save your life. Honour and life are two things which are worthy, as it seems to me, of attention. If you were to deny or disguise your religion, you would save neither, were you to present yourself to me. One must live and die a Catholic; if you fail in this, you will be unworthy to be servant of mine. Let not the threats of the King of Sweden astonish you: do not consider them, but come back to me . . . Don't dare to return unless you can give evidence of never having swerved in your faith."

Davison returned accordingly, and Christina remained without money. She is *said* to have frequently complained of the folly of Charles in engaging in a war disastrous for Sweden, and to have asserted that if the Emperor and the Elector would give her an army, she would lead it against Charles herself, and take Pomerania and Bremen from him, on condition that she should enjoy their revenues during her life : to revert to the Emperor on her death. And she sent Sentinelli to Vienna to ask for an army of twenty thousand men under General Montecuculi for that purpose. The Court of Vienna is said to have lent an ear to this strange proposal; though it came to nothing, as Christina changed her mind.

In the pecuniary difficulties which now harassed

her, she was assisted by the Pope, who gave her
an income of 12,000 scudi a year, and assigned
Cardinal Azzolini to her as intendant of her
domestic economy.   His skill succeeded in introducing a better state of her finances, and his
qualities were such as to extract her admiration ;
all through her life she preserved an extraordinary
esteem for him.   He was a fine-looking man, of
very great culture and universal abilities, one
of the chiefs of the " flying squadron," and had
taken a prominent part in the election of the
Pope.   Christina writes of him to a friend as
" the only man she knows equally above flattery
or envy.   He has," she says in another place,
" the mind and cleverness of a demon, the virtue
of an angel, and the great and noble heart of an
Alexander ": " the Cardinal is a divine and incomparable man."   Much as she admired Condé,
Cromwell, and one or two others, she seems to
have placed Azzolini above them all.

   Freed by his assistance from immediate difficulty, she devoted herself to study and literature.
Her house was the resort of the most cultivated
men in Rome.   She augmented her collections of
medals, statues and paintings, and took great
interest in chemistry and astronomy.   Her enemies
have accused her of leanings to alchemy and
astrology ; even were this true, her age might be
her excuse.   Wallenstein believed in the stars,

if in nothing else, and even Richelieu in his difficulties lent an ear to the promises of one who was to make him gold. But we shall see reason in the sequel to doubt the truth of these accusations.

Her intellectual pursuits were varied by quarrels with the Pope. In these squabbles it has always been assumed that Christina was in the wrong, but the facts point otherwise. Pope Alexander VII. was a man of Liliputian mind. Cardinal de Retz, a judge of character, calls him " a man of *minutiæ:* a sign not only of a little mind, but of a mean soul. Speaking one day of one of his youthful studies, he told me that he had written for two years with the same pen. This is but a *bagatelle,* but as I have often observed, little things often tell more than big ones." Furthermore, the Spanish faction was continually attributing to Christina designs of which she was entirely innocent, and this not unnaturally irritated her. Hence the attempt to thwart her in trivial matters. She wished to marry Sentinelli to the Duchess of Ceri. The Pope endeavoured to dissuade her; but failing in this, he sent the Duchess into a cloister, and banished Sentinelli from Rome. This annoyance was soon succeeded by others. Rumours were spread about that Christina wished to raise forces for France against Naples : the Pope accordingly published an edict, that no one should raise forces of any kind on pain of death, and placed guards round her palace. Excessively disgusted, Christina exchanged all her Italian servants for foreign ones, and, perceiving the origin of all these pitiful suspicions, withdrew from Mazarin's palace, and took up her abode at a convent; whence the Parisian gossips bruited about that she was intending to take the veil. Here the Pope caused her to be spied on by the monks and ecclesiastics. This *espionnage*, the crowning proof of his womanish pusillanimity, at once outraged Christina and convinced her that she did not well to be angry; she kept her temper, and appeared in public with a serene and cheerful countenance, endeavouring to appease the jealous Spaniards by causing some of her attendants to adopt a Spanish fashion of wearing their accoutrements, and taking revenge on the Pope by the means best suited to his nature, satirical contempt. The papal arms were six hills; Christina appended the appropriate motto : *Parturiunt montes, nascetur ridiculus mus.*

In this state of things, two pieces of news arrived from Sweden which drew her thoughts away to that country. The first was that a certain woman, of the name of Anne Gyldener, had given herself out to be Christina, and deceived a few people at Norköping, though the fraud was speedily discovered, and the impostor punished and banished from Sweden. The second, of more importance, was the death of Charles X., on February 13, 1660. During his five years' reign he had found time to give proof of his daring military audacity, as well as of an entire want of policy; the glory of his victories over Poland, Brandenburg, and Denmark was soon effaced by his subsequent failure in his last attempt on the latter country, arising from his inability to let well alone. The Swedes found themselves left at his death with little but the hatred of Europe and the exhaustion of their finances. But if among the people there were found some who regretted the peace policy of Christina, such was by no means the opinion of the noble oligarchy. Now at last they felt they had their chance.

Duke Adolphus, who, with, among others, Magnus de la Gardie, had been appointed one of the Regents by his brother, the late King, informed Christina of his death. She replied in a letter, recommending to his care the good education of the young King, and intimating her intention of coming to Sweden to settle the difficulties in her own affairs. She left home on July 20th, and arrived in Hamburg on August 18th. There, hearing that her visit to Sweden was not pleasing to the ruling faction in that country, she wrote letters to her agent Bååt, and

Brahé, one of the Regents, assuring them of her intentions, and hoping that the Swedes would support her claims. She then passed through Denmark, and was received in great state by the King, who sent her on to Helsingborg in one of his own vessels. In answer to a letter from Brahé, warning her not to come to Sweden, she wrote again, saying she could not comply with his request, and congratulating him on being a liberator of his country. This was an allusion to his share in getting Duke Adolphus excluded from the Regency; the violent and altogether abominable character of the Duke made this a real necessity for Sweden, though the struggle to get him put aside nearly caused a civil war.

Meanwhile her approach filled the Regents with apprehension. Her French enemies, fearing she might interfere with their designs, secretly accused her to the Swedes of coming to try and introduce the Catholic religion. But in fact she had no such design; nor was there any need of adding to the hostility against her: although she was still very popular with the people, the nobles and the clergy were her bitter enemies. Chief among these were Brahé, who went so far as to propose to shut her up in prison at Åland, and her old *protégé* Magnus de la Gardie. It was decided to send Baron Linde, to meet her and prevent her from coming to Stockholm; but he did not succeed ; Christina arrived on October 1st, and was received with great attention by the young king and his mother ; she was lodged in rooms in the castle which had once been her own.

With regard now to those reports that were spread about, that she was aiming at regaining possession of the crown, at being appointed guardian of the young king, and so on, the following extract from a letter of Algernon Sydney to the Earl of Leicester, dated September 8th, 1660, proves that they sprang entirely from the fears and suspicions of her enemies :—

" I left the Queen Christina at Hamburg, with a design of going into Sweden, before the time of the Diet, which is to begin the 22nd of this month at Stockholm. She is thought to have great designs, of which every one judges according to their humour ; some think she will pretend to the Crown, others, that she would be content with the Regency, and there doth not want those that say she is employed from Rome to sow divisions in Sweden, and to make use of the Prince Adolph his discontent ; others, to marry him. I have conversed a good deal with her and do not believe a word of all this. She hath a great aversion to the Prince Adolph, thinks him not to be trusted with anything, nor capable of any great business ; when she resigned the Crown she did publicly advise the Senate not to admit

x

that Prince unto the Crown in case his brother should die without sons, he being unfit for government, of an evil nature, and of understanding nowise able to bear such a weight: upon which by an act of the Senate, confirmed by the succeeding Diet, it was declared that the Crown should descend only to the heirs male of the King's body, and these failing the power of election should revert unto the Senate and Diet. This is the obstruction unto Prince Adolph his pretention to be Constable, lest, that he having the power of the Militia in his hands might either attempt something to the prejudice of the young King, or if he died strengthen his own pretensions. Notwithstanding this he did write to the Queen Christina, earnestly endeavouring to engage her, and offering great services if she would favour him. The contents of this letter were reported to me, and I saw the answer, which if he is not absolutely out of his wits will take from him all hope of advantage from her. A day or two before I came from Hamburg, talking with her of the opinions people had of her pretensions to the Crown, or Regency, she told me plainly there was but one place for her in Sweden, and having resigned that, she could neither pretend again unto it, nor content herself with any other. I do not believe this merely because she said it (for I am in this year's employment grown much less

credulous than I was), but because the impossibility of effecting anything is so plain that she,
who has a great deal of wit, and as good counsel
as any is perhaps in Europe, cannot but see it.
For besides the aversion that is to her religion,
and the little appearance that the jealous Swedes
would give credit to her change, if she left it, the
Senate and nobility like no government so well
as while the kings are in minority ; for now they
have the power in their own hands, whereas before
they depended on the will of a king, and will
more hardly be brought to innovate anything
perhaps than when their last King was living.
This and many other reasons do convince me
that her only business is to procure of the Diet
the settlement of her yearly revenue of two
hundred thousand dollars, reserved out of her
resignation, of which for the last five years she
received but the tenth part, and this being done
to return to Rome where she hath great designs,
of which I may speak more hereafter, and there she
intends to live and die. The French ambassador
hath order to serve her as much as he can, and
she hath been persuaded to stay at Hamburg
until he could have an answer to the letters he
sent to Stockholm, concerning her reception,
which caution is very necessary, for though all
the principal persons of the Senate owe their
fortunes to her, no man can undertake that if

she should go there without an engagement for her security, she may not pass the rest of her life in some castle in Sweden, instead of her palace at Rome."

The last hint was, as we have seen, not unfounded, for there was some talk among the Regents to that effect; yet want of courage was not Christina's failing, and she went to Stockholm unconcerned by the warnings her friends gave her.

The Diet was held on October 19th, and she sent a memorial to the Senate, asking for the confirmation of the act relative to her abdication in the past reign, and claiming her revenues. The other Orders found her demands reasonable, but not so did the clergy. Their rancour towards Christina was redoubled on seeing that she had Mass celebrated every day at a room in the Castle fitted up as a chapel. They demanded time to consider, and employed the interval in fulminating against her from the pulpit, and endeavouring to rouse the popular religious prejudices against her. Their answer to the memorial was to the effect: That by reason of her change of faith, she had forfeited her rights; which nevertheless they were willing to continue, not in virtue of the former act, but purely as a recognition of the merits of her ancestors; yet they could not permit her to exercise papistical idolatries in sight of the apartments of the young King. To this sentiment the other Estates gave their sanction. A deputation waited upon Christina and forbade her to perform the Catholic services. Her entreaties and expostulations were of no avail; after a stormy interview, Archbishop Lenæus said, on going away, "We know well what the Pope is aiming at, and how he wants to get our souls." "I know him better than you do," retorted Christina; "he would not give four dollars for all your souls put together."

On December 23rd, her chapel was pulled down, and her priests and Italian attendants banished from the country. In spite of this, she continued to attend the Catholic service at the house of M. de Terlon, the French Minister, who had accompanied her to Sweden, and she sent to certify this to the Pope, to parade the fact that her faith was her first consideration. She now withdrew to Norköping, thinking that she might be less molested there while her affairs were being settled. Having at length received this confirmation of her revenues, she sent to the Estates a declaration, that in the event of anything happening to the young King, the right to the Crown would revert to her, nor could they settle the succession without her. But they would not hear of it; the Senate returned her declaration within an hour, and she had to sign another act of abdication renouncing *in toto* all claims to the throne of Sweden. She did so willingly; nor is there anything to show that her declaration was anything more than a protest against what she feared might come to pass, in the event of the death of the delicate young King. Luckily her forebodings were not realized. The action of the clergy left her no doubt of their real fears. They pursued her at Norköping, and prevailed on the Senate to forbid her to perform Mass in her own house. This, as they foresaw, was to banish her from Sweden. The final outrage on her feelings was her discovery that Terserus, Bishop of Åbo, had boasted in letters written to Germany of having seen her weeping and sobbing over her change of religion, and heard her bitterly repent of having done so: Terserus, whom she had protected when accused of taking part in the Messenius conspiracy! She wrote an indignant letter to the King, asking that the Bishop might be punished for his scandalous allegations, and reproaching him for his ingratitude; for this charge touched her 'more nearly than anything else. The Regents promised to look into the matter, but Terserus excused himself, and nothing was done. As to the interdiction placed upon her from exercising her religion, Christina wrote a biting letter to Bååt, praying him to send her her money, and let her go. This seems to have produced the desired effect, and her enemies perhaps felt a little ashamed of themselves. Thereupon she returned to Hamburg on May 16.

She remained here more than a year, occupied principally in the settlement of the never-ending difficulties in her money affairs. From a minute by Texeira, her business man, we learn that instead of the 200,000 crowns due to her, she received but little more than half. The pensions, however, which she bestowed on various persons, such as Matthiæ, her old nurse, Anna von Linde, and others, were always punctually paid. She amused herself by making occasional visits to neighbouring states, and by chemical investigations, with the assistance of one Borri, an alchemist, who combined the usual trades of gold maker and beggar. That she did not, as her enemies asserted, become a convert also to alchemy is proved not only by her known views on that study, but also by the fact that Borri, who left her suddenly and met with better success with Frederick III. of Denmark, disliked and abused her; he subsequently fell into the hands of a Papal Nuncio and died in the Castle of St. Angelo. She befriended the unfortunate scholar Lambecius, who by her aid and recommendation went to Rome, became a Catholic, and librarian to the Emperor.

If the charges of Terserus needed refutation,

they would find it in the attempt she made to
secure free exercise of their religion to the
Catholics in Denmark and Holland, writing letters
for that purpose to all the continental courts,
though her efforts were unsuccessful. She failed
also in her attempts to rouse the European Powers
to assist Venice against the Turks, sending Count
Galeazzo Gualdo, her envoy, round with circular
letters. But the accuracy of her political foresight was proved by the events of a few years
later, when John Sobieski saved Europe from the
danger she feared.

In April, 1662, she left Hamburg, and arrived
in Rome on June 10. Two months later some
disputes in Rome, which threatened to produce
serious disagreement between France and the
Pope, afforded her an opportunity of playing her
favourite part of peacemaker.

The Duc de Créqui, the French ambassador at
Rome, partly owing to his own self-importance,
partly perhaps to differences with the Papal
Court, originated the quarrel. He and his suite
fought openly in the streets with the Pope's
Corsican police and body-guard. The latter
being severely handled in a street fray, retorted
by besieging the Duke's palace, the Farnese, and
firing on his wife and attendants at the moment
they were returning home. The insult was keenly
resented by Louis XIV.; he withdrew his

ambassador from Rome, expelled the Papal
Nuncio from France, and sent a threatening
manifesto to the Pope; at the same time he
seized on Avignon, and threatened to march into
Italy. The Pope, who had not considered the
matter in so serious a light, was obliged to send
his nephew, Cardinal Chigi, and Cardinal Im-
periali to Paris to apologise, besides getting rid
of his Corsican guard, and erecting a monument
to commemorate the fact. Christina attempted
by repeated letters to Louis and his Minister,
M. de. Lionne, to mollify his anger and mediate
between him and the Pope; her trouble was however thrown away, though the latter showed his
appreciation of her attempts by paying her a
complimentary visit soon afterwards.

The perpetual confusion in her revenues caused
her to think about revisiting Sweden, with the
view of trying whether her presence could effect
what was apparently impossible by letter, and
getting her money paid with at least a show of
regularity. She informed her Swedish agents of
her intention; this at once renewed the jealous
suspicion of the Lutherans, that she was the
agent of a scheme to introduce Papistry into
the country. Such a thing never entered her
head. When proposals were entertained at Paris
and Rome for sending Jesuits for that purpose
into Sweden, "It would only be to send them to

their deaths," said Christina, "for as to converting the regular Swedish Lutherans, it is an
absolute impossibility." But it was with her
designs as with the whereabouts of the Caliph
Vathek—"nothing being known of them, a
thousand ridiculous stories got about." She
left Rome in 1666, and arrived in Hamburg
towards the end of the year. Here she remained
some time, corresponding with Båät, and pro-
posing various means of improving her supply—
such as letting some of her domains on lease, of
which the Swedish Government did not approve.
On April 29, she left for Sweden, *via* Denmark,
and was again transported by the Danish King
to Helsingborg, where Pontus de la Gardie was
awaiting her. But they had not gone further
than Jonköping when they were met by a courier,
forbidding her to bring a Catholic priest with
her, otherwise he would be dealt with according
to law—a measure adopted in consequence of a
meeting held by the Queen-dowager and the
Regents, to provide for the safety of religion
and the State against Christina's supposed
designs. Christina at once declared that after
such an insult she would not only not dismiss
her priest, but herself leave the country. In
answer to the entreaties of de la Gardie, she
consented to wait at Norköping till a courier
could be sent to the Senate and return. The

Senate, however, had foreseen the effect this would have upon her, which was exactly what they wanted; they sent back the messenger reiterating their first injunction, with the addition that if she proceeded she would not be allowed to hear Mass at all, either at the house of the French, or any other ambassador. Upon this, Christina no longer delayed her departure, dismissing the escort that had been sent by the King to escort her. At the towns through which she passed the people thronged around, expressing their sympathy, and declaring that during her reign the land had been crowned with all kinds of blessings, but had since been worn out with all sorts of misfortunes. She only took four days in going from Norköping to Helsingborg, a distance of three hundred miles; young Pontus de la Gardie was unable to perform such rapid marches as herself, being laid up with fatigue on his arrival. She arrived again at Hamburg in June, 1667.

The Regents had gained their end for the moment; but their harsh usage worked in her favour; the country was generally ashamed of the scant ceremony shown to her by the ruling oligarchy, and as we shall see, even the clergy relaxed their zeal a little when they found their suspicions of her designs were without foundation.

While she waited at Hamburg, uncertain

what course to adopt, Pope Alexander VII. died,
—an event that had been for some time expected;
Christina wrote in September, 1666, "that she
did not believe the Pope would remain so well
as his relations, nor so ill as the rest of the world
hoped." She expresses in another letter her
doubts as to the intentions of the "squadron,"
and the chances of the election of various cardinals. In fact, she felt considerable anxiety as
to who would replace him; she feared it might
be Farnese, with whom she did not stand well.
It was accordingly with no small delight that
she received news of the election of Rospigliosi,
Clement IX., her most particular friend. She
did not confine her joy to letters of congratu-
lation. On July 15, she celebrated Mass in
honour of his accession in the Great Hall of her
palace, which had been decorated with special
illuminations, representing, among other things,
the arms of the new Pope: the Eucharist adored
by angels in the clouds; and the Church trampl-
ing on heresy, with VIVAT CLEMENS IX., PONT.
MAX. To the crowd which assembled to assist
she caused a fountain to flow with wine from
nine different spouts at once, wherewith "all the
world got drunk for six hours, and the noble
ladies at the windows looked out upon the scene."
The copious streams having at last ceased, the
illuminations were all set alight; and the im-

pious spectacle added rage to the drunken ex-
citement of the mob.   Just as the Queen was
thinking of going to bed a quantity of large
stones broke her windows; learning what was
the matter, she gave orders to extinguish the
illuminations and shut the gates of the palace ;
she also armed her domestics, but in spite of the
attacks of the populace, and their menacing shouts
of " kill! kill! " assisted by the discharge of fire-
arms, she would not allow any return of the
shots, till on repeated attempts to force the
gate, real danger seemed to be imminent ; a
volley was then fired on the crowd, which killed
a good many and wounded others.   Christina
escaped by a back-door to another house, and the
arrival of the commandant and the military put
an end to the disturbance.   Next morning, she
went at nine o'clock, in spite of remonstrances,
at which she laughed, to look at her palace :
although she found several thousand people assembled before it, and was attended by only two
or three persons, no violence was offered her.

We might suspect that the liberal supply of
wine had most to do with the violence of the
crowd ; but we are told that the whole town knew
of her design a week before, and various friends
endeavoured to dissuade her from it.   " The
preachers did all they could to arouse the populace against it ; but the Queen, who was informed

of all this, laughed at them, and let them preach,
paying them no attention, which enraged them ; "
they are probably to blame for the attack, as
the mob was found possessed of the necessary
weapons ; and " some of them were on the spot,
haranguing, at the time." Christina distributed
money for the benefit of those who were wounded
in the affray ; but nothing further came of it,
though she remained at Hamburg for more than
a year after to settle her money matters before
returning to Rome.

At the Diet of 1668, all orders in the State
were favourable to her demands, which she sent
by her agent, Rosenhane. They decreed that
the original terms of her act of abdication should
be observed; that her arrears should be paid;
and that she and her suite should be allowed the
free exercise of their religion when she visited
Sweden. This, however, she did not do again :
partly because it was now no longer necessary ;
partly because of the dissuasions of her friends,
who feared lest violence might be employed
against her ; partly again, because her attention
was turned in other directions. The course of
events sufficiently proves what she wrote to her
friend Azzolini, " that the people loved her ; only
the ruling faction hated and feared her, of which
time would give him the proof."

A letter she wrote to Bourdelot at this period

shows, among other things, how correctly she estimated Louis XIV.

"You gratify me by not sending me all the rubbish that has been made upon the Flanders' campaign. I can imagine the sort of thing; I pity those poor Cyruses, Alexanders, and Cæsars so much that I can scarcely think them worth more than to be mere musketeers. I love great actions as much as any one, but I don't like panegyrics; and my taste for satires is so great that I am fond of reading even those against myself (the number is large enough, thank God!) to amuse myself at my own expense, after having done so often at the expense of others. I say, at my own expense, because all I have seen as yet are so silly and impertinent that it would have been impossible to read them if they had not spoken ill of me. . . . As to the transfusion of blood, I think it's a fine invention; but I shouldn't like to try it on myself, for fear of turning into a sheep: if I must be metamorphosised, I should much prefer to become a lioness, so as to avoid being eaten. I'm well enough, and laugh at all doctors and medicines; but to enjoy perfect health my sovran receipt is to go to Rome. At any rate in case of need, to show you that I understand more than you animals about the transfusion of blood, I am determined to make use of a German, who bears of all the animals I know the least likeness to a man."

# CHAPTER IX.

In October 1668, Christina took leave of her friends with a grand farewell banquet, and left Hamburg for Rome, which she entered for the last time on November 22. The new Pope met her with a train of fifty carriages, each drawn by six horses, an augury of what was to come ; during his brief two years' reign the stream of various and cultivated enjoyment flowed on so easily and gently that this has sometimes been called the golden age of Rome. No disputes interfered to break the harmonious friendship between him and Christina, who from this time ceased to be a rolling stone, but contented herself with gathering moss, becoming, as she afterwards told Burnet, one of the antiquities of Rome.

She made, however, one attempt to gain a more important position in that same year. The abdication of John Casimir, while she was still at Hamburg, in September, offered her a chance of obtaining a crown not hampered by Lutheran tenets. Her family connection with Poland gave her, if we forget her sex for the moment, advantages over the other candidates such as Condé and the Czar of Russia. She applied herself to her canvas with energy and skill. She sent Father Hacki, a Cistercian, himself a Pole and her chaplain, as envoy to the Papal Nuncio at Warsaw. He was instructed to emphasize the fact, that she was the last surviving representative of the royal line of Sweden and Poland ; that she would never have quitted the throne of Sweden had it been a Catholic country, or had there been any hope of its ever becoming such; that it would be to their interest to elect her, inasmuch as, she being neither of an age nor an inclination to marry, the succession would be left free at her death. The Pope wrote strongly to the Nuncio in her favour, saying that the matter was of the first importance with him, and that he would have him use all means possible to make it succeed. In opposition to the objections made on the score of her sex and unmarried state, she pleaded two precedents in Polish history as to the first ; as to the second, nothing, she said, not even the empire of the world, would make her yield ; on this point she desires her envoy to avoid committing himself, but use ambiguous language and raise hopes in the Poles that she might accede after the election. The Pope wrote personally to recommend her to the Diet. But neither Christina, nor the rivals she most feared, were ultimately successful. The Poles, who had their own reasons for wishing for a weak king, elected Duke Wisnowiski, a Pole, whose

Y

three years' reign was nothing but a sea of troubles with which he was incapable of coping. Christina sent her congratulations to the new King, and accepted her failure with unconcern.

Her enemies have always pointed to this canvas for the throne of Poland as evincing her repentance for resigning the crown of her own country. But this rests on a misunderstanding. Her own abdication was no sublime contempt for earthly things, but, as she thought, necessitated by the claims of religion; all the evidence we have goes to endorse her statement to her envoy, that had it been possible for her to become a Catholic and remain Queen of Sweden, she would have done so; the key to the apparent incon- sistencies of her career is to be found in her conviction "that one must live and die a Catholic." Those who insist upon interpreting her motives in the light of their own fancies rather than the facts, can, of course, make out inconsistency and contradiction wherever they please.

For the remaining twenty years of her life she lived in Rome, observing with interest the course of European politics, as a critic and spectator; her own time she divided between the social intercourse and amusements, and the study and patronage of science and literature. Her hand was always open to assist eminent men in distress. She was constantly engaged in writing to Sweden, and sending messengers to look after her money matters, which were a source of perennial annoyance to her. It would not repay our efforts to follow out these wearisome negotiations in detail; it is sufficient to say that her revenues were always in arrear. "I wish," she writes to her agent, "you would send me money, or teach me how to live without it. No one pays me, but every one expects me to pay them." This may be taken as her chronic position; owing to the perpetual disturbances in the North it could hardly have been otherwise.

In the literary society of Rome she became a prominent figure and influence. Out of the receptions held in the garden of her palace arose the celebrated Arcadian Academy; although it was definitely constituted only after her death, yet it took its origin from her, and its members always recognised her as their founder, celebrating her anniversary with poetical funeral rites. Each member represented and was named after some shepherd of Arcadia; their annually elected president was the *Custos*, or Guardian of the flock; the arms a syrinx, crowned with pine and laurel. The qualifications for membership were nobility, whether of rank or nature, ladies not being excluded, provided that they showed a taste for poetical culture; and the principal Academy had various colonies affiliated to it in Italy. Its aim was to promote the cultivation of poetry, especially Italian, and to purify style. Moral and æsthetic questions were favourite subjects of discussion, but no topic of philosophic interest was excluded ; only satire, mutual admiration, or panegyric, especially of the Queen, was expressly tabooed. Any one of Landor's Imaginary Conversations will give us an idea of what went on.

If we are inclined to think little of academical patronage, and the literary hothouse growth it produces, we must not forget that such things were in the taste of that age. The French Academy was founded by Richelieu in 1635, and arose from very similar beginnings. In Italy, they were so to speak indigenous. They spring naturally out of the soil, wherever, as in Greece or Italy, hot afternoons and plane trees invite two or three to gather together in the name of philosophy; and their influence has been great, if not in original creation, yet in stimulating and inducing a higher level of culture. "I think," says Ranke, "we may venture to affirm that Christina exerted a powerfully efficient and enduring influence on the period, more particularly on Italian literature, and in substituting a purer and more masculine style for the labyrinth of perverted metaphor, inflated extravagance, laboured conceit, and vapid triviality into which

Italian poetry and eloquence had wandered;" "we meet in the Albani library of Rome with essays by Italian Abbati, with emendations from the hand of a Northern Queen." Crescembeni spoke with admiration of her Italian style. She continued to add to her collections of pictures, medals, and manuscripts: it was by her assistance that Spanheim was enabled to produce his valuable treatise on medals. "The Correggios of her collection have always been esteemed the choicest ornament of any gallery into which they might pass;" "the Vatican owes much of its reputation to her MSS.," which it purchased after her death.

The generosity she showed in assisting people in difficulties was doubled by the way she gave. To Archbishop Angelo della Noce, a member of the Academy, a very learned and very poor man, she afforded the means of living according to his rank. Hearing one day of his great immediate need for money, she sent him 200 ducats, with a note: "I send you 200 ducats, which do not come up to your deserts or my desire; but you have your revenge in my blushes; do not mention a word of it to any one, if you would not mortally offend the Queen." Nicolas Pallavicini wrote an enthusiastic panegyric upon her, which was never published on account of fifty-four heresies discovered in it. Menzini, another member, was indebted to her for his livelihood, which he gratefully recorded in his poetry. Alexandro Guidi she assisted both with her purse and her advice; a pastoral entitled Endymion is still extant with corrections from her hand. He became a member of the Academy in 1683, and obtained by her influence a situation in the Pope's household. Filicaja she assisted in a still more material way—paying for the education of his two sons, on condition that no one should know of it, and put her to the blush, as she said, for having done so little for a man she esteemed so much. In return, Filicaja begged to be allowed to sing her praises in an ode; but Christina earnestly dissuaded him. "I should not like you to think I wished you to praise me; those who gave you such an idea have done me great wrong; do not waste your time and talents on me."

Her dislike of flattery is worth noticing, for no one was ever so much belauded as she was, and it has done her almost as much harm as the abuse of her enemies. To Holsteinius, who arranged and catalogued her library at Rome for her, she wrote from Pesaro in 1657 :—

"Mr. Holsteinius: I should be offended at the things you have written of me to Cardinal Omodei, if I did not consider that you have done more harm to yourself than to me, in wishing to pass me off as learned. My ignorance will always give you the lie; you can only justify yourself by confessing you wished to flatter me, and thereby again you incriminate yourself. What good do you derive from all the study you have given to the ancient philosophers, if you have not learned from their writings to instruct Princes rather than to flatter them? If, however, you have abandoned the school of the divine Plato for that of Aristippus, at any rate do not quit the Vatican; flatter the Roman patrons, instead of wasting your time in flattering those who have need of being, not flattered, but instructed by you. What is the use of giving me out as learned, if I am not? Remember, too, that Aristippus only flattered those from whom he thought he might get something ; in like manner he believed it allowable for the wise man to become thief, liar, murderer, adulterer, if occasion required. It is not your flattery, then, that I blame, but that you have addressed it to the wrong person, for in giving me out for learned, who will believe you, if I do not myself?"

Again, she writes to de Court, a member of the Academy, in 1679 :—

" I wish the fine passage in your letter of the 10th instant was better applied; though it does not suit me, it applies admirably to one of my friends, who is well-known to you, Cardinal

Azzolini; he alone is worthy of your praises for his admirable qualities. But I see you are incorrigible, and that it is useless to quarrel with you on this head. Yet you are also insincere: you say you know incense does not please me; if so, why do you lavish it on me by the handful, as you do; you see you are caught."

In addition to literature, mathematics and astronomy were subjects that took up much of her time. She used to sit up at night with her astronomer, Cassini, who discovered a comet in the Chigi palace in her presence in 1664, and predicted its route. She befriended the celebrated mathematician and physiologist, Borelli, in his poverty; his treatise, " *De Motu Animalium,*" a most important contribution to physiological science, she caused to be printed at her own expense.

Occasionally she perpetrated a harmless jest at the expense of the *savans* with whom she came in contact. She was always fond of medals, and thought of arranging the great number she had struck of herself in biographical series (which has been done since). She had one medal struck in Rome containing on the one side her bust; on the other a phœnix rising from the flames, with the word ΜΑΚΕΛΩΣ. It was not till the antiquaries had puzzled their heads for some time over this strange Greek word, that she revealed it was a

Swedish word in Greek characters, meaning both "incomparable" and "virgin."

Panegyric was not the only language in which she was addressed; sometimes we find her expressing her contempt for her hostile critics, whose name was legion. "How ridiculous," she exclaims, "are all these absurdities about Monaldeschi! All Westphalia may persist in believing him innocent if they choose; it is quite indifferent to me." Another time she found a treatise, written to lay bare the motives of her conversion to Rome, and wrote on the fly-leaf words that have become proverbial : "*chi l' ha sa, nò l' ha mai scritta; e chi l' ha scritta, nò l' ha sa*"— *i.e.* "The knower writes nothing, and the writer knows nothing"; or we might translate it best by her hero Condé's remark to the Cardinal de Retz : "These rascals make us talk and act as they would have done themselves in our place."

In 1674, in spite of her claims to indifference, she was greatly annoyed by the publication of Chanut's *Mémoires*, by Linage de Vanciennes; she writes to Bourdelot, complaining of the great injustice done to herself and Chanut :—

"The age we live in consoles me; no one is spared, and calumny fastens chiefly on the worthiest. What vexes me is, that the book should bear the name of Chanut. I am convinced that he never wrote it, and I am sorry that such a dark stain should be fixed on the memory of so honest a man. For if God had abandoned me to such an extent as to permit me to be capable of all the baseness imputed to me, it is certain that it would be the last misfortune for me; from which His mercy has preserved me. That does not prevent any man capable of publishing such things from being unworthy to live; and he must be the most utterly degraded of men. I will on this head give the definitive judgment which an Italian author once gave *à propos* of slanders on the Pope—'*Il Papa è Papa, e tu sei furfante.*'" *

Meanwhile her health continued good, with occasional relapses; Bourdelot still continued to be her medical adviser, in so far as she took medical advice. He seems to have recommended her to eat less on one occasion in 1679—to which she replies:—

"You are vexed because your verses are not sufficiently appreciated, and by way of penance you try to dock people's ordinary meals. You must be a perfect Jansenist, to assign such harsh penance; for it cannot be as a doctor, but as a confessor, that you are determined to make people die of hunger. The advice you give me would be good if you were my steward, and it was for economy, at a time when money is scarce; yet

* "The Pope is Pope, and you are a scoundrel."

it would be laughed at, and all the misfortunes of Sweden do not drive me to such despair as to be anxious to die by diet. If you knew how much I eat, most assuredly you would say there was nothing to retrench; a man may be as temperate as he likes—he can't eat less than I do. You tell me I have done well to give up wine, which I have not given up, for I never drank it, as you know. As to my *embonpoint*, it does not afflict me. I have only got fat enough to cover my bones; the way I live, I am not afraid of getting any fatter. I eat little and sleep less, since I'm rarely more than five hours in bed when I'm well. You know I used to sleep much less, but in my complete leisure, mistress of all my time, I sleep a little longer, in order to cool my constitutional fire and flame. I am surprised at what you tell me, that MM. Arnauld and Nicole have gone to Rome. They are people of great worth for Jansenists, but were they devils one must give them their due. There are no Jansenists that I know of at Rome; if there are any at all they are only fools, and people of no account. As for me, I am blindly pledged to the sentiments of the Church of Rome, and believe without reservation all that its chief commands. The peace you speak of is still an enigma. I see peace made in many places, but executed nowhere. I believe true peace is only to be found

in this world in the hearts of those who despise
everything."

Some of the allusions in this letter, such as
that to the peace—the Peace of Nimeguen of
1678—make it necessary to glance at contemporary events, especially as it was owing to
them that Christina's reserves were never
forthcoming. The "flare-up" of Sweden in
Charles X. had died away, only to leave her
in still blacker gloom than before, internal
and external. By the treaty of Oliva in 1660,
she obtained peace, but the only gainer was
Brandenburg, whose "Great Elector" was now
laying the foundations of Prussian history.
Left to themselves during the minority of
Charles XI. the oligarchy at last got their
chance. The State was administered entirely
in their interests, the Crown lands recklessly
squandered, the young King brought up as
much as possible in ignorance, to obviate the
possibility of creating another Christina. The
dominant party, led by Brahé, Wrangel, and
Magnus de la Gardie, turned their backs upon
peace, advocated by the opposing faction as the
only way of salvation for Sweden; which might
be true enough, but was not the aim of their
opponents, who desired quite other things,
chiefly money. They unwillingly took part in
the Triple Alliance of 1668 between England,

Holland, and Sweden against France. Both
with England and Sweden, however, the gold
of Louis XIV. was a more potent influence than
honour; the latter country agreed, in consideration of huge bribes, to despatch an army against
Brandenburg under Wrangel. The indecision
of the Swedish general, who kept receiving
contradictory orders from home, proved fatal
to him against the prompt action of the Elector,
who speedily and completely defeated him at
Fehrbellin and expelled the Swedes by a series
of victories from Pomerania. The Danes seized
the moment to attempt to recover their losses
by the Treaty of Copenhagen. But in spite of
his neglected education, Charles XI. proved
his abilities by the victories of Lund and
Landskrona, though they were balanced by the
success of the Danes at sea. The Peace of
Nimeguen in 1678, the Treaty of St. Germain-en-
Laye of the following year, and that of Lund,
put an end to hostilities; but "as Louis XIV.
proved a gentleman to his Swedes," the Elector
had to disgorge all his winnings in Pomerania.
The knell of the oligarchy had sounded;
Charles XI. with the nation at his back took a
terrible vengeance upon them. The Crown lands
alienated since the time of Gustavus Adolphus
were resumed at a blow, and enormous fines
were imposed on many nobles, or where they

were dead, on their heirs, of whom many were
reduced to beggary. The power of the Senate
was annihilated, and that body reduced to a
complete dependence upon the King. The war
policy of Charles X. was reversed ; Charles XI.
sedulously maintained peace during his reign,
and Sweden in consequence took a less important and more natural position in European
affairs.

Now at length Christina began to receive her
own revenues with more regularity, which
enabled her to restore to her Court at Rome
something of its original brilliancy. But her
relations with the Pope had also changed with
the times. Clement IX. had long been dead,
nor did his successor, Clement X., live long ;
in 1676 Cardinal Odescalchi became Pope as
Innocent XI. He immediately set himself to
reform the existing evil state of things ; nepotism,
in full swing under his predecessors, was stopped ;
the finances, which showed an increasing deficit,
scrutinized with care, and abuses of all kinds
abolished. But a more striking opposition to
his predecessor's policy was shown in the strong
attitude he took up towards Louis XIV., to
whose bullying and imperious mode of treating
ecclesiastical questions he became a strenuous
antagonist. In these disputes between France
and the Pope Christina was mixed up.

The quarrel arose out of the claim of Louis XIV. to the right of *régale*, the right, that is to say, of enjoying the revenues of vacant bishoprics and appointing to all their dependent benefices. This he wished to extend to four districts, Guienne, Languedoc, Provence, and Dauphiné, in which it had never obtained before. Two Jansenist bishops, of Pamier and Alais, protested and appealed to the Pope, who forbade Louis to proceed. The consequence was that Louis, who hated the Jansenists, and was supported by the Jesuits, got a convocation assembled in 1682, which pronounced the celebrated four decrees, that the temporal power is independent of the spiritual, that a general council is superior to the Pope, that the Papal authority cannot alter the Gallican usages, and that even in questions of faith the decision of the Pope is not final without the sanction of the Church. In spite of this fatal blow Innocent remained inflexible, and refused to concede spiritual ordination to the nominees of Louis; this position he retained during his life. Nor was the dispute settled till 1693, under Innocent XII., when Louis withdrew his decrees.

With this was closely connected the affair of Molinos, a Spanish priest, who preached a doctrine of mystical quietism. Innocent was not himself inclined to deal hardly with him.

"If he is in error," he said, "nevertheless he is a worthy man;" and some of the Cardinals, Azzolini for instance, were favourable to him. But the Jesuits abhorred him, as well for his doctrine as his influence, and went so far as to accuse the Pope of leaning to his heretical opinions; by the influence of the French Cardinals he was condemned by the Inquisition to recant, and be imprisoned for life. Christina, who was ever as ready as Voltaire himself to defend the persecuted and oppressed, took up his cause, and supplied his wants in prison, for which her enemies accused her of quietism; and they were, strangely enough, though quite accidentally, for once nearer the mark than ever they were before or after, for Christina's own views, as has been already pointed out, show a distinct vein of mysticism, though this was by no means her reason for befriending Molinos. Burnet says, that her tact and charity established harmony among the members of the Sacred College. Molinos died in prison at the age of seventy.

Christina saved two other Spanish gentlemen from the Inquisition; but the finest proof of her noble intolerance of persecution is to be found in a letter she wrote to the Chevalier de Terlon, on February 3, 1686, telling him her views upon the Revocation of the Edict of Nantes, by which in 1685 Louis aimed at crushing the Huguenots, and only succeeded in inflicting a lasting injury on France.

"Since you wish to know my sentiments upon the pretended extirpation of heresy in France, I am delighted to tell them to you on a subject of such importance. As I profess to fear and flatter no one, I will frankly own to you that I am not much persuaded of the success of this great design, and I cannot rejoice over it, as a thing advantageous to our holy religion ; on the contrary, I foresee many prejudices that will arise everywhere from so novel a proceeding. In good faith, are you well assured of the sincerity of these converts ? I hope they may obey God and their king sincerely, but I fear their obstinacy ; and I would not have at my door all the sacrilege which will be committed by these Catholics forced in by missionaries who treat the sacred mysteries too cavalierly. Military men are strange apostles. I think they are better suited to kill, ravish, and rob than persuade ; and, in fact, accounts we cannot doubt tell us that they are performing their mission quite in character. I pity the people abandoned to their discretion. I bewail so many ruined families, so many honest folk reduced to beggary, and cannot look at what goes on in France without compassion. I am sorry for these un-fortunates having been born in error, but they

z

seem to me more to be pitied than hated; and as I would not for the empire of the world share in their error, so would I not be the cause of their distress. I consider France to-day as a sick man, whose arms and legs are cut off to cure him of a disease that a little patience and gentleness would have cured completely; but I fear lest this disease may grow more acute, and become finally incurable; lest this fire hidden under the ashes may not blaze forth some day still fiercer than ever, and heresy become all the more dangerous that it is masked. Nothing is more praiseworthy than the design of converting infidels and heretics, but this method of doing it is quite new; and since our Saviour did not adopt this way of converting the world, it cannot be the best. I wonder at, and do not understand, this zeal and these politics; they are above me, and I am glad of it. Do you think this is a moment to convert heretics, to make them good Catholics; an age when attempts so noticeable are made in France against the respect and submission due to the Roman Church, which is the sole and unshakable foundation of our religion, since it was to it that the Saviour made the magnificent promise, that the gates of hell shall not prevail against it. Still, never has the scandalous license of the Gallican Church been pushed to greater lengths against it than now. The late propositions, signed and published by the clergy of France, are such, that they have given only too obvious a triumph to heresy, and I think its surprise must have been without parallel, on seeing itself so soon after persecuted by those who have on this fundamental point of our religion dogmas and sentiments so much akin to their own. There are powerful reasons to keep me from rejoicing over this pretended extirpation of heresy. The interest of the Roman Catholic Church is without doubt as dear to me as life, but it is this same interest which causes me to see these things with grief, and I tell you that I love France well enough to mourn over the desolation of so fine a kingdom. I hope with all my heart I may be wrong in my conjectures, and that all may end to the great glory of God and the King your master; I am sure you will not doubt my sincerity."

This letter, a rock upon which all the accusations of her enemies split, will always constitute Christina's next title to immortality, after her part in the Peace of Westphalia.

It was soon published and circulated about. The philosophic Bayle so far forgot his usual acumen on this occasion as to term it " a remnant of her Protestantism." This made Christina justly very indignant; after some explanations he wrote her an apology, which she accepted graciously, and wrote him a reply, in which she says that the accusation of Protestantism had touched her nearly, as casting a slur upon her conversion ; she laid upon him the penance of sending her any new and curious books he could find.

Were there needed any further proofs of the sincerity of her conversion, they could be furnished in hosts. She refused to print the book of one Wasmuth, as she had undertaken to do, till he convinced her that there was not the least expression in it derogatory to the Church of Rome, otherwise she would not contribute to it in any way, nor suffer it to bear her name ; she even spoke of it as an outrage that he should ever have imagined that she would. To an account in which she is described as a Roman Catholic, not of the French school, but of that of Peter and Paul, she appended a note : "This is divinely put ; ay, so I am, and by the help of God will always remain." To Count Wasanau, a son of Ladislaus of Poland, whom, being left in destitution, she had provided for in her own service, she wrote to recommend him to assume the cowl, and consecrate himself to the service of God, adding, that she envied him that station in life and unhampered position which permitted him to do so.

In 1682, being informed of rumours of her own

death spread about in Stockholm, she writes to Olivekranz, her agent in Sweden :—

"I am not surprised at the news of my death. There are so many people who long for it that I don't take it ill if they sometimes flatter themselves by anticipation. It will come when God pleases, but up to now I have not been sufficiently favoured to hope for it. I am in the best health and vigour I have ever enjoyed in my life; however, that is no reason why I shouldn't die, yet according to appearances plenty of people will die before me who don't think it. I am waiting for death in great peace of mind, and neither fear it nor desire it ; I assure you I shall never die of the evil things published about me in Sweden ; if I only die of fear or interest I shall be immortal."

She felt more anxious about another report that came from Sweden, of injuries sustained by Charles XI. in a fall from his horse. Visions of the nobles fighting for the crown haunted her, which were dispelled by the news of the birth of an heir, afterwards Charles XII. The year before her death, 1688, when he was five years old, he wrote her a letter, which she answered, assuring him of his " good aunt's " best wishes for his success, and pleasure at hearing of his talents.

An event of more immediate importance was

the relief of Vienna by John Sobieski, who defeated the Turks with vastly inferior forces, on September 12, 1683. Christina's endeavours to provide against the danger in this quarter have already been related. Since then she had written to Sweden on the instigation of the Pope and her own fears to try and persuade the government to take some decisive action against the Turks, but without success. She welcomed the deed of Sobieski with great joy.

"A great and rare spectacle," she writes, "has your Majesty given to the world in the memorable and victorious day of the relief of Vienna; it must be immortal in the annals of the Holy See and the whole world. It behoves each of us to give his separate thanks. Your deeds show you to be worthy not only of the crown of Poland, but of the monarchy of the world. I wish I could express my sentiments on this occasion; yet I may boast of knowing the value of this victory over the Emperor of Asia better than others, since I realized better than any the danger hanging over us in Rome. I owe your Majesty the preservation of my independence and peace, yet I must confess to feeling ungrateful, because I feel envious, which sentiment was till now a stranger to me. I do not envy you your kingdom, nor your treasures and spoils, but your title of Liberator of Christianity."

The otherwise peaceful current of her life was broken in 1686 by disagreements with the Pope, arising out of the question of the "Freedom of Districts." This was a privilege of the palaces of foreign ambassadors; they and their household were exempt from the jurisdiction of the Roman law and police, and the immunity was extended to a considerable radius all round the palace precincts. Persons of the same nationality claimed the same privilege as the ambassador's suite, and took up their quarters in his vicinity; hence these protected quarters became asylums for the offscourings of every nation. Innocent XI. determined to apply his new broom to these Augean stables, by restricting this freedom to the actual palaces of the ambassadors and the members of their household. Those of the Emperor, and the King of Spain at once agreed to renounce their right, conditionally on France doing the same. Christina, who enjoyed the same privilege, at once wrote to the Pope to follow their example. But not to mention the existing feud between France and the Pope, such an opportunity was meat and drink to the vanity of Louis XIV. The French refused to do as the others had done; when, therefore, the new French ambassador arrived, the Pope refused to see him till he renounced his " district privileges." The " Grand Monarque" retorted that he was accustomed to set, not to follow an example; that the signal services of France to the Holy See were well deserving of some recompense, and that he would maintain his right. Thereupon the Pope excommunicated his ambassador.

Meanwhile a certain brandy vendor, who was being hunted by the police, took refuge in a church. The sbirri discovered his whereabouts by means of a spy, seized him, and were conducting him to prison, when, being a young and powerful man, he broke away, and ran to take refuge in Christina's stables; finding these closed, he seized hold of the padlock so tightly, that they could only tear him away by putting a cord round his neck to strangle him. It was Easter Day, and Christina was in her chapel. Hearing of what was going on, she was very indignant at the insult, and sent to command the police to release their captive, which they did. The Pope, excessively irritated, ordered his Treasurer to proceed with the utmost rigour in the case, and the latter published a decree, condemning Christina's officers concerned in the release to death. Thereupon she sent the following letter to him :—

" Dishonouring yourself and your master you call doing justice in your tribunal; I am sorry for you now, and shall be still more so when you are a Cardinal. In the meantime I give you my word that those whom you have condemned to death shall, please God, live yet a little longer; and should they chance to die by other than a natural death, they shall not die alone."

Some of the Cardinals were on Christina's side, and considered she had been hardly used. After some ineffectual negotiations, in which the Pope refused to make any concessions, she proceeded to brave him openly by going to the Jesuits' Church with her whole suite armed, among whom were the two condemned officials. "I am," she wrote to a friend, " like Cæsar of old, in the hands of pirates, and like him I menace them, and they fear me." Innocent, in fact, now made some attempt to appease her ire, sending her baskets of fruits. But she distrusted these gifts; "I am not," she said, " to be deceived by these politics." To this the Pope replied by two words, " È donna," " 'tis a woman ; " and added to his epigram by depriving her of her pension of 12,000 crowns, which she still received from the Papal Treasury. On this she wrote to Azzolini, who informed her of it :—

"I assure you you have given me the most pleasant news in the world. I entreat you to do me this justice. God, who knows the depths of the heart, knows I do not lie. The 12,000 crowns allowed me by the Pope were the sole blot on my life, and I took them as a mortification from the hand of God in order to lower my pride ; I see well He is taking me into His grace by His singular favour of removing them."

The French, pleased to see themselves not alone in their opposition to the Pope, supported her, and Louis XIV. wrote to mark his approbation. The Elector of Brandenburg offered to give her an asylum in his dominions, and send her assistance, if necessary. At first she asked him to send her a guard, but finding the French would back her up, she withdrew her request. In this situation Innocent waited to see what time might do for him, and thus the matter dragged on ; in fact, both Christina and himself died before any settlement was arranged. Louis' subsequent difficulties in other quarters left him little leisure to stand on his dignity at Rome ; in the end the French ambassador resigned his claims.

In a letter to Mademoiselle de Scudéry, in 1687, Christina deplores the death of Condé, which took place in that year, not without a touch of good-humoured satire. "Why did you, who write so well, let the Prince die without doing something for him in verse or in prose ? " She began to feel that her own death could not be far off; a feeling that she expresses in her letters of this time, especially in one she wrote to the Marquis del Monte, whom she had sent to Sweden on her economical affairs, to inform him of the death of his father at Rome :—

"Yesterday your father was in health as perfect as a young man of your age could enjoy; he was with me till three o'clock, and went away in good case, pleased with himself. This morning at eleven he was taken ill, and died at sundown. What things we are! dust, cinders, ashes, nothing at all. God grant that we all live and die in His grace; all else is vanity. I am sorry you are without a Mass, where you are, but God is everywhere, and He is enough. We are all to disappear like shadows; life is a dream—it vanishes and fleets like a momentary flash—we all run to eternity."

At the close of her life public affairs again awoke her keen interest, and she showed her political sagacity in her criticisms on the principal actors. In 1688 Louis XIV. made his sudden onslaught upon Germany, and achieved a temporary success. But Christina saw further :—

"There is Germany once more in fire and flames; the King of France has made a master-stroke. If he had acted thus fifteen or twenty years ago he might have done great things. My chief curiosity is to see what attitude Sweden will take, and the disclosing of the Prince of Orange's great designs. Personally, I fear for the King of England. Pray heaven

I may be mistaken. The Prince of Orange is clever and brave; I don't think he has entered the business lightly, without being well assured of his *coup*. The taking of Philipsburg will decide all here. I hardly doubt of its capture. But we must wait for the event."

"Every one here trembles," she writes again, "except me." The event soon justified her prevision. Philipsburg was taken, and Louis was master of the four Electorates of the Rhine. But William of Orange seized the opportunity afforded him by this diversion, and soon carried all before him in England. Christina writes again to Olivekranz, Dec 5, 1688 :—

"I am convinced that the best thing for Sweden is to remain neutral. I am very impatient to see what it will do. English affairs are in a pitiable condition. Bigotry, Jesuits, and monks have done for the King; I predicted his ruin long ago. If the Prince of Orange succeeds, as I believe he will, England and Holland will be a formidable power, conjoined under one head, and such a head as that of the Prince, whose abilities are extraordinary. I am much mistaken if he does not give France her work to do, and show her the mistake she made in persecuting the Huguenots."

And again, a week later :—

"The Prince of Orange is and will be King of

England all his life, and no other; I predicted all that would happen to the former King; the Huguenot business has been the fatal stroke for this poor King, too much of a bigot and too little of a statesman, who has got ruined by letting himself be governed by the accursed race of Jesuits and monks, who always spoil everything they touch."

A fortnight later she expresses herself more plainly: "If you had heard my predictions for the last three years, of which all Rome is witness, you would admit that I am a greater astrologer than the English, and that terrestrial astrology is worth more than celestial. I will make another prediction to you. England and Holland united will make all Europe tremble, and give stern laws by land and sea. Remember my words."

In addition to this expressed contempt for astrology, on which her enemies have accused her, she says in another place, "I am not of those who believe in astrology, but it is my curiosity which would know all things!" "One must know enough," she says in her maxims, "of medicine and chemistry not to be the dupe of doctors and astrologers." How correct her terrestrial astrology was is matter of history. As soon as William was established in England she wrote to him to ask his protection for the Roman Catholics in England: "They are but a little troop, who will not interfere with your designs, and are but too happy to be allowed to live; you have nothing to fear from their weakness."

She was a centre of attraction in Rome in the last years of her life. "At the Queen of Sweden's," says Burnet, "one learns all the news relating to Germany or the North. This Princess, who will always reign among those who are endowed with wit and learning, keeps up in her antechamber the finest court of strangers in Rome. The civility and great diversity of matters furnished by her conversation makes her among all the rare sights of Rome the rarest, not to say among all the antiquities, which is the term she made use of in doing me the honour to speak to me." She is described at this time much as we have seen her in her youth, only, at sixty-two, she was "very small, fat, and round, with a double chin and a laughing air, and very obliging manners." Her tongue was as sharp as ever. "The Church," she told Burnet, "must certainly be governed by the Holy Spirit, for since I have been at Rome I have seen four Popes, and I swear not one of them had common sense."

In February, 1689, she was suddenly seized with an attack of erysipelas and fever; she surprised everybody, including herself, by re-covering.

" God has snatched me from the arms of death

against my hope. I had already resigned myself to the last journey, which I thought inevitable. Still, here I am, full of life, by a miracle of grace, nature, and art, which have conspired to give me back health and life. The strength of my constitution has surmounted a malady capable of killing twenty Herculeses. I hope to be quite well by Easter, and out of the hands of the doctor, who scolds me when he sees me writing."

But in April she fell ill again for the last time. Just before the attack, she wrote her last letter :—

" I can only answer your letter by approving all your thoughts; I am impatient to see you, and am waiting for you like the Jews for their Messiah. I have a hundred things to say that can't be written. I hope you will find me quite well when you arrive."

Feeling, however, that the end was approaching, she sent to ask the Pope to forgive her for any harsh expressions which her hasty temper might have allowed to escape her. Innocent sent her absolution. She died at six o'clock in the morning, on April 19.

By her will, dated March 1, 1689, after certain legacies to the Pope, the Emperor, the Kings of France and Spain, the Elector of Brandenburg, and other private persons, she constituted Cardinal Azzolini sole heir, " for his incomparable

qualities, his personal merit, and the services of
so many years ; " directing him to pay her debts,
if there were any, and provide for twenty
thousand Masses being said for her soul.   Her
legacy to the Pope was the statue of Christ by
Bernini, which she admired so much that she
refused to buy it of the artist, saying that she
could not afford to pay him what it was worth.
Bernini left it to her at his death.   As Cardinal
Azzolini died himself two months afterwards, his
nephew succeeded to his claims; but he did not
get much out of them, all her money being
consumed in satisfying the legacies in her will,
while her furniture and personal effects were
eagerly bought up by Cardinals and noble
families, who, we are told, never paid for them.
Her fine library and collection of manuscripts
were bought by the Pope to enrich the Vatican ;
her unrivalled collection of medals was purchased
by his nephew, Cardinal Odescalchi.

   Her body was embalmed and lay in state for
some days, first in her own palace, then at the
Church of St. Dorothy.   She had left special
directions that there should be no pompous
celebration of her funeral rites, nor any epitaph,
other than

D. O. M.

VIXIT CHRISTINA ANNOS LXIII.

But herein the Pope disobeyed her. Her funeral was celebrated by a magnificent procession to St. Peter's, led by the literary and scientific men, followed by the long series of religious Orders, the Cardinals, and the Pope. Her coffin was laid in the Basilica. A monument was afterwards erected, which Innocent did not live to complete : it was finished, and an epitaph added, by Clement XI., in 1702, who also struck a medal to commemorate the fact.

The Swedish Court went into mourning, and Charles XI. sent round to the other European Powers, asking them to do the same.

Strange irony of events, that the Basilica of St. Peter's should receive the daughter of Gustavus Adolphus! Or shall we not rather consider it as emblematic of a new *régime* which should substitute mutual toleration for the old uncompromising antagonism, closed at least in theory by the Peace of Westphalia. It is because Christina showed herself fully conscious of this great change, and was its ardent pioneer, not only by the prominent part she took in shutting the door on the past epoch by bringing about the Peace of 1648, but also by her openly expressed and heartfelt abomination of persecution, that she deserves a niche in the temple of humanity. And this is, too, the secret of her enemies' abuse,

2 A

that she stood above and outside of the religious and political animosities of her age, disregarding and even contemning the smaller formal conventionalities. None of her great and brilliant qualities, her political genius, her eagerness for the progress of all branches of learning and science, her ready generosity, her humane sympathy with all oppressed minorities, could in their eyes atone for this.

By her abdication she deprived herself of the true field for exercising her abilities, and of the power of realizing her great conceptions. Hence, from the utilitarian point of view, she has been condemned for having done so little. She foresaw this herself. "Those who examine this action according to the maxims commonly established among men will blame it, without doubt." A critic of a different school, when he observes her capacities, and all she did during her short reign, will regret it indeed, but will also give her all the credit which is her due, for acting up to her religious convictions.

# CHAPTER X.

ALTHOUGH Christina is not, strictly speaking, to be classed among authors, she has left some more or less fragmentary writings which have an intrinsic interest apart from their biographical value. These are, the History, or Memoirs of her own life; Reflections on Alexander the Great, and Julius Cæsar; and some detached Aphorisms, or Maxims, of which there are two different collections (many of the thoughts being the same in both), arranged in centuries, or groups of a hundred.

Even if we had nothing else from her pen, her letters, many of them masterpieces in that style of writing, combining feminine ease and grace with a masculine vigour and satirical point that recalls those of Byron, would give ample proof of her literary power. They won the admiration of Leibnitz, and show that had she chosen to apply herself to a complete work, she might have become a French classic, for French was the language she preferred, though she wrote easily in many others. Hence it is all the more to be regretted that she never finished her Memoirs, the most important of the writings named. This most curious piece of self-analysis

2 A 2

has already been characterised, and frequently quoted. There is nothing exactly like it in literature. Judging from what there is of it, it is not too much to say that, if complete, it would have taken its place among the half-dozen world-famous autobiographies. The essentials in this *genre*—a peculiar genius, a varied experience of life, and an admirable style—are here, as rarely elsewhere, conjoined. It is a sort of personal confession to the Deity, to whom it is addressed : " I consecrate to Thee, Lord, in this work, such as it is, my past life ; " and displays throughout a strong mystical vein. What has, in fact, been said of a very different person applies also to Christina, that no one will appreciate or understand her who has not a certain sympathy with mysticism.* After the dedication, she gives a rapid sketch of Swedish history down to her own time, and then dwells at length on her education and character, speaking of herself very

---

* This will be all the plainer if we compare, *e.g.*, the unsympathetic external way in which Voltaire criticises Madame de Guyon, and Parkman's very different method of dealing with Marie de l'Incarnation, a character in many points akin to that of Christina: to whom also his remark, that such cases are a problem, not only for the theologian and philosopher, but also for the physiologist, applies. Her ardent and impetuous nature, finding no legitimate object on which to expand, threw back upon the bottomless abyss of mystical yearning; though her strong intellect preserved her from the extravagance usual in such cases.

frankly both in good and bad. It breaks off
suddenly at the point where she is about to be
removed from her mother. Internal evidence
seems to shows it was, at least partly, written
in 1681.

The Reflections on Alexander are of capital
import for her own character; a better idea of
what she was, or, perhaps, what she would have
been, is to be gained from this essay than from
any other source. In describing the nature of
her hero she lays bare her own : " We acknowledge
that the imitation of this incomparable model
is difficult and almost impossible ; but no matter,
it is good to propose to oneself so perfect an
ideal, and the despair of not succeeding should
not hinder any one from making the lofty
attempt." Had she been a man, we might have
been more struck with the resemblance of the
copy to the original : there is a heroic magnanimity discernible in some of the House of Vasa,
though in Christina it was disguised by her sex
more than in others. " He had a fiery spirit
which rendered him indefatigable to the day of
his death ; his liberality exceeded the conceptions
and wishes of his friends and enemies; . . . he
distributed all his money and his patrimony to
his friends before passing the Hellespont, with a
greatness of soul of which he alone was capable,
reserving only the pleasure of having given all, *a*

*thousand times more worthy of him than,* &c.   (The
italics are ours.)   She describes his genius, his
skill at all physical exercises, his personal charm,
*his continence,* and the divine fire of his heroic
soul, *which made smaller minds tax him with
madness.*"   "But Alexander was a man, and on
this account we ought to pardon his faults for his
great virtues.   Nature has placed spots on the
sun, which do not prevent it from being the
most glorious luminary in the world."

Just so Disraeli, in describing Bolingbroke,
gives us his own aspirations as to what he would
himself wish to be; the fervour of the portrait
drawn springs out of the feeling of kindred with
the subject.

The little sketch on Cæsar is of less moment,
and wants the sympathetic bond which gives that
on Alexander its interest.

The Aphorisms, or Maxims, are not all of
equal merit, though some of them have an
epigrammatic and caustic incisiveness not unworthy of Chamfort himself.   A selection of
some of the best, with others that illustrate
Christina's peculiar opinions, is subjoined.

Did men understand the duties of princes, they
would be less anxious to become one.

One is, in proportion as one can love.

Fools are more to be feared than knaves.

Modesty is a sort of sincerity.

Men are unknown to themselves, as well as to others, till occasions arise to test them.

There is a sort of pleasure in suffering from ingratitude known only to great minds.

Extraordinary merit is a crime never forgiven.

People are wrong in blaming Cæsar for having made himself master of Rome, if it was the most important service he could have rendered it.

Great men and fools are sometimes the same thing, only in a different way.

Vainly do men oppose changes in states and republics; there is a fatal point, which once reached draws all along.

The oracle which bade men refer to the dead, was doubtless referring to books.

There is a star which unites souls of the first order, though ages and distances divide them.

One rises above all, when one no longer esteems or fears anything.

However feeble a prince is, he is never so much ruled as is believed.

At the moment Justice is punishing some rascals, others steal the purses of the spectators.

Small princes can do little good and much harm.

A man's merit is often the greatest obstacle to his fortunes.

To undeceive men is to offend them.

The Salic law, which excluded women from the throne, was a good law.

More courage is required for marriage than for war.

All expenditure on arms or troops is economy.

We must submit ourselves blindly to the Catholic Church, the only oracle of God.

When one is a Catholic, one has the consolation of believing all that so many great minds have believed, who have lived for sixteen centuries; a religion authorised by so many millions of martyrs; which has peopled the deserts with those who by a secret martyrdom have sacrificed themselves to God; a religion fertile in admirable virgins, who have trampled upon their sex and their age, to consecrate themselves to God.

How can one be a Christian without being a Catholic?

In vain do the heretics usurp the fine title of Catholic, which does not belong to them.

Interest is a god, unknown to many who sacrifice to him.

We must not be the dupes of confessors and directors.

Nothing is so disgusting as external devotion. To love God and one's neighbours is the true devotion; all the rest is but grimaces.

Bigots hate all who are not their dupes; but they never want money or wives.

The famous "know thyself," given out as the source of human wisdom, is only that of its misery.

Philosophy neither changes men nor corrects them.

He who loses his temper with the world has learned all he knows to no purpose.

Genius is always a paradox to those who are without it.

# APPENDIX.

## A.—Peace of Westphalia.

Readers may find it convenient to have some further details as to the territorial changes made at the Peace. France acquired Alsace, the Sundgau, and Brisach; and the definitive possession of the Bishoprics of Metz, Toul, and Verdun. Brandenburgh received the Bishoprics of Camin, Halberstadt, and Minden, with the prospect of Magdeburg. The Bishoprics of Schwerin and Ratzeburg were given to Mecklenburg - Schwerin. Saxony retained Lusatia, and Bavaria received the Electorate with the Upper Palatinate; the Lower Palatinate went back to Charles Lewis, son of the Elector, and an eighth Electorate was created for him. Switzerland was made independent of the Empire. Other changes were made of minor importance.

The charge usually brought against the Peace, that it destroyed the unity of Germany, is based on an insufficient grasp of the position. For its long disunion, Germany has rather to thank its connection with the Empire, its religious and political divisions, and especially the war. Unity is good, but to be united a nation must first exist. Existence, rapidly becoming impossible for Germany, was ensured by the Peace; unity was achieved only at a later day.

## B.—Contarini Fleming.

The curious identity of the idea of Disraeli's novel, and Christina's own history, especially as conceived by Voltaire, whose influence on Disraeli was very strong, is perhaps more than a co-incidence; many of the very names we meet with in the history are repeated in the fiction.

## C.—Sigismund III., p. 7.

Had Sigismund had but the rudiments of policy he might not only have retained Sweden, but added Russia to Poland and Lithuania united at Lublin. What an opportunity, and how clumsily improved! A striking instance of the influence individual character may have on the history of the world.

## D.—Whitelocke's Embassy.

For a fuller consideration of this than can be given here, see Ranke, ' History of England,' iii. 123.

## E.—On the Calendar.

The dates have in general been left in the
old style, ten days behind our own; but in a
few instances of special importance, as *e.g.* that
of the Peace of Westphalia, they have been
reduced to the modern method of reckoning,

# INDEX.

## A.

Åbo, College founded at, 147; made a University by Christina, 170

Abdication of Christina, reasons for, 109, 225; account of, 238; judgments upon, 243; of John Casimir, 320

Academy, the Arcadian, 323; Academy, the French, when founded, 324; Christina and the, 297

Adolphus, Gustavus. *See* Gustavus.

Adolphus, Duke, 60, 202, 303; on Christina's dislike of marriage, 107; his character, 306

Alexander the Great, Reflections on, 357

Alexander VII., Pope, elected, 255; De Retz on him, 255, 301; his dispute with Christina, 301; with Louis XIV., 313; death, 316

Alexandra, Christina assumes name of, 260

Alliance, Triple, 332

Amalia Elizabeth of Hesse, 46

Amaranta, Order of, 193

Amazon, Christina as an, 259, 260

America, colony established in, 132

Anatomy, school of, established, 150

Anne of Austria, 275, *sqq.*

Aphorisms of Christina, 358, *sqq.*

Arcadian Academy, 323

## G.

LONDON.
PRINTED BY WILLIAM CLOWES AND SONS, Limited,
STAMFORD STREET AND CHARING CROSS.